The Mage From Alira

G.L. WATTERS

CHAPTER ONE

There was only one thing the people of Alira hated more than anything, and that was magic. They simply disliked what wasn't ordinary, scared of what they couldn't explain.

Through no fault of her own, Olivia grew into being one of those people that was hated by everyone. It didn't matter that she was widely liked throughout the kingdom as a child, nor that she had grown up beside the prince like an honorary sister.

They didn't care that her magic had presented itself in desperation to save the lives of innocent animals, who were being burned alive by a young stableboy. He had accidentally knocked over a candle while tending to them. As soon as Olivia had doused the flames, the Kingdom had turned its back on her.

Her only saving grace had been her father, who was well respected as Court Mage and a valued assistant to King Alroy. Had it not been for him, Olivia surely would have been run out of Alira, chased by the very people who had cared for her so dearly only days before.

"Careful with that, Olivia."

Osmond shook his head with a smile as he turned back to his work. He was an older man, with tanned skin and little hair, and an odd amount of muscles for a man his age. He was one of the few that didn't abandon her after the fire. Even Renly, the prince she had grown up beside her entire life, refused to spare her little more than a glance these days.

She hadn't even known Osmond's name before he offered her a position working with him in his forge. She hadn't understood why he was doing it at the time, but she was grateful. He had given her a job, a purpose, at a time when everyone was scared of the little eleven-year-old with emerging magic. In the six years that followed, the public hatred of her had not waned.

"Here." He held out a hammer to the boy standing beside him.

Osmond indicated towards where he was holding a red-hot piece of metal over the flames. He gingerly took the hammer and swung, almost missing the metal completely. Osmond just laughed and encouraged him to try again.

Cassius was new to the Kingdom, having moved with his father a week or so before. He never spoke about the reason why he moved, or where he had come from. She had barely even known he had arrived before Osmond had dragged him into the forge.

It was in such a similar way to how he had taken Olivia under his protection that it had her wondering, until she had seen him before work one morning, laughing with a small group of men outside the forge's doors. He was too well-liked to have a single drop of magic in his blood.

He was barely older than her, but he hardly acted like it. He was much too nice, happy even on dreary days when everyone else around him wore a frown. He walked around like he hadn't a care in the world.

Everything about him infuriated her.

For the longest time, the only person Osmond paid any real close attention to was her. It had barely been three days and it was like Cassius had always been there.

A loud clang sent sparks flying across the room, the hammer sliding to the floor out of Cassius' grip. They both laughed, and Cassius grinned brightly when Osmond clasped his shoulder in a fond gesture.

Olivia snatched an apple from Osmond's work desk and walked out, calling out over her shoulder that she was taking an early break.

Distant laughter floated over the training fields as Olivia climbed the fence and perched on the top rung, legs swinging down the other side. The field stank of sweat and dirt, but It smelt like her childhood.

She watched as the knights trained together. It reminded her strongly of when she sneaked into training sessions as a child. The young prince was always glued to her side as they copied the stances of the much older knights. The only knight who remained from those days was much older now, grey sticking out of his dark beard.

Renly noticed her with a frown. He was usually the first to spot her, and he always acted the same. Barely sparing her a glance before turning back to his knights – and they were his, now that he was of age to command them.

He had his father's dark hair and crooked nose, and his mother's round blue eyes and dimpled cheeks. When he was younger, the strange combination made him look different, always appearing much younger than he really was. The look suited him well now that he's older, his straight hair curling slightly at the ends.

It certainly gained him a lot of attention from potential suitors.

"So this is where you disappear to."

Olivia jumped in surprise as Cassius appeared behind her, climbing the fence to perch on her left. He looked over the training field and his eyes grew in size, an excitable grin sliding onto his face.

She hummed in response and took a bite from her apple.

"Why do you eat out here?"

She scoffed and tried to glare at him, but he didn't see it, still watching the knights in wonderment. "None of your business, Cassius."

He shrugged. His mood didn't dampen, even when she was rude, and obviously didn't want his company.

She resisted the urge to shove him, his constant beam of positivity begging her to lash out. It was unfair that he was older than her and was allowed to be so happy when she wasn't. She resisted, knowing it would only anger Osmond if the boy showed up that afternoon with a broken shoulder. Instead, she lashed out with her words.

"Gods, why can't you just leave me alone?"

Her words didn't have the desired effect she had hoped they would. Instead of growing angry and leaving, or perhaps yelling back at her, his beaming smile slid off his face and he went unnaturally quiet. It felt odd. She hadn't seen him so quiet, so still, since she first laid eyes on him.

She didn't like that look on him.

Chewing her lower lip, she held out her half-eaten apple toward him in a peace offering. Who knew Cassius finally shutting up would be so unsettling? She scrunched up her nose when he took it happily and chewed over the part she had already eaten.

"I've watched them train since I could walk," her cheeks grew warm at the thought of being intentionally kind to Cassius. "Reminds me of when I was a kid. When things were good."

Merek, the eldest knight apart from greying Robard, caught her eye as she looked back over the field. He had been standing closer to them than the others and, judging by the glare on his face, he had heard their conversation.

He laughed, but it seemed to lack mirth. "Don't you have anythin' better to do?"

"Not really," she shook her head. "Watching you flail is entertaining enough."

Cassius laughed, hiding his smile behind the apple as he took another bite.

Merek grinned cruelly and spat so far that droplets landed by her feet. "Jinxflinger."

Her smile dropped and she averted her gaze. Shivers wracked her body as Merek cackled.

Sometimes, she wondered why she watched them anymore. It was foolish to want something so far out of reach. Her dreams of becoming a knight had long faded from the realm of possibility.

"C'mon," she nudged Cassius gently with her boot. "Let's get back to Osmond."

She spotted the grin slide off Renly's face as she jumped off the railing and turned her back, slinking back to the forge with Cassius right behind her.

Chapter Two

A week had passed, and Cassius was growing on her. They weren't friends, exactly. She liked him well enough, but he was naïve, and much too happy.

She tried not to let him under her skin, but she wasn't sure it was working. He just kept smiling at her, as if he were happy to see her each morning. She hated it.

Olivia tried to avoid him as much as possible. It was hard, though. He just kept appearing, all lopsided grins and wild hand gestures, making his presence almost impossible to ignore.

She sighed as she turned away from Cassius, who was playing around with tools she knew he had no idea how to use. Osmond was fretting over the final details of a sword he had been commissioned to make. He hadn't let her touch it since it came into the forge, glaring her into submission every time she so much as looked at the thing. She hadn't seen him this worried over his work in a long time.

With one final polish he lifted the sword and inspected it closely, running his hand down the blade to feel for any inconsistencies. He held it at eye level to ensure every small detail was perfect, turning it in every direction to make sure.

She loved watching him work with such passion. He was so driven for perfection with every order he made that it was almost impossible to guess who the order was for.

Osmond hummed as he placed the sword at the edge of his workbench and dug through a pile of scraps from a box in the corner. Seconds later he appeared holding a beautiful piece of cloth, and very carefully wrapped the sword before he held it out to her.

She looked between him and the sword and back again, not shifting an inch. If the client didn't come to the forge, Osmond was always sure to hand deliver it to them, brimming with pride and a need to know his work was well-received.

No matter what, a delivery never involved Olivia. Everyone knew she worked there, and they were happy to look the other way if they never had to see her, because Osmond's quality was just that good.

Osmond sighed as he held the sword right in front of her face. "Take it."

Olivia scanned Osmond's face carefully, looking for anything out of the ordinary. Fear, maybe, or perhaps nerves so powerful he couldn't bear to look the client in the face. But she saw nothing. Just a tired man, one that was overworked and underappreciated, but nothing unusual.

"Why me?"

"Don't see no-one else," Osmond snorted as he placed the sword in her lap before she could object more.

Olivia cocked her head to the side, regarding the older man with curiosity. "You aren't going to deliver it?"

"Got lots of orders," he shrugged with a smirk. "'m a busy man, Livvy."

She remained silent as the older man walked back to his workbench and pulled out plans for his next project. His back was to her, as if he thought avoiding her eyes would avoid her questions. "But–"

"Besides, you been more lazy than usual." He cut her off with a sharpness to his voice, one that warned her against protesting, that almost begged her to just do as she was told.

Cassius snorted from his corner of the room, where he was working on what looked to be a small knife. It didn't look very well made. "Which is an achievement in itself."

Olivia smiled at the boy, tight-lipped, and raised a finger to flip him off.

"Fine."

She turned back to Osmond, who looked relieved she had finally agreed. It wasn't like she had much of a choice anyway. He looked tense as he rubbed a hand over his tired eyes and stifled a yawn. When was the last time that man slept?

"Where's it headed?"

Osmond avoided her gaze as he looked intently at the plans in front of him. "Sir Nicolas."

She froze at the mention of the knights. It explained why he was so focused on his work the last few days, why he was so intent on keeping everything perfect. There was always the underlying worry that if Renly didn't like the work he had done he would tell his father, and Osmond would have his business run into the ground.

He knew she didn't like the knights, which she was sure was the reason he looked so guilty. He had never asked her to deliver something before. Even just thinking of the knights made her blood boil and her palms sweat, equally nervous and enraged.

"Explains the behaviour," she snapped.

He flinched a little at her harsh words. "Watch it."

He pushed himself back from the workbench and spun around to face her. He seemed truly apologetic for asking such a thing from her, and she immediately felt bad for snapping. "Take Cassius with you."

Olivia tried to object, but one pointed look from Osmond had the words dying in her throat. She knew he was concerned, he always was when it came to her. Perhaps that was why he was sending Cassius with her. He knew the boy couldn't defend her, but having someone else there seemed to deter the more... weak-willed townsfolk from approaching her.

She supposed she should be thankful he was forward-thinking enough to suggest it, but she would rather take her chances with the townsfolk than be trapped showing Cassius around the castle.

She didn't have a leg to stand on though, not really, so she grumbled out an agreeance and stood, holding the sword with one hand as she gathered her things with the other. Cassius was already standing before her as she turned around, beaming from ear to ear. She bit back a groan.

Great.

She turned and left, satisfied to hear Cassius clumsily stumble after her, smirking as she heard him trip over something and have it come crashing to the ground. He was beside her in a matter of seconds, and she assumed he left whatever mess for poor Osmond to clear up.

Cassius beamed at her, but she refused to look his way.

"So, Liv—"

"It's Olivia," She snapped, ducking under an overgrown tree branch that hung over the footpath, smiling to herself as Cassius ran straight into it a moment later.

To his credit, he took her mood in stride. "Olivia, then." He glared at the branch as he scrambled to match her pace, grin still in place despite himself. How he could be so happy in a place like this was beyond her. "How do you know your way around the castle so well? I mean, I know you've lived in Alira all your life, but you don't really see many people just wandering the halls, do you?"

Olivia hummed as she narrowly avoided a nervous-looking servant, precariously balancing a tray of food in one hand, as they entered through the castle doors. The young girl didn't even spare her a glance, just re-balanced her tray and continued on her way.

Cassius didn't give her time to respond before he was pushing for an answer. "Olivia?"

She paused in her stride, stopping in the middle of the corridor, and looked at him. It wasn't often someone asked her about herself with such honest curiosity. Usually, the people who asked just wanted to know the gory details and wanted a reason to hate her more than they already did.

With Cassius, though, his eyes held nothing but sincerity.

She continued to walk, eyes anywhere but on him. "My mother worked in the castle."

"Really?" Cassius asked. "She still work here?"

"Not since I was a kid," she shook her head.

Cassius hummed. "She quit?"

"Something like that."

She barely moved out of the way of a fumbling servant, one who glared at her as she all but pushed past him in an attempt to escape Cassius' questions. She knew bringing him along was a bad idea.

Cassius didn't push, just nodded and kept walking beside her with the same pep in his step. He was looking through the large windows adorning the walls and peering through the rooms with the doors left open, a large grin on his face the entire time. He seemed so much like a little, excitable kid that she couldn't help a small smile as she watched on.

Not that she'd ever admit it.

It took a while, peering into empty rooms and sneaking a look at noon-time festivities, before Olivia finally gave up. She thought she'd be able to track Sir Nicolas down through the old methods she used as a kid whenever she was trying to find Robard, or whenever Renly had snuck off. It seemed the castle had changed a lot since she was last here. That, or the people had.

She rather liked the first thought better.

"Are you lost?" Cassius asked, all curiosity and no malice. He didn't seem to blame her, but he did seem confused.

"I'm not *lost*," Olivia bit back, rubbing the back of her neck in embarrassment. She ducked her head into the closest room, knowing before she opened it that it would be empty, but still disappointed when she was correct. She closed the door with a soft click before looking at Cassius.

"Why don't we ask her?"

Olivia turned to find him approaching a girl. She was around her age if not a bit older, scrubbing at a mark on the floor. She was hunched over, a wooden bucket filled with soapy water sitting to her right, and an old scrubbing brush in her hand, the type to have splinters coming off into your hand. She was on her knees and scrubbing as hard as she could at the mark, but it didn't seem to be making much of a difference.

Cassius reached a hand out to get her attention. The girl flinched, just a little, but enough to make him withdraw his hand with a blush. "I'm sorry, miss. I didn't mean to frighten you."

The girl smiled as she turned. She reached up a hand and tucked the flyaway strands behind her ear. "It's not a problem."

She knew that voice.

The girl was a lot older than Olivia remembered. Granted, Olivia herself was a lot younger at the time too. They hadn't spoken often back then, only in passing, but she seemed nice. Happy. A far cry from the flinching girl she saw before her now, with a smile that barely reached her eyes. Cecily, her name was, the daughter of the cook. The one that would always let her steal the first baked treat of the day, or sneak her a small loaf of bread straight from the oven for her to share with Renly.

Cassius ran a hand through his hair, as if trying to show off his muscles. She giggled at the action, all but melting into a puddle under his gaze. Olivia barely repressed a snort at the events playing out in front of her. Since when was

Cassius interested in anything but his work and being as much of a pain as possible?

"I was wondering if you could help me?" He grinned down at Cecily. "Only if you have time, of course."

Cecily peered up at him through her falling strands of hair, matching his grin with her own. "I have some time."

"Great!" He waved his arm in a lazy gesture toward Olivia, an action Cecily didn't track, still fixated on Cassius. Maybe that's why she hadn't become proper friends with the girl in the first place. "Me and Olivia here were looking for Sir Nicolas. Have you seen him today?"

The bashful, playful demeanour shattered as quickly as it came into being. At the mention of Olivia's name, Cecily turned quickly to face her. Cecily met her eyes and properly flinched, scrambling backwards a few paces until she nudged the bucket, which shook but didn't fall. Not that she was paying it much attention anyway, not with the wide-eyed look of pure *fear* as she locked eyes with Olivia.

She didn't say anything for a long time, seemingly stuck in a trance of horror. Olivia flinched at the unspoken accusation. She broke eye contact quickly, looking anywhere but at the scene playing out before her.

"Miss?" Cassius sounded confused, unsure of the mistake he had made. "Have you seen him? Sir Nicolas?"

Olivia didn't have to see Cecily's face to hear the shaking in her tone, to know the fear that was still there. "I... I think I saw him head to the armoury w-with some knights. I don't know. I'm sorry."

Cecily scurried away, knocking over the bucket as she went. Olivia watched as the water slowly pooled and trailed along the floor, bubbles being left in its wake.

Cassius didn't say anything about Cecily's sudden exit, but she could feel his eyes on her as she turned and left. She understood the fear that the public held, the fear of the unknown, but she *knew* Cecily, and she was still scared enough to run away from her.

They weaved through hallways, avoiding eye contact with anyone they passed, and down a few flights of stairs until they reached the armoury.

Olivia paused outside the door, hovering with a hand half-raised in a knock, but she couldn't bring herself to actually do it.

Cassius noticed her inner turmoil and nudged her out of the way to knock in her place. He opened the dark oak door with a soft creak as a voice called out for them to enter.

Sir Robard sat on a long bench, his Broadsword in his lap as he ran a cloth along its edge. Sir Merek lent against the weapons rack, openly laughing at Sir Nicolas, who was fumbling with a tin of something, which was of obvious amusement to Merek.

Cassius paused as the door reached its full swing, smacking gently against the wall. He shuffled in place, eyes widening, in fright or wonderment, she wasn't sure. She supposed he had never been this close to nobility before.

Robard looked up with a small smile, which grew as he made eye contact with Olivia. He opened his mouth to speak, but closed it again upon noticing Cassius next to her, his grin fading into a confused, polite smile.

Despite everything, Robard had always made sure to keep in touch with her. They used to be close when she was a child, closer than she was with her own father. He made sure that she knew, no matter what, that he wasn't going to let a little sway in public opinion stop him from loving her.

Olivia regained her confidence at seeing Robard and walked toward him, gently nudging Cassius on the way, as if to jolt him back into reality.

"Mornin', Liv," Robard eyed the bundle in her arms. "Brought me a gift?"

"You wish, old man." She turned, trying her best to ignore the glare Merek was sending her way. "It's for you, Sir Nicolas, from Osmond. Said you have been expecting it."

Nicolas abandoned the tin in his hand as he made his way to Olivia in haste, a polite smile turning into a broad grin as he kept his eyes on the bundle in her arms, completely disregarding her in the process. She stifled a laugh at his excitement, knowing he was going to get a talking to once she left about his lack of chivalry.

He halted as he reached her, hands outstretched, as if suddenly remembering the company he was in. He cleared his throat and took a step back, eyes shifting from her arms to her face, his cheeks reddening.

"Thank you, miss."

Nicolas wasn't much older than Cassius and seemed to share his same wonderment of the world. He wasn't like the other knights, who were mostly all hardened and brash, but he was still quite new. He had only joined the knights a few months prior.

He still had the boyish charm about him. Much too eager to prove himself to everyone around him, but too nice to trample others to do so. He had wide, youthful eyes that made him seem entirely too innocent.

She bit the inside of her cheeks to stop any smart retort from spilling, feeling the same warning glare on her as she was sure Nicolas had felt. Instead, she smiled politely and held the weapon in her outstretched arms for Nicolas to take.

He grinned once again, his nervousness about his sudden rudeness dissipating, and all but snatched the weapon from her arms, letting the cloth fall to the floor without much thought.

"Did you work on this yourself, miss Olivia?" He was holding the sword in his palms with all the care in the world.

"Olivia is fine." He smiled gently at the response, eyes reflecting the smile, so unlike the response she usually got from any of the knights. "Osmond wouldn't allow anyone but himself to touch it."

Merek snorted from where he stood at the back of the room. He was eyeing the exchange with a smirk that was jarringly different from the look that Nicolas was giving her, not that she was surprised. Judging by the interactions she had witnessed over the years, she has a sneaking suspicion that Merek had replaced her by Renly's side.

"'Course she didn't touch it. You're old enough to know someone with tainted hands like hers could never make something of quality." He flashed his teeth at her, the whites of them gleaming across the room, and his eyes sparkled with a kind of mirth that made her squirm.

She felt a graze along her arm as Cassius' small frame shifted into her line of sight by her right, his head held high. It was laughable to see the bouncy, overly-excited boy trying to appear threatening against a fully-fledged knight. A knight with muscles on his arm that were bigger than Cassius' head.

She reached out a hand to grab his wrist, tugging softly until Cassius took a step back and deflated. She hadn't taken her eyes off of Merek, who smirked wider at Cassius' actions, as if he had won some unspoken battle against her.

"You mean like the blade you're holding?" Olivia smirked. "The one these tainted hands personally crafted? You seem to like that one well enough."

Robard snorted loudly at the comment, flicking his amused smile at Merek when his face turned a few shades brighter. "Stand down, Merek."

Her attention was drawn back to Nicolas when he gripped tightly on the leather bind of his sword's handle, bringing it closer to inspect it better. He let out a small, gleeful sound at what he saw, grinning boyishly as he eyed the small engraving that Osmond made. The etching of a flame emerged from the binding and wrapped its way around the blade.

He took a few steps back and drew the sword outward from his body, shifting his feet into a combat stance. He waved the sword around a little in his grasp, turning around to face Merek and Robard as he did. "It's well balanced."

Merek scoffed, the tone much lighter than the one he had used on her. "Do you even know the words comin' out of your own mouth?"

Nicolas turned back to Olivia and Cassius, a faint dusting of pink to his cheeks, but a broad smile still on his face. "Thank you both for overseeing its safe passage here. I'm very grateful. Please tell Osmond that I love his work."

Olivia smiled gently at his words. Robard had always encouraged her to speak to Nicolas since his knighthood, and now she understood why.

She prepared herself to respond in kind, scrambling for words that sounded polite enough to exchange with Nicolas, who was obviously struggling with his formality but was trying so damn hard to impress her.

Just as she felt she found the right words, the door behind her burst open.

Renly strode into the room, head held back in a bark of laughter. Sir Maddox trailed behind him, eyes bright with happiness he so obviously felt at causing such a reaction from his prince.

The laughter quickly faded as Renly's gaze fell on Olivia. His gaze flicked from her to Cassius, head cocked to the side in confusion.

"You are?"

A moment or two passed before Olivia looked over at Cassius, who had yet to answer. He was frozen in place, eyes wide and mouth clamped shut. If she had known all it took to get him to shut up was to parade him around the castle she would have done so much earlier.

She nudged her elbow into the flesh on his side, making him jump a little. He turned to her, a dazed-out look still adorning his face, and only turned back to Renly at the pointed look she sent him. He was practically shaking, half bent over in a bow he seemed unsure he was supposed to give. She reached out and clasped his shoulder, pulling gently to get him to stand. She pointedly ignored the look on Renly's face as her hand remained, a grounding action to get Cassius out of his own head.

"I... m-my name is Cassius, Your Highness." He smiled shakily. "I work in the forge under Osmond."

Renly narrowed his eyes. "I haven't seen you around before."

"I moved recently, Your Highness." Cassius was shaking still, a gentle movement she could feel under her hand, but he seemed more coherent with his thoughts. "I haven't been in Alira long."

"Hmm."

He bodily turned away from Cassius, as much of a dismissal as his words would have been, and settled his gaze on her. It was as if his entire demeanour changed the moment their eyes met. He straightened his back and held his head high, as if trying to intimidate her, challenging her to become the stuttering mess that Cassius had reverted into. "And what are *you* doing here, Olivia?"

Her grip on Cassius's shoulder tightened, a subconscious movement, only releasing at the soft hiss of pain he let out. She crossed her arms across her chest and fought to keep a neutral expression on her face. She refused to let him intimidate her.

"Didn't know it was a crime to be in the castle."

The anger practically radiated from Renly, bubbling up inside of him and leaving him leaking at the seams. Olivia knew she shouldn't antagonise him, but he made it so easy.

Before either of them could decide on their next move, Nicolas approached the pair, sword held out toward Renly with a boyish grin, seemingly unaware of the dangerous conversation he had interrupted.

"They came to deliver my new sword! Osmond must have spent an age on this, look at the carvings!"

She couldn't help but think of the slight chance that Renly would take Nicolas' new sword and send it straight through her chest.

"Lad's been droolin' since they came in," Robard grumbled from behind her.

She appreciated Robard's efforts, she really did, but it didn't help. Renly didn't smile and didn't turn his attention on Nicolas, who was so obviously trying not to beg for it. He kept eye contact with her for what felt like hours until his lips curled over his teeth. "You've done your job. Now leave."

Despite expecting it, the dismissal still stung. She remembered a time when Renly would beg to spend time with her, would do anything to make her smile. The rage all but drained out of her.

She looked away from Renly before she let too many of her emotions show. She reached out a hand to grab hold of Cassius' shirt and tugged, dragging him out of the room with her. She didn't chance a look back, couldn't see the satisfactory look she knew to be on Renly's face at how easily she had given in.

Her mother always told her that she wore her heart on her sleeve. It was something she was trying to work on, but she hadn't quite been able to grasp yet. There was nothing more humiliating than for Renly to know how easily his words could affect her.

She clenched her fist, digging her fingernails into the palm of her hand, leaving behind half-crescent moons as she unfurled them. The slight pain grounded her, reminded her that slipping up in a place like this wasn't worth the consequences.

Cassius didn't say a word as they made their way back to the forge. He trailed beside her, silent but never wavering from her side, and she found herself profoundly confused by this boy. He knew she didn't like him, but he still attempted to defend her against royalty in a place he had only just arrived, supporting her when he had no obligation to do so.

The moment they stepped out of the castle walls, she breathed in a deep breath of fresh air. The silence that clung to Cassius didn't last long once they left the castle. The fresh air that calmed Olivia's mood seemed to be the same air that hyped Cassius' up.

"It was pretty exciting to meet the prince!" He chanced a look at her. "Must feel pretty good that he knows you by name."

A small shiver ran down her spine at his words. She was still amazed how quickly Renly could dampen her mood, even when he wasn't around.

Olivia grimaced as she turned away from Cassius. "Don't get your hopes up. Ren isn't as nice as you want him to be."

Cassius cleared his throat, as if trying to defuse the sudden tension that fell over them, but spoiled his attempts with a single word. "Ren?"

She tucked a strand of hair behind her ear with a blush. "Prince Renly."

Cassius snorted, the lilt in his tone teasing. "You called him Ren."

Olivia rolled her eyes as she fell against him, digging her elbow into his side. "Shut up."

She absolutely hated how this boy was starting to grow on her.

CHAPTER THREE

Olivia's palm tingled as she gazed into the fireplace, her arm outstretched toward the warmth of the flames. Her back twinged in pain at her slouched posture, legs criss-crossed on the hard floor underneath, but she paid it no mind.

The flames gently licked upwards off the thick log resting at the bottom of the fireplace. Heat roared off the wood in bounds, making her forget all about the biting winds outside.

Above the log, atop the rising flames, rest the image of a dancer. As Olivia wiggled her fingers, the dancer followed her movements. It raised itself onto the tips of its toes and twirled around, getting lost in the flames for a few moments before leaping back out and continuing the slow dance.

If she concentrated hard enough, she could hear the soft rushing of the river outside the front window. She tried to make the dancer follow the gentle music of the water, but it gets lost in the shifting of the wood in the fireplace, and the sudden whoosh of flames the small movement produced.

Olivia's lips quirked in a fond smile as she gazed at the dancer. She always liked this side of her magic, where she could make something simple, something beautiful, out of something ordinary and mundane.

" ... so the Council voted against me."

Olivia startled, having forgotten her parents were in the room with her, sitting together on the bed behind her. They had been there when Olivia had arrived home, cheeks flushed from the cold, still in a bad mood from seeing Renly earlier. One look at her father's harrowed, worn-down features told her all she needed to know, and so she skirted past the pair to plop herself down in front of the fireplace.

Her mother sighed, "of course they did."

"It's not as though they intend to be ignorant," her father said. "They don't know any better."

"That's why they have you though, isn't it?" Her mother questioned. "So they *do* know better."

She heard her father sigh and the sound of rough scratching, and she could almost see him running a calloused hand through his beard in frustration. "It's fine, Thea."

"It's not fine!" Her mother bit back. She must have heard her tone, because her next words were much gentler. "You're exhausted, William. How many days have you come home looking so drained? I've lost count."

The silence that followed was almost deafening, the only sound coming from the crackling of the flames. The silence was heavy, as if there was something unspoken hanging in the air between her parents, something Olivia herself wasn't privy to. She wasn't sure she wanted to find out what it was.

"You know about the growing concerns, Thea. People are scared of a magical attack. When people are scared they get desperate." He huffed. "Ironic that I'm the only one they trust on the matter but they hardly listen to my words, isn't it?"

An attack? A *magical* attack? On Alira?

She turned away from the fire, letting the dancer drown in the flames. Her father was already looking at her when she met his gaze. She couldn't decipher the look he held but she could feel the energy radiating from him. The exhaustion, the desperation, was almost tangible. There was something else too, something darker that she couldn't place.

"William!" Her mother hissed. "You shouldn't be discussing these things in front of Olivia. You know that."

He held Olivia's gaze for a few more moments before he blinked and turned to face her mother. She could no longer sense his emotions, but his shoulders tensed, as if he were readying himself for a fight.

"She's 17, Thea. She's old enough." He looked back at Olivia with a calculating gaze. "The rumblings are getting louder and she can't ignore the growing threat they will bring."

Olivia turned back to the fire, but didn't make another attempt to make anything appear from the flames. She ignored the whispering behind her, the gentle creak of the bed and the sharp closing of the front door.

If what her father spoke of was true, she was in for a world of trouble. She had a tentative grasp on her magic, and she didn't know any sort of magic that would be helpful in the event of an attack.

How had she not heard of any of this before? It was obvious her father had been discussing it with the King and his council for a while.

"Livvy, darling? Are you okay?"

She was out the door before she even realised she had stood, desperate to avoid her mother's questioning. She loved her mother, she truly did, but she just didn't understand. Not for lack of trying, though. She tried so hard to understand magic, to grasp the intensity and the reality of it all, but she didn't have the same hum under her skin, didn't feel the same warmth through her veins. She didn't know what it was like to be looked down on, spat on, simply for being born.

The wind howled as she walked, whooshing in her ear and causing the hairs on her arm to stand on end. Shivering, she hunched her shoulders and stuffed her hand in the pockets of her coat, burrowing her chin as far into the warmth as she could.

The air fogged in front of her as she choked on a laugh. If she had been thinking, she wouldn't have left the warmth of her home in the first place. It was what her father always did, storm out of the house in a huff to avoid a fight with her mother. Maybe she was more like him than she thought. More like him than she wanted to be.

Walking around Alira once it got dark was something she has come to cherish in the years since the fire. She always loved the city, with its cobblestone streets and imposing buildings lining the paths. Once night fell upon the city, its people abandoned the streets in search for somewhere warmer, hauled up in their homes or the tavern until the light filtered through the windows once more. When the people were gone, Alira was more like the place she remembered, the one she had once loved. It was once more the place that left her thinking she could be whatever she wanted to be.

Olivia continued to walk until her legs burned and her breathing became ragged. She sighed and took in her surroundings, gaze landing on the tree just off the side of the training fields. It would make a good place to rest a few minutes, just until she could feel her legs again, before she made her way back home. Hopefully her father had already returned and would be fast asleep by the time she made it back.

She sat with a dull thud, feeling the dew on the grass slowly seep through her pants, but she paid it no mind. She stretched out, the back of her head hitting the trunk of the tree with a thunk as she closed her eyes, relishing in the soft breeze that played with the ends of her hair.

The darkness she was met with when she opened her eyes slid a smile onto her lips, and had warmth spread under her skin. The conversation with her father slowly slid to the back of her mind as she watched the flames from the street lamps dance around in their glass boxes.

The leaves on the branches above her head rustled with the arrival of stronger winds, leaving Olivia shaking. She looked up and saw the half-crested moon high in the sky. It was later than she expected it to be. She always seemed to lose track of time when she was running from her thoughts.

Heaving a sigh, she pushed herself up from the grass. She shook her legs a few times to get the blood flowing again and started the trek back home.

She hadn't made it very far when she heard shuffling on the cobblestone street behind her. Her skin prickled as her body went into high alert. She walked faster, suddenly wanting nothing more than the warmth of her fireplace and the soft comfort of her bed.

She rounded the corner a few streets from her home when she slid to a halt. Two men, dressed all in black, stood blocking the path. The footsteps behind her grew to a stop too, and she wasn't surprised to find two more men standing behind her as she turned. She was in the middle of town, houses lining the streets to either side, effectively blocking any chance of escape.

Great.

"Well, if it isn't little miss Shaw." The man on the left sneered.

The one beside him laughed, "don't you know it's dangerous to wander by yourself at night?"

Olivia shivered as the laugh rang through her ears, the danger it promised evident. "I - I was j-just–"

"Y-you were j-just," someone spoke directly against her ear, the teasing tone being cut off by the man's own laughter. "Just what? Hmm?"

She felt a soft pressure against her back as the ghost of a breath tickled her ear. She didn't dare look back, but the glinting smiles of the men in front of her told her all she needed to know. She felt fingers flit across her hip and she couldn't help but shiver at the cold contact.

The man let out a low laugh directly into her ear, "you like that, huh?"

The men in front of her took a few steps forward until she could see their faces under the streetlamp. She didn't recognise the man on the right, the one that towered over the others. He has a sharp glint to his eye, as if he were enjoying the show set out in front of him.

The man on the left, however, she did recognise. She didn't know his name, but she remembered the dark curls sticking to his forehead. She remembered his stocky build and the way he could put away beer after beer in the tavern without getting tipsy. She remembered once being impressed with him.

He chuckled before he lent forwards and spat. She watched as it flew through the air and landed mere centimetres in front of her boot.

She could smell the alcohol on his breath as he spat the next words into her face. "Jinxflinger."

Before she could fight back – or, more likely, cower at their words and beg they let her go – she heard more footsteps in the distance.

More of their friends? Civilians who would walk right past them and avoid her pleading gaze? Both scenarios had happened a few times in the passing years and she didn't know which was worse, didn't know if one even was worse than the other.

She let out a sigh of relief when she saw the glint of a crest under the street-lamp. No matter how much the knights hated her, they never let anything bad happen to her if they could help it. Something about having to uphold their chivalrous code, probably.

"Hey!"

Her shoulders tensed as she recognised the voice. With a few more quickened paces, Renly swam into her view, only just visible over the curly-haired man's shoulder. He was just as likely to be there to join in the fight than he was to break it up. It was only once the men in front of her took a step back, turning to see who their intruder was, that she spotted Nicolas standing by Renly's side.

"Prince Renly," Curly stood to attention. "I didn't expect to see you out so late."

"Evidently." Renly peered around the two men in front of him to look at Olivia, searching for something in her gaze she couldn't place. Without saying a word to her, he looked over her shoulder at the man she could still feel plastered to her back. "Would you mind stepping away from her?"

The pressure was immediately gone, and she felt like she could breathe for the first time since the men arrived.

Renly hummed and flicked his attention back to Olivia. He didn't look her in the eye again, instead he inspected her body, as if searching for any injuries she may have obtained. Once he deemed her fine enough, his attention turned on the taller man in front of her. "You should leave now. All of you."

"But–"

"I said leave." His gaze landed on Curly with such intensity that even Olivia flinched back at the severity of it, the anger seeping off of him in waves. It was only when his hand moved toward the sword on his hip that the men made any move to leave.

Before they left she could feel breath against her ear once more, the whispered threat that followed sounding more like a promise than anything else. "You won't get so lucky next time, Jinxflinger."

She heard his retreating footsteps a moment later, and it was only when she turned to watch the men disappear from sight that she allowed herself to relax.

"You okay, Olivia?"

She turned and found a gentle, concerned look on Nicolas' face. "I'm okay, Sir Nicolas. Thank you."

His posture slumped and relief crossed his face, as if he hadn't truly believed in her safety until he heard her say it. He was much too nice to be a knight, she thought idly. Much too good to be around the knights he was stuck with.

Renly seemed angry still, but his gaze was fully focused on her, as if he were angry with her for getting ambushed. Before she could defend herself, before she could even think about why she even needed an excuse for what happened, he shook his head at her with a scoff.

"You know you shouldn't be out here this late."

"Ren–"

"Go home, Olivia."

The dismissive tone hurt more than the words that came with it did. He didn't even care that she was almost beaten up by those men, or worse. He didn't even offer to walk her home, to make sure she made it there safely. It wasn't that long ago when he would wrap her in a bundle of blankets and force her to spend the night with him in the castle if anything even remotely like this had happened to her.

With that said, he walked away, almost bumping his shoulder against hers as he passed.

She mustered up a comforting smile as she saw the unease in Nicolas' features. Renly may be rough with her, but he was a good leader, and she didn't want to know what would happen to Nicolas if he started to doubt him.

"Goodnight, Nicolas."

She walked past him, lingering a moment to rest a hand on his shoulder, before she continued down the path.

CHAPTER FOUR

The rumblings her father spoke of spread quickly.

She passed a few people on her way to the forge the following morning. They all stared at her with a little more anger than their usual distaste. She heard them whisper about attacks and threats, but she wasn't entirely sure what was truthful and what was gossip born from fear.

Osmond must have heard his share of the news, as she only spent the morning in the forge before he told her to take the afternoon off. He would never usually allow her to leave so early, claiming he had too much work for her to ignore her duties and run amok instead, so she's positive he must have heard something.

She found herself at the training grounds, as she always seemed to, even though she was too early for any of the knights to be around. There was something about that place that gave her comfort, a feeling of safety that she didn't often feel these days.

Her peace didn't last long. She didn't know why she expected it to.

She heard chatter in the distance, coming from the side entrance of the castle. Someone let out a snort and a loud, high-pitched laugh. Robard appeared with Sir Nicolas hot on his heels, the younger carrying an armful of training weapons as he tried not to trip over his own feet.

They didn't seem to notice her sitting on the fence. If they did, they ignored her. It wasn't unusual. If she was there before the knights started training, they wouldn't even spare her a glance as they went about their duties.

This time, no other knights trickled out after the pair.

Nicolas unloaded the training weapons onto a table, spilling from his arms in a messy heap. Where Renly would have demanded they all be neat and presentable for appearance's sake, Robard just told Nicolas to pick one up, getting one for himself in the process and leaving the others where they lay.

It wasn't long before she heard the familiar sounds of wood hitting wood, of sudden yelps of pain and a sharp retort to *"move faster"* or *"strike quicker"*. Nicolas flailed under Robard's harder strikes, and fell to his quicker movements. He stood just as quickly as he fell though, and it was a testament to his training that he simply rubbed at his aching spots and went straight back to it.

It brought back memories of when she was a child, running around the grounds with Renly as Robard tried desperately to teach them the knightly ways of fighting. She remembered bruised skin from being too distracted to block a strike, and Osmond scolding them through a fond smile. She remembered Ren's beaming face when he finally beat her to the ground, hard enough for her to tap out...

Renly, she sharply reminded herself. He hadn't been Ren for a long time.

She pulled herself back into the present to find Robard watching her with a raised brow, Nicolas panting beside him with his hands on his knees, groaning about being bested by an old man.

He watched her for a few moments before he decided to approach. The moment Robard turned his back, Nicolas collapsed onto the ground, panting.

Robard stopped beside her, resting his back against the fence as he looked out over the training fields. He was silent for a while, but he was standing so close to her that his arm brushed against her leg every time he moved.

"Remember when you were like that?" He gestured over at Nicolas, who had just managed to pull himself up into a sitting position before collapsing onto his back again, groaning. "Half his age but you'd run 'round like you were possessed, you and Ren tuggin' at my arm to teach you more." He paused to let out a soft chuckle. "Not that your mother's were very impressed, comin' back all dirty and bruised."

She grimaced at the mention of Renly. It irked her that he was still Ren to him. She shook the thought – it was something stupid to be jealous about. "Robard–"

The elder looked up at her then, a concerned frown pulling at his lips. "Been hearing rumblings lately. Little things, 'bout–"

"Magical attacks?" Robard raised his brow at her interruption, but simply nodded in response. "There's a lot of those rumblings going around, it seems. Scaring a lot of people."

He hummed as he turned away from her. "You gotta be careful, Olivia. Watch your back." He waved a hand in the general direction of the castle. "I'll do what I can, but Ren's been high-strung lately."

She glanced back down at Robard and felt warmth bloom inside of her. He was like her second father to her, always had been, and she knew he didn't stop caring for her after everything that happened, but she was always pleasantly surprised when he spoke so freely of his care for her.

Robard tapped his fingers against the railing as he looked around the training yard, flitting his gaze to the castle entrance and to the path behind them. He was always vigilant, always seemed to be on guard, especially around her. It seemed as though he was looking for someone through. Or, rather, the lack of someone's presence.

Eventually, he looked back at her and offered his hand. "Follow me."

She took his hand and jumped down without a second thought. Who was she to question him? So much had changed in her life, but Robard never had.

He dropped her hand and led her toward Nicolas, who was clambering onto his feet the moment that he spotted the pair. She stopped in front of him just as he brushed the last of the dirt from his pants.

She bit back a smirk as she bowed to him. "Sir Nicolas."

He blushed, smiling nervously. "It's good to see you again, Olivia."

Robard snorted at the stifled interaction as he took a few steps away from them. He leaned over to rummage through something on the table, his back turned to her. Before she had the chance to ponder what he was looking for, he turned to face her again, a wooden training sword in hand.

He smirked as he threw the sword at her, not waiting to see if she caught it before turning to face Nicolas. She's glad he did, so he didn't have to watch as she fumbled with it, having to jerk her head out of the way to avoid the hilt hitting her in the cheekbone.

That would have been embarrassing.

Robard waved a hand in Olivia's general direction as he approached the pair again. "Spar."

Nicolas sputtered, eyes growing wide as he looked between Olivia and Robard. "Is this some sort of chivalry test?"

"I'd be surprised if you can lay a hand on her." He crossed his arms over his chest and raised a brow. "Prove me wrong."

Olivia looked down at the sword in her hand and didn't move, no matter how much every fibre of her being wanted to instantly follow Robard's command. It would be the first time she trained with someone like this in years. It was distantly familiar, the foggy memory of childhood not clear enough for her to grasp.

What if she hurt him? What if she failed and disappointed Robard?

Robard clapped her on the shoulder hard, grounding her. She turned to look up at him, only to find him frowning down at her. "Just let your trainin' take over. I got faith."

She nodded, warming at his words, before she turned to face Nicolas. She couldn't help the smile that took over at how utterly terrified he still looked.

"No magic, Liv." Robard laughed. "You'll scare the poor lad to death."

She didn't strike hard. Her movements felt stifled, unpractised. Nicolas deflected her strikes easily but didn't go on the offensive, his features still unsure and apprehensive. She knew she could fight harder, fight stronger, if she just let her training take over, just like Robard had said. If she surrendered herself to what she already knew, Nicolas wouldn't be able to put up much of a fight.

Even if she wanted to, she knew it wouldn't be the smart thing to do. She knew what would happen to her if she got too carried away and Nicolas ended up getting hurt.

She landed with a *thud* on the ground, stomach stinging from the sharp jab that Nicolas managed to land. She rubbed at the spot idly and cursed herself. She only meant for him to win, to land a finishing blow so Robard would finally call it. She didn't mean for him to land something so sharp in the spot between her ribs.

Robard sighed heavily, and she felt a prickle of shame run through her. In her efforts to save Nicolas' face, she had insulted Robard's training, inadvertently proving to him that she wasn't worthy of his teachings. She chanced a look up, only to find no anger or regret on his face.

"Get up, Liv." She did as he commanded, wincing a little at the sting as she stood.

She avoided looking over at Nicolas, as she could practically feel his guilt. Instead, she focused on Robard, who was rubbing at his face with a deep sigh. He dropped his hand and gave her a look, one that dared her to question him.

"Stop holdin' back. It's *me* watchin'. Not the prince, not the king, not your father." She shrunk back at how easy he could still read her. "I know you haven't practised, but I know you're better than this."

The next round she beat Nicolas, but not easily. Robard's faith pushed her forwards, and she slowly let her training take over. It was hard work. She hadn't fought in years, and Nicolas was training almost every single day, but she was still strong. She knew she had more inside of her, knew she was more than just some girl with magic, and in this moment she was damned if she was going to let Renly, or her father, or anyone else take that away from her.

Nicolas landed on the ground harshly, panting against the dirt as he rubbed idly at his chest, where she delivered her final blow. She sighed heavily. She knew she should have been able to do better, knew she was able to do better when she was training as a kid.

She avoided Robard's eye as she reached down to help Nicolas stand. "Sorry, Robard. I know I can do better."

"Better?" Nicolas took her hand gratefully and stood, a beaming grin plastered on his face, despite one hand still rubbing at his chest. "That was amazing! Why aren't you a knight? Or a guard, at the very least? What are you doing hiding away in the forge?"

She frowned as she dropped his hand and took a step back. His words were innocent, and she knew he didn't intend to cause any harm, but she felt something sour coil in her gut. She should have been a knight by now, if what Renly swore to her as children was supposed to hold any sort of value. They were all empty promises.

"You should ask your dear prince that question."

She turned to face away from Nicolas, only to be faced with a sharp look from Robard as he approached.

"Watch yourself." He picked up the sword she had dropped during her fight and held it out for her to take. "I'm impressed, considerin' how long its been since you last trained."

He turned away from her and approached a blushing Nicolas with a smirk. "Don't be ashamed, lad. She's a lot tougher than she looks."

Nicolas grumbled something she couldn't quite catch, but made Robard laugh heartily.

"Teach him some techniques. *Slowly*." Robard waved her closer to the pair. She raised a questioning brow at the request, but he crossed his arms across his chest again. "I want to know how much of my trainin' you still remember."

Nicolas looked between them, confused at the exchange, but didn't say anything. He just kept smiling at her with this dumb hopeful grin that reminded her entirely too much of Cassius. Nicolas was not much older than her, and he still had this sweetness about him, something soft and youthful that hadn't been washed away from battles and conflicts, from any kind of proper service. When he smiled like that... Gods, it was like she was staring straight at the sun. The corners of his eyes crinkled with the force of it.

She did exactly as Robard told her to. One look at Nicolas, shaking slightly as he gripped the handle of his sword tightly, with such a determined look on his face, had her caving.

Robard worked hard with her when she was a child. He didn't have to help her, could have easily sent her running from the fields and no-one would have cared, but he made sure to take the time to carefully teach her. He was determined to make her stronger and braver, to mould her into a fighter who wouldn't need anyone else's protection, simply because she wanted him to. It was about time she paid him back.

If she could help Nicolas in any way, for Robard, she would do it.

It didn't turn out to be as much of a chore as she thought it would. Robard interjected a few times, adjusting either one of their stances before allowing them to continue. The young knight was kind, laughing at her mistakes and groaning good-naturedly when he was tossed to the ground at one of her well-aimed blows. It was almost like sparring with a friend.

She came out of training a few hours later, the back of her shirt damp and her hair sticking to her forehead with sweat, but her mind was a lot clearer than it had been in weeks. She found a new friend in the form of Nicolas, who swore not to tell Renly about what they were doing if she promised to come back and spar with him again sometime.

Olivia strolled back into the forge with a spring in her step and a smile clinging to her lips. Osmond looked up as she waltzed through the door, brow raised at her sudden change of mood, but didn't say anything. He smiled fondly as she perched on the bench beside Cassius and refused to do any work as she watched him.

Osmond shook his head fondly and threw a chisel in her direction.

"Get to work."

CHAPTER FIVE

Things seemed relatively normal over the next few days. Other than a few glances, no-one seemed to bother her.

Olivia had made sure to train with Nicolas and Robard every day since, and a lot of her training as a kid came back to her easily. Nicolas held himself well, being beaten so ruthlessly by a girl he barely knew.

Osmond seemed pretty pleased with her new arrangement, even if it meant she had to take a few hours off work to attend training. Apparently it had made her more tolerable, and less argumentative to actually do her job.

Much to Osmond's annoyance, however, Olivia had managed to injure herself during her latest training. She had let Nicolas get a hit in, but tripped over some uneven ground and somehow twisted her ankle. It hadn't hurt badly, not after her father fixed her up once she arrived home that evening, but the phantom pain was hard to shake.

She had taken to resting her leg as she perched on the workbench by Cassius, dragging him into whatever insignificant topic that popped into his head at any given moment. She poked and prodded at him even as he worked, trying to waste as much time as possible until Osmond finally had enough and either put her to work or kicked her out.

Cassius was pleased to have her undivided attention for the first time since they met, but Osmond's annoyance was almost palpable from the other end of the room.

His decision was made for him when the doors to the forge burst open to reveal a small boy, about half her age. His hair was wild and he was puffing slightly, as if he had run all the way there.

"You alright, lad?" Osmond quirked his lips at the boy's haggard appearance.

He bowed towards Osmond when he finally had control over his breathing. "His Majesty The King requests an audience with Olivia Shaw."

The kid didn't look over at her as he spoke, although his gaze did drift towards Cassius, who stood to her right. He snapped his gaze back to Osmond as soon as Olivia shifted to slide off the table. It was definitely not something that she expected on such a sunny, normal morning. The king usually preferred to pretend that she didn't exist at all.

Osmond seemed to think it an odd request too, as he frowned in confusion, but waved Olivia over anyway. "Away with you. You're no help today anyway."

Olivia snorted as she slid past Cassius with a grin, "You love me though."

"Hmph." Osmond shoved at her shoulder as she got closer. "Get out."

She laughed as she followed the kid back to the castle. He didn't look back at her once, his shoulders tensed and his back ram-rod straight. She's sure she hasn't seen him around Alira before, but she wasn't that surprised he was afraid of her. Rumours of her flew about the city so quickly she could hardly keep up.

One of the guards standing outside the great hall pushed open the heavy oak doors as she arrived, gaze boring into her as he did. The boy scampered off the moment he saw her delivered safely to the king.

To her credit, she only stumbled a little as she entered, only to find the hall filled with important people – her father, the king and queen, even the king's entire council. Renly was there too, standing in the middle of the room with his back to her, facing them all. She hadn't been summoned in front of this many people in years.

"Ah, Olivia." She bowed deeply to King Alroy as she approached, standing a respectable distance away from Renly. "Glad you finally decided to show."

She bit her tongue to avoid snapping back like she wanted to, and winced at the metallic taste. Her father gave her a warning look before he turned away from her.

A man from the council, one with a round belly and thin-rimmed glasses, hair balding and a scowl on his face, turned to face the king. "Now that everyone is present, may we begin?"

King Alroy nodded as he turned to face both herself and Renly. "I'm sure you've both heard the rumours of magical attacks that have been circulating lately."

Renly nodded, "I've heard rumblings among the townsfolk on my patrols."

"It's more than rumblings, Renly." The king sighed as he ran a hand over his face. He seemed tired, as if he had been worrying for days. It would explain why her father had been more absent than usual. "I've received concerns of an upcoming attack in a village a few days' ride from here. You and your knights will go make sure that attack doesn't happen." He flicked his gaze over to face Olivia. "Olivia will go with you as protection."

She felt Renly glare at her as she lifted her gaze to stare at her father. He avoided looking at her, almost as if he had known about this plan or. It would have been nice to have some warning.

"Father, I don't think that's necessary." Renly let out a groan. "Another person to look after is just going to slow us down." He turned his glare back on her. "Having *Olivia* is going to be nothing but a hindrance."

She winced as he spat her name out like a curse, like even the suggestion of having her with them was laughable.

"Renly!" Queen Raina gaped at him, her tone scolding. "Be quiet until you suddenly find your chivalrous code. It's not up for discussion."

Renly huffed, knowing nothing he could say was going to make much of a difference in their decision. He grit his teeth as he spoke, and she could sense the anger he was radiating, even if she didn't have a clear view of his face. "When do we leave?"

"Best to do it sooner rather than later." The king frowned. "You leave within the hour. Gather your men and ready your horses."

Renly gave a messy bow and stormed out of the room, knocking hard into Olivia's shoulder as he passed.

She rubbed at her shoulder and turned to her father. Why hadn't he told her? This decision had obviously been spoken about frequently. She knew the King wouldn't dare send her out with his son if he had any other choice, and he wasn't about to risk his own court mage to investigate.

"Why didn't you tell me?"

"You didn't need to know."

Queen Raina shifted in her seat, demanding attention. Olivia obliged, and a warmth filled her heart when she saw the motherly look that the queen sent her. Even after everything, she had never dismissed her like the others. "Pack warm for the journey, Olivia. Stay safe."

She smiled, only a small upturn of her lips, at her concern. "I will, Your Majesty." She turned to face the room as a whole, bowing as she settled on King Alroy. "I will keep your son safe."

She left before anyone could say any more. She jumped as the doors opened for her, only to find Renly waiting on the other side. He leant up against the wall with something akin to a pout. He looked up when he heard the doors open, and his pout quickly turned to anger, making her flinch at the intensity.

"If it were up to me, you wouldn't be coming at all." He took a step toward her, crowding her as she slowly backed away. Her back hit the brick wall, the harshness sending a twinge down her spine. "If you slow us down, if you're *anything* but helpful..." He smirked as he leaned forwards, one hand on the wall beside her head, and whispered in her ear. "I *will* leave you behind."

The comment stung, and she shivered at his words. She was sharply reminded of a long time ago, back when they were best friends, making promises to each other that they swore to keep no matter what. They were happier then, she supposed, and Renly had a lot less on his shoulders.

His gaze flicked between her and the wall behind her, and he frowned as he withdrew his hand. He seemed skittish, almost scared, as he turned to stride up the staircase, no doubt towards his chambers.

She didn't go back to Osmond and Cassius after her interaction with Renly, instead heading straight home. She wanted to see them, but it would be harder to leave if she did. She knew that having a taste of companionship, of friendly interaction, before leaving for a few days with the knights was just going to remind her how much she didn't want to go.

Her mother was still at home when Olivia arrived, not having left for work at the tavern yet. She smiled as she watched her mother flit around the room, humming under her breath. She was packing things into a saddle bag sitting by the fireplace.

Her mother glanced up as a strong wind blew, knocking the open door against the wall. She smiled gently at Olivia before she turned back to rearrange what she had packed in the saddle bag.

"Close the door will you, my darling?"

Olivia did as she was asked, taking a couple of steps into the room so she could shut the door behind her. She watched her mother cram a bulge wrapped securely in a red-and-white chequered cloth on top of a large waterskin, before she closed the bag securely and handed it to Olivia with a soft smile.

Before she had the chance to question it, she drew Olivia into a tight hug, lasting only a few moments before she pulled back. Her hands were still on her shoulders as she held her daughter's gaze.

She raised one hand to gently cup her cheek. "You'll be okay, my darling." Olivia closed her eyes and leaned into her touch. "Renly will be there to protect you."

Olivia laughed as she shook her head and averted her gaze.

Her mother gripped her cheeks with both hands and forced Olivia to look back at her. "Renly's not a bad man, Livvy. He's just confused. He still cares about you, and he will never let anything bad happen to you. Not if he can help it."

Olivia smiled sadly at her words, but decided not to tell her mother any different. She didn't see the need to mention Renly's last words to her in the hall. Her mother didn't need that sort of anxiety before she left. Olivia was frightened enough over his words as it was.

She was going on the mission to protect Renly, to protect all of the knights, against an unknown threat that no-one knew to be true. What if they did happen to run into magical trouble? It would be entirely down to Olivia to protect everyone there, to defend the Kingdom, to defend her people...The fear began to rise in her throat, choking her.

"What if I'm not good enough?" She asked her mother. "What if something happens and I can't save them? What if I fail?"

Her mother tuts and draws her in for a long, lingering embrace. She held her there as she ran her fingers through her daughter's hair, shushing her. "I believe in you, Olivia."

"You should go before they leave without you."She withdrew from the hug, holding Olivia outstretched from her body. She gave her a soft smile, squeezing her shoulder once before dropping her hands. "Shadow is already waiting for you at the stables."

She took the bag with a forced smile and walked out the door without a backwards glance. If she lingered any longer, she would never be able to convince herself to leave.

Gods, this wasn't going to end well.

Chapter Six

Most of the knights were already gathered by the time she made her way to the stables.

Renly frowned as she approached, "nice of you to finally join us."

Merek snorted loudly from Renly's side, sharing an amused eye-roll with the prince before turning his attention back to Maddox.

She shook off their words and fetched her horse from the stables. She was already saddled and ready to go, no doubt her mother's doing. Shadow had belonged to her since before the fire, and she usually remained in the stables by her home, along with her father's horse.

Olivia double checked that everything was in its right place before she attached her saddle bag. She didn't trust any of these idiots not to have tampered with Shadow, even though she's positive that she would have kicked them if they had tried anything. It was better to be safe than sorry.

She whirled around at the sound of a yelp, only to find Nicolas fumbling over his own feet as he rushed to the stables, much to the delight of the others.

He hunched over as he reached them, hands on his knees as he drew in harsh breaths. He must have run all the way from his chambers.

"Sorry, I was—" Nicolas drew in another sharp breath, sputtering as he inhaled.

Renly laughed loudly, the corners of his mouth quirked in amusement. "Packing, were you?"

Nicolas nodded, drawing in one final, long breath before standing upright. She could see the sweat forming on his brow, from the heat of the late morning or the exercise she wasn't sure.

"What could have taken you so long to pack? Did you take your entire wardrobe with you?" Maddox snorted as he pointed at the bag slung low on his shoulder, overpacked and bursting at the seams. "Look! It's going to combust!"

The other knights laughed as they continued to poke fun at Nicolas, and Olivia was about to jump to his defence before she saw it. He was blushing as he turned away from their jibes, but he was smiling, just slightly, as if he were actually enjoying the teasing. She couldn't help the sharp jolt of jealousy she felt as the teasing dialled down to friendly banter.

She watched as Nicolas struggled to get his horse ready, smiling softly as his saddlebag fell twice before he managed to secure it properly. She bit back a laugh as he tried to mount his horse, only for the heel of his boot to get stuck in the stirrup.

Looking back at the others, she saw them climbing onto their own horses with ease, not paying their youngest any attention.

Olivia approached an obviously struggling Nicolas, laughing softly enough for only the both of them to hear. "You're gonna twist your ankle like that, you fool."

"No shit," Nicolas huffed as he turned to Olivia with a pout. "Help me?"

She wasn't about to let him suffer, and his pout was strangely endearing, so she easily obliged. She nudged his foot out of the stirrup, corrected his positioning and shoved the reins in his hand as she hoisted him up. He let out a yelp, righting himself just in time so he didn't slip and fall down the opposite side.

Nicolas shifted until he was upright and looked down at her with a blinding grin, one that made her blush and look away. "Thank you, Liv."

She mounted her own horse and took off after the group that were slowly fleeing into the forest. She dutifully ignored Robard's smirk as she rode past him.

Olivia was quiet during the first day's trek. She wasn't spoken to, not that she minded. The knights were all teasing each other, babbling about whatever came to mind, or giving Nicolas a hard time. None of them were paying much attention to their surroundings.

She kept herself on guard as they ventured further into the woods. The knights weren't taking the threat very seriously, if the amount of noise they were making was anything to go by. Even if the magical threats were just rumours, the woods still held hunters and bandits, people who wouldn't hesitate to rob them no matter who they were.

Perhaps it was just the way she was brought up, always taught to keep on her toes, no matter the safety she thought she was in. She was surprised that these men, these protectors of Alira, weren't the same. Renly was on alert, but only enough to point out passing rabbits for Arley to shoot, too focused on their food to be truly on guard. Arley was quiet too, but he flushed every time the others congratulated him on his sharpshooting, riding too high on their compliments to care.

They only stopped riding once the sun began to set. She didn't know how far they were from where they needed to be, but she couldn't feel any magic around her, so she was sure they were relatively safe.

She groaned as she stretched until her limbs didn't feel quite as stiff, her back popping as she dismounted. The ride wasn't that long, but she was used to walking, so the journey had caused her legs to seize until it hurt simply to stand.

She watched in amusement as Nicolas slowed his horse to a stop, looking well out of his comfort zone, and all but fell out of his saddle. She swore that even his horse was laughing at him.

Renly dismounted with practised ease, handing off the reins to his servant. "We'll camp here tonight. Peter, get things ready for some food and build a fire. Olivia, take the horses and tie them up." He turned to face her with a smirk. "Make sure they don't escape, will you?"

"I'm not your servant, Renly." She barely held back an eyeroll.

He gave her a cold, steely glare at her objection. It almost made her shrink back from the force of it, reminding her painfully of their conversation earlier that day. "Are you refusing an order from your prince?"

Olivia held his gaze, despite how much her legs were shaking, and every fibre of her body screaming *danger*. She knew she shouldn't push things, but he made it so easy to fight against.

She sighed, tearing her eyes away from Renly as she held her hand out to take the reins of Renly's horse from Peter.

Nicholas frowned and took a step forwards, opening his mouth as if to object, but she caught his gaze and shook her head sharply, stopping him before he could do something stupid. He shut his mouth with a click, almost pouting as she left, but he didn't comment like he obviously wanted to. He was still new, still needed to really earn the respect from the other knights, and standing up for the one person that Renly hated was a terrible way to do that.

She walked the horses to the edge of where they made camp, by the treeline of their perimeter. Far enough away that Renly and the others wouldn't complain, but close enough that they could watch over them during the night in case someone came to steal them, or worse.

She could feel Peter's glare on her as she tied them up. He was collecting firewood just past the treeline, but he never said anything. She had the feeling that he hated her, but she had no idea why. They hadn't properly met before today, but the hatred he seemed to hold so strongly behind his gaze made her hesitant to find the reason why. Perhaps it was Renly or Merek that influenced him with tall tales about her. Peter was around them enough for it to have at least made him wonder, if not convinced him entirely.

Peter hurried past her and back to the campsite, arms almost overflowing with firewood. He quickly built up a fire before he began to ready the meat that Arley had caught on their ride there.

She turned back to the horses and absentmindedly ran her hands through the manes of the closest ones. She briefly wondered if they had names, if the knights had ever bothered to give them some, to look after them. She knew they probably didn't. Not like she took care of Shadow.

Closing her eyes, she concentrated on the forest surrounding them. She relished in the feeling of innocent wildlife, the happiness radiating off the knights in the clearing behind her, the calmness of the horses. She could hear the gentle flow of a creek nearby, and the wildlife that were there too. She couldn't hear any danger, couldn't sense any other magic apart from her own. As far as she could tell, they were safe.

Renly had, annoyingly, chosen a pretty good spot to rest.

When she opened her eyes again, she saw Peter dishing out the food to the hungry knights. She must have lost time, being in the comfortable companionship of the horses. She took a few moments before approaching for her own dish, for what little remained in the bottom of the pot after Peter took his own serving.

Renly stared, and after a few moments of eye contact, he turned to the pot and poured the rest of the food into his own bowl. "Looks like you were too slow, Olivia. I'm sure you can magic something up though, right?"

She scowled and glared at the prince. He knew very well that wasn't how her magic worked, he had been present when her father had explained it to the court, to the entire royal family, that first time after the fire.

She turned back to the horses and settled in against the trunk by Shadow. Reaching into her saddlebag, she gently lifted the chequered cloth that her mother had packed for her. She grinned as she unwrapped it to find freshly baked bread, still warm from being wrapped so tightly. She must have made it for her while Olivia had been busy in the forge.

She was suddenly grateful to be sitting so far from the others. The bread seemed much better than whatever rabbit stew Peter had managed to cook up. Besides, the company of the horses seemed to be far superior than the company of the knights.

The loneliness didn't last long.

After eating half of her bread, she wrapped up the remnants, not willing to waste her food so early on in the trek. She didn't look up at the sound of footsteps approaching, not in the mood for dealing with more teasing, until whoever it was cleared their throat. She glanced up to find Nicolas smiling unsurely, holding his bowl out to her. There was a decent amount left at the bottom, the spoon was wiped clean and resting on top.

Was he wanting her to clean his dirty dishes, to bully her like the others had just to get their approval?

Olivia scoffed. "I'm not cleaning your scraps, Nicolas. Despite what Renly says, I'm not actually a servant, and—"

"No! I didn't mean, I just... I thought you must be hungry." Nicolas blushed. "I'm still full from breakfast, and it would be a shame to waste the rest of this food, so if you want some..."

She watched him for a few moments, trying to decipher if he was teasing her or not, but when all she found was nerves and kindness she knew he was just trying to be chivalrous. At least one of the knights had remembered his code.

"I'm okay," She waved the chequered cloth in front of him before turning to place it gently back in her saddlebag. "Packed my own. Thank you, though."

He didn't move from his spot, standing over her with a nervous smile, so she reached out her foot to tap against his own. "Sit."

He sat beside her gingerly with a small laugh. He continued to eat as he looked back over at the knights. She followed his gaze, but they were all too busy laughing with each other to pay them any attention.

She could feel Nicolas turn back to her, and she eventually looked over. He seemed more fidgety than usual, and he kept opening and closing his mouth like he wanted to ask her something, but shoved his face full of food before he gathered the courage to speak.

"You can ask me anything you want, Nico."

He blushed deeper at the nickname but didn't speak up. Eventually, as he was nearing the bottom of the bowl, he found his words. "What's it feel like to have all that power?"

It wasn't the question she expected, and sure as Hell not a question she had ever been asked before. It wasn't something she spent much time thinking about. She didn't want to give him some half-arsed answer, something just to pacify his curiosity like she probably would have with anyone else who asked. He was nice to her, despite everyone and everything telling him not to be.

"It's not something I usually notice. I just feel it in the background, like it's a part of me, like another limb." She nervously chewed on her lip. "It makes me feel alive, fills me with warmth." She bit her lip hard enough for it to bleed and frowned. "But sometimes it just hurts."

"Hurts?"

She nodded, watching as he slurped the remainder of the stew. She used the break in the conversation to think of a better way to phrase her words.

"When I heal, it feels like my bones are stitching themselves back together. I can sense animals from a mile away, and sometimes that range makes my head throb, everything becoming a little overwhelming." She glanced at the forest around her. "Sometimes it feels like my entire body is attuned to the lifeforce surrounding it."

His eyes widened, "oh, I didn't know you could do all that." Before she had the chance to defend herself, he fiddled with his bowl and moved to stand. "I'll clean this in the stream so Peter doesn't have to."

She felt something inside her glow with his kindness, and she couldn't help the fond look that came over her face. She waved her hand over the bowl, watching with amusement as Nicolas' eyes grew wide at how clean it suddenly was. She had never been more glad that a cleaning spell came to her so easily.

His face split into a wide, innocent grin. It was easy to see how young he really was when he smiled. "That's amazing! Is there anything else you can do? Anything wonderful like that?"

He looked so bright-eyed and innocent that she found she just couldn't refuse him.

In that moment, he reminded her a little too much of Renly's little sister. Lorelle was always this giddy when she watched her perform magic. She couldn't help but think that Cassius would probably react in kind.

She busied herself with gathering some twigs around their little spot at the edge of the clearing, binding them together with blades of grass until it formed something that resembled the figure of a person. With a deep breath, and one quick look back at Nicolas, she squeezed her eyes shut.

She pictured the image of the stick figure in her mind, and imagined exactly what it would look like if it began to move. She could feel the creak of the bark as each part came to life. Opening her eyes, she waved a hand over the top of the stick figure. It leapt up from its position in her hand and landed in front of Nicolas with a flourish of its arms. It then began to dance around in front of them.

Nicolas' eyes lit up as he giggled, eyes even brighter than they were before. She beamed as she watched him, his eyes glued to the figure, giggling a little herself when Nicolas beamed wider as the figure stopped to bow in front of him.

It had been so long since she had seen someone this happy to see her use magic. Not since–

A loud, booming voice carried over the clearing, startling Olivia out of her thoughts.

"What do you think you're doing?"

She flinched and snapped her head up. Renly was glaring at the pair of them from across the clearing, anger radiating from him. The other knights were looking too, and Robard was frowning at her. She flinched at the weight of their gazes and quickly looked away.

She reached for her stick figure and quietly picked it apart. She could feel the weight of Renly's stare until it was entirely dismantled.

Without another word, she got up and left, making camp as far away as she could.

CHAPTER SEVEN

Olivia was jolted from sleep by the uneasy tingle under her skin. She was slow and groggy, still half asleep when she realised something was wrong. She yawned and she slowly sat up, rubbing the sleep from her eyes, and stretched as well as she could while still seated.

The more awake she became, the more she sensed magic in the air. She took a quick look around and frowned. Everything looked and felt the same as the night before. Perhaps she was just on edge.

She did, however, find a few people missing from camp. Robard, Maddox and Renly were gathered around the unlit campfire but they seemed content, if a little tired. Surely they wouldn't be so calm if everyone else was missing.

She stood, groaning at the feeling of stiff muscles, and sat herself heavily beside Robard. He gave her a fond smile as he reached over to ruffle her hair, sliding a bowl of food towards her before she had the chance to complain.

Renly didn't even look at her.

Nicolas appeared shortly after, yawning and rubbing his eyes, his clothes dishevelled. Robard shoved the rest of his breakfast at him, tousling his hair as he pouted into the bowl. She had to look away quickly before the fond look in Robard's eyes killed her.

The rest of the knights slowly trickled over to them as she and Nicolas ate. Arley seemed as though he had to drag a still-asleep Merek to the campfire by his ear. She let out a breath she hadn't realised she had been holding when the last of them sat heavily beside her.

As everyone settled in and began to eat, Renly told them of the plans for the day. They would make it to the village by mid-afternoon, where they'd get something proper to eat, have a look around, sleep in a proper bed, then they would leave the following morning.

It didn't sound like he was taking the threat very seriously. It seemed more like he had only gone to appease his father. In his defence, the king hadn't seemed too worried about it either.

"Where are we going?" Nicolas asked around a mouthful of food, ignoring Robard's look of disgust.

"The report came from inside the village of Drerimas."

Olivia paused with her spoon halfway to her mouth and looked up at Renly. The name sounded familiar, but she couldn't quite place it. Had she read it somewhere? Heard it in passing? It made the tingling feeling under her skin buzz even more and she couldn't deny that it meant something.

What it meant, though, she didn't know.

Renly spared her a glance, narrowing his eyes in confusion, but didn't say anything. Not that she'd have an answer for him if he asked.

She looked down and continued to eat, the feeling festering under her skin. The more she thought about it, the more she became wary of this Drerimas, a nervous feeling bubbling under her skin. It was on the tip of her tongue, an answer she could taste but couldn't speak, and it was starting to drive her mad. Even though she didn't know what this feeling was, she knew it was something the others should be aware of. Something that Renly should be wary of, at the very least.

When Renly stood to go to the bathroom, she decided to follow him. They needed to talk, and she knew he would listen to her more if he wasn't around his knights, the people he felt the need to impress.

He was in the middle of peeing when she slid up to the tree beside him, leaning her back against it so she didn't have to watch him, thunking against it dully. Renly jumped in surprise, swearing as the movement made him redirect his stream all over his shoes. She barely suppressed a snort, but settled with a smirk at the glare he sent her.

"Christ, Olivia." He turned back to the bush. "What do you want?"

Olivia sighed, "it's Drerimas."

"What about it?" He scoffed. "Getting scared, little Livvy?"

"Shut up."

She took a moment to close her eyes and really feel her surroundings, to listen to what her magic was trying to tell her. "Something's wrong, I can feel it. It's like I know this place but I can't put my finger on it." She ran a hand over her face in frustration. "I can sense it, Renly."

There was silence for a long moment. Neither of them spoke, and neither of them moved.

"You're delusional, Olivia." Renly sighed. "We're only here to appease father. There's nothing waiting for us other than food and ale and a proper bed."

"Ren—"

"Don't speak of this to my men." His voice was sharp, leaving no place for argument. He zipped up his pants and boxed her in against the tree. She gulped and shrunk back as the fight drained out of her. "You're not going to spook them over some hunch you know nothing about. Keep this to yourself."

She gulped as she watched Renly rake his gaze over her. He scoffed, and left without another word. She ran a trembling hand through her hair as she watched him disappear back to camp.

It hurt that he didn't believe her, that he was so convinced it was all some test by his father that he didn't seem to care about the consequences if it all turned out to be real. He should have more sense. If it was some sort of test, there's no way the king would have sent her along with them.

She leaned back against the tree trunk. It didn't matter if he believed her, she knew what she felt. Her father always lectured her to keep her wits about her when she left the safety of Alira's walls, that the world was a dangerous, unforgiving place full of things that wanted to hurt her.

She trusted her father a hell of a lot more than she trusted the uncaring, snivelling man that Renly had turned out to be.

Shrill screams floated over the clearing to where she remained by the stream.

She jolted and looked around wildly for the source of the noise, frowning when she saw nothing. Heart racing, she ran in the direction she heard the screams coming from, mentally running through all the possibilities, and of the magic she would need.

She breathed out a sigh of relief at what she found.

Nicolas was being tackled to the ground by Maddox, laughter bubbling from the both of them as Nicolas tried desperately to wiggle out of his grasp. The others were around them, grinning and laughing at the pair.

It seemed she was the only sane one there.

She caught Renly's eye, who was now smiling warmly at his boys from a few trees over. She shook her head in disappointment and turned to walk away. Right after she warned him of her bad feeling, too.

As she was leaving, she felt a sharp pain in her temple, as if someone was stabbing her through her skull. As if her magic was trying to warn her of something.

She gripped onto her head with a whine and looked around, trying to catch whatever it was that her body was warning her about.

Renly straightened up, leaning off the tree as he watched her closely. He seemed mildly alarmed when she caught his eye, but the ache was softening into a dull throb and was fading as quickly as it came.

She rubbed at her temple and turned away to make her way back to camp.

The sooner they hit the road, the sooner they got to Drerimas, and the sooner she could find out what the hell was going on.

Chapter Eight

The ride to Drerimas wasn't as eventful as she had feared.

Olivia kept quiet the entire time, eyes peeled on the trees and shrubs surrounding them, and ignored the soft chatter of the knights. She felt Renly watching her every so often from where he rode beside her, but he never said anything. He may dislike her, most of the knights he surrounded himself with may hate her too, but she wasn't about to let that hatred keep her from protecting them.

She hadn't felt the sharp pain again, but the hairs on the back of her neck had been standing on end ever since they left their campsite. It was as if she could feel something, or someone, watching them.

She never saw anything.

The ride was a short one compared to the day before, taking only a few hours, but she was glad they had waited another day to arrive. If this was the feeling she got now, she didn't want to think about what would have happened had they arrived the night before, too exhausted from a full day's ride to pay as much attention to her surroundings as she needed to.

She could sense the magic again as soon as they rode into the village.

Even though she had known, on some level, that she was riding into a magic-filled area, it still shocked her when she felt it. The magic itself felt odd, though. It felt like old magic, settled into the very soil of the earth, but she knew it wasn't a place full of mages. They wouldn't have been sent there if it was.

Renly spared her a glance when she tensed up beside him. She looked back, wide-eyed and alert, and a small part of her was glad to see him straighten up in his saddle. He may hate her, but he wasn't stupid.

At least they knew one thing for certain now. Whatever was waiting for them in that village, it definitely had something to do with magic.

They rode into the village with little fanfare. The villagers didn't seem suspicious or scared, something that confused her. Most of them spared them little more than a glance before continuing on with their work, some lingering longer on the Bayard crest on Renly's chest before shying away. They didn't seem to be scared. If they were, they weren't keen on Renly and his men finding out about it.

They made it to the village centre before anyone seemed to really give them any proper attention. A small man, late in his years with a greying beard and little hair, emerged from a small house and walked up beside Renly's horse, his grin a little too wide to be natural. Renly slowed to a stop with Robard hovering closely beside him.

The man smiled widely, showing off the gaps in his teeth. "To what do I owe the pleasure..." he glanced down at the crest on Renly's shirt. "Prince Renly?"

Renly shared a look with Robard before turning back to the man, obviously confused. "You are...?"

"Oh!" He bowed. "My name is John, and this village is under my care." He slowly stood, smile fading into a confused frown. "I wasn't expecting a visit today."

The confusion seemed genuine, if a little nervous. He definitely wasn't their informant. Perhaps it was someone in his village, someone that didn't trust John to deal with the threat they believed they were under. Strange, though, to bypass the man that was supposed to be in charge to go straight to the king.

Renly glanced back at her, as if unsure how to proceed. Should he inform John as to why they were really there? Or should he keep it under wraps, and try to discover the real reason they were called without tipping anyone off?

Olivia glanced around at the mingling villagers. There must be a reason, even if they were just scared and the magic she felt was merely old.

She turned back to Renly and shook her head, trying her best to warn Renly to keep as much as he could to himself.

Renly turned back to John and plastered on the big, fake smile she came to associate with diplomacy. "Don't be alarmed, John. We were travelling through the area, checking on my people." Renly gave John a look, as if daring him to question his authority. "On behalf of the king."

Mentioning the king made John stand straighter and clear his throat, looking away to avoid Renly's gaze. No matter who he thought he was, John was in no position to question orders from his ruler.

"Well, we welcome you to our humble little village." He spared the rest of them a glance, gaze running straight past her in order to give better attention to those wearing armour. "You and your men must be tired from your journey." He gestured down the road, towards a large, sprawling building that seemed to ooze warmth. "We have a tavern you could rest in. Hot food and cold ale, and a place to rest."

She could hear Arley and Maddox cheer quietly from behind her, muttered whispers of joy drifting over to her. If they were this picky after only a single night in the woods, she shudders to think of how prickly they'd be after a long journey.

John smiled at their cheers, "I can take your horses for you."

Renly shook his head, "that won't be necessary, thank you." His smile wavered as he sent a warning glare at the men behind her. "Peter, Arley, Maddox. You can handle the horses, can't you?"

The sounds of a grumbling agreement made her smirk.

Olivia didn't know if they should really leave the horses unattended, not when John seemed this twitchy, but she didn't say anything. She knew Renly would only argue, and would probably just make her stay out with the horses all afternoon. She wouldn't mind if she wasn't so wary of this place.

She frowned as she watched Robard and Renly dismount, and slowly slid off of Shadow. She held out the reins to Peter, but he didn't even spare her a glance, tugging the reins harshly out of her grasp before pushing past her, shoulders colliding roughly.

A sting ran up her arm and she rubbed idly at her shoulder, glaring at his retreating figure as she left, following the others into the tavern.

The tavern wasn't anywhere as nice as the one back home. It didn't seem nearly as friendly, either. There was a plump lady polishing glasses behind the counter, who didn't even look up as they entered, despite their rowdy entrance. The place was rather large, with an abundance of tables littered throughout the room. The outside definitely looked more inviting than the inside. The village seemed to heavily rely on their farms to keep them running, and she's sure that didn't leave much money leftover to beautify the place.

She sat herself quietly beside Robard at the end of one of the longer tables, across from Renly and Nicolas. Merek stood by the bar and flirted with the barmaid who, she noted with mirth, did not look the slightest bit impressed by him.

The others filed in and sat at the table beside them. Merek slid in last, finally having enough of the barmaid's rejection.

They were brought bowls of soup and mugs of ale, the barmaid trying to charm everyone but herself and Merek. She jumped when the bowl was all but slammed onto the table in front of her, the liquid close to spilling over. Her mug never came. Olivia frowned at the missing cup, glancing at the others to see if she was the only one missing a drink. She was. She glanced up at the barmaid, only to be met with a shrug.

"Got nothin' for no girl to drink."

Robard snorted from beside her, laughter tapering off with an 'oomf' when she nudged him in the ribs with her elbow.

She pushed the soup around with her piece of bread without actually eating anything. Her stomach was rumbling, but she didn't trust the food. She didn't trust the people, nor the way John hovered by the back of the room, never leaving them alone.

The others ate without her, not having the same hesitation that she did.

Renly sent her a sharp glare, as if he knew what she was thinking. "Eat up, Olivia. It's rude to not indulge in the meal John graciously provided for us."

He kicked her shin under the table, and kept doing it until she gave in and nibbled at the bread. It was good, though not quite as good as her mother's baking, and she didn't eat any more than she had to.

John kept watching over them from his place by the door, sipping slowly on the ale that the barmaid had handed him as soon as they walked through the doors. His gaze lingered on Renly the most, a frown on his face the entire time.

There was definitely something suspicious about that man.

Chapter Nine

Renly asked if John could show him around Drerimas after they had all been sufficiently fed.

He told the others to take a look around and report back to him if they saw anything out of the ordinary. He took Peter and Robard with him, dismissing Olivia when she tried to stay by his side. She was nervous and didn't trust anyone, but especially not John.

"I'm fine, Olivia." He rolled his eyes at her. "I *am* a prince, remember?"

She watched his back until he turned the corner and faded from view. Merek and Arley quickly disappeared down the path to her right, laughing obnoxiously as they did.

"Come on, Liv!" Nicolas threw his arm around her shoulder and pulled her towards where a grumbling Maddox stood. She smiled at his enthusiasm but allowed herself to be dragged away.

They didn't find anything, much to her annoyance. The kids played in the fields, laughing happily as they chased each other around, while their parents watched on with fond smiles. By all accounts, they seemed content. The most disturbance probably came from the knights. She could hear Merek's laughter from the other side of the village, while Maddox and Nicolas messed around with each other more than actually paying attention.

She couldn't exactly blame them for not taking any of it seriously. Not with Renly acting as he was, and with the villagers all seeming normal. Everything was in its place.

Olivia lingered as they passed the local forge. She was surprised that Nicolas and Maddox allowed her to, although they seemed quite uncaring either way. It was a lot cosier than the one she worked at back home. Where she worked in a forge that was mostly indoors, with solid walls and upscale tools, this Blacksmith had most of his work tools outside under a patchy roof. His tools had seen better days, the anvil covered in deep dents and his tongs scorched from overuse, but the finished work he had lying against the walls were a testament that he didn't need anything flashy to make tools and weapons of quality.

She definitely had to tell Osmond and Cassius about this place.

The blacksmith looked up from where he had been plunging something glowing into his bucket, the steam hissing before slowly dissipating. "Who're you?"

She avoided his gaze as she moved around the forge. Talking back to the man would only antagonise him, especially since she wasn't dressed in armour or wearing the Bayard crest like the others were.

Nicolas took one look at her before he turned and grinned at the blacksmith. "We've come from Alira with Prince Renly." He made his way towards him, practically oozing boyish charm. "This place looks great!" He fiddled with various pieces of equipment as he passed. "What do these do?"

She watched with amusement as the brash blacksmith smiled at Nicolas' purity and answered any questions he had for him. It was almost endearing. No-one was oblivious to Nicolas' charm, it seemed.

She felt a sudden sharp, stabbing pain in her temple as she continued to poke around the forge, the exact same one she felt back in the forest. She grit her teeth and clutched at her head, shuffling away from where Nicolas was distracting the blacksmith.

Gratefully, Maddox helped guide her further away from the building with a warm hand on her shoulder.

"Are you okay?" He spoke close to her ear, so as not to raise unwanted attention.

She shrugged off his hand as they made it a safe distance away, the pain trickling away slowly, leaving her groaning and rubbing at her forehead. She'd never had pulsing headaches like this before.

Her father had told her about these. He said it was like another mage was trying to poke your brain to get your attention, but she never really believed in it. His stories definitely didn't tell her it would hurt like this.

Then she heard a whisper.

She looked up at Maddox, who seemed just as confused, clearly having heard it too. Glancing over at Nicolas, it appeared he was too engrossed in whatever the blacksmith was teaching him to have noticed anything else.

Glad for the distraction, she allowed herself to walk towards the sound. She was surprisingly glad to find Maddox following closely behind.

A young girl was standing in the narrow alleyway connecting the forge with the building beside them, one that didn't appear to have been open for some time. The girl was a few years younger than herself, with a hood over her head and her face hidden from view.

Olivia could feel the pull of power as they approached. She reached out to grab Maddox's arm on instinct, to try and hold him back, but he shook out of her grasp and kept walking.

"I *am* a knight, you know."

When he was finally in front of the girl, just a few steps away, she took off her hood to reveal her face. She was young, with a round face and a sharp jawline, her red hair long as it flowed beneath her hood – and she had glowing eyes. Violet, just like every other mage. Suddenly Olivia could feel the magic in the air like lightning.

Olivia darted forwards to grab a hold of Maddox and pulled him back harshly. He went easily in his confused and surprised state, evident in the way he allowed her to touch him without argument.

The girl simply watched as Olivia stepped in front of Maddox, but didn't make any move to run. Olivia's head throbbed as the girl stared. She grimaced but didn't make a move to clutch at her head, in case it scared her off. Perhaps she didn't realise she was doing it? Or maybe she was waiting for Olivia to act first, to judge if she could trust her.

She didn't blame her. After all, the king was notorious for his less-than-kind treatment of mages, and she was travelling with the prince and his most trusted men. It was smart to be cautious.

"We won't hurt you," Olivia smiled kindly at the girl, and took a few more steps until she was sure the girl could see the violet in her eyes.

She seemed to relax almost immediately, her stance retreating to something far more vulnerable and safe. Olivia relaxed a little too, allowing Maddox to stand beside her rather than behind, but stopped him from properly approaching the girl again.

"I'm sorry." The girl sounded meek, eyes downcast and fingers twiddling with each other. She seemed well out of her depth, and even though she was a mage she didn't seem like she would be ruffling enough feathers for someone to go straight to the king because of her.

"Why are you here?" Olivia asked.

The girl scrunched up her nose, as if the words were unpleasant to even think of. "I'm here with some other mages." She looked up to meet Olivia's eyes. She seemed fearful. "They came here for the people. Told them how King Alroy only supported those he could control and left everyone else for dead." She sniffled. "I - I don't know what's happening."

Maddox tensed beside her, "you don't dare speak ill of the king!"

The girl raised her hands above her head in defence. "Not me! No, I - I have nothing against the king, nor his family or his people." She turned back to Olivia, seeming desperate. "You *have* to believe me!"

Olivia glanced over at Maddox. She wasn't sure if she should believe this girl, but she seemed genuinely frightened enough for at least some of what she spoke of to be true. "These mages you're with, you said they came for the people. What do you mean?"

"Poison," the girl shuddered, voice coming out small. "They said they would poison anyone that supported a tyrant leader instead of encouraging freedom. Like all the other villages. Said the poison wouldn't draw any attention to their magic.

"They said they were doing it to prove that King Alroy would do nothing, that he didn't care that whole settlements and villages were dying, so long as no-one else heard about it."

It sounded far-fetched, even to her own paranoid brain. She's sure she would have heard something about this, especially if they had done it before. How had she not heard about it? Entire villages being wiped off the map, and for what? To prove a point?

"Only the two of them?" Maddox snorted by her side. "You expect me to believe that?"

"It's not just them." The girl said. "There's a whole lot of them. Call themselves Uprisers, or so I've heard."

Things were a lot worse than she thought. If there were only a couple of them they might have stood a chance in snuffing out the idea then and there, but a whole group of them? They wouldn't all be in Drerimas, she definitely would have sensed that much magic in the area. Even if they managed to change the minds of the few that were there, it wouldn't do much in the grand scheme of things.

"Why are you telling us this?"

The girl seemed almost reluctant to answer, opening and closing her mouth a few times but no words flowed through. Eventually she straightened, looking poised to finally answer Maddox's question, when there was a disgruntled grumble coming from behind them.

"Olivia? Maddox? C'mon guys, this isn't funny!" She could practically hear Nicolas' pout as his voice rang through the alleyway.

The girl quickly pulled her hood back over her head and seemed ready to run. She looked up and met Olivia's eyes, held steady for a few moments before she cocked her head to the side, as if in thought. "This is one fight you can't sit out of, Olivia Shaw."

The girl disappeared before Olivia had even processed what she had said. Nicolas rounded the corner a moment later.

Maddox blinked after the girl, trying to process what had happened, before he turned to face her. "Do you know her?"

Olivia shook her head, eyes still glued to where the girl had been standing. How had she known her name?

They quickly made their way back to where Renly had told them to meet. They didn't speak, not to each other and not to answer Nicolas' pressing questions. Her mind was swirling with unanswered questions – who was that kid, and what had she meant by her last words? Was she telling the truth about the other mages and the poison? If they really did have an uprising on their hands, this all became a lot more complicated.

Renly had laughed in their faces when they recounted what had happened.

"Did you guys find some special plants? Sneak back to the tavern to drink your weight in ale?"

His laughter died down when neither Olivia nor Maddox laughed with him.

He sighed as he ran a hand through his hair. "Say you aren't trying to make me look a fool. It's quite a tale, you have to admit. How much trust should we put on the words of a little girl?"

Maddox gulped. "She was magic, Sir."

"Magic?" Renly looked at Olivia. "You're sure?"

Olivia nodded, "definitely."

"And we're sure she's not a threat?" Renly hummed, gaze never leaving hers.

"Fairly certain," she nodded. "She was definitely scared of something, and it wasn't us."

Renly seemed doubtful, but she didn't blame him. She wouldn't have believed it herself if she wasn't there, if she didn't see the look in her eyes. The girl wouldn't turn in another mage, and definitely not to someone who directly served the king. Not unless she was terrified of them.

Robard began to speak, but Renly rubbed at his face and held up his hand. "Save it, Robard. I don't wanna hear it."

She could hear Merek and Arley approach before she saw them, all laughter and bright smiles, completely oblivious to the serious nature of their current conversation. They were shoving each other as they appeared in view.

Merek straightened when he saw the small gathering around Renly. He was still grinning, though. "Nothin' to report. Everything is as normal as can be."

Olivia had to bite her tongue so she didn't outwardly laugh, especially after what she and Maddox had just witnessed. This place was anything but normal.

Renly let out a frustrated groan, "you two are little more than useless." He rubbed at his face and looked to the sky, closing his eyes as Merek spoke proudly.

"Thank you, Sir."

Renly grumbled and looked back to his gathered knights, frown deepening as his gaze flicked past her head.

Olivia turned to see what had caught his attention. John was approaching, as if he had a sixth sense as to what they were discussing. He looked more jumpy than he had earlier, seeming to grow more nervous as he met the various gazes of the knights.

He cleared his throat and motioned behind him, "The villagers heard you were here and wanted to put something together in the tavern, Your Highness. It's not much, but they wanted to welcome you."

Renly, ever the professional, smiled at the man. "Thank you, John. That's very much appreciated."

John smiled, tight-lipped, and bowed a little. "Food will be served soon, Your Highness."

Renly nodded and turned to face the knights, "go on, join John and the villagers for some food and ale."

They didn't need any more convincing, especially Merek and Maddox. Everyone but Olivia, Robard, Renly and Peter scurried after John, asking him about the types of food that would be served and how many women would be there.

Renly waved Peter off towards the disappearing group. "Join the others, Peter. I don't need you hanging off my arm all day."

Olivia raised an unimpressed brow at the way he spoke to Peter, but the kid didn't seem to mind. He shrugged off the comment with a smile before jogging to catch up to the others.

She waited until they were all well out of earshot before she turned back to Renly with a frown. "Do you believe her? The girl?" She took a step closer to Renly and Robard, lowering her pitch. "That there's some sort of uprising forming against your father?"

Renly sighed, deeper this time. "I don't know. It's just some little girl, and I know I shouldn't believe the words of a child, but..." His gaze seemed desperate, confused. "She knew your name. You have no idea who she is but she sure knows you."

Renly's eyes never wavered from her own, and he muttered a curse. Before either of them could say any more on the subject, he turned away from her. "Go join the others."

She was going to protest, but Renly's shoulders were hunched and his brows drawn, a clear sign of being too tense to have a proper discussion with him. She caught Robard's warning gaze and decided they could discuss things on their own. She trusted Robard's opinion.

She turned and left with a sigh.

What the hell was going on?

CHAPTER TEN

The feast that John promised them was grander than she was expecting. There was more variety of game to eat than she could even name, along with seemingly endless bread and soups. Perhaps it had to do with the good woodland that surrounded Drerimas, or maybe a spread like this was usual for visiting royalty.

Whatever the reason, the food was amazing. Peter's eyes seemed to bug from his head as he ate whatever he could get his hands on.

It was chaotic and crowded in the tavern. The whole village seemed to be in attendance. There were kids giggling and running around, their laughter heard through the open doors after their parents told them to take it outside. Maddox was kissing some girl in the corner of the room, and Nicolas was laughing with a group of villagers that none of them knew, while the rest of them remained seated.

Renly was occasionally dragged into conversation by the people around him, but he didn't seem overly pleased with having to leave their table to converse with them. He looked a little more uncomfortable and on edge than he did as they rode in that morning, but no-one seemed to take much notice the second that food and ale was mentioned.

Even Maddox, who had seemed concerned over the girl in the alley, had forgotten all about the danger they faced the moment a woman took any notice of him.

The girl from the alley was there, standing in the corner of the room, as far away from everyone as she could get. She was standing behind a table, where a couple of older women were nursing mugs of ale. They seemed to be the only people in the room to not be engaging with everyone else. They must have been the mages that the girl had warned them about.

She caught Renly's eye from across the room and pointedly looked at the little group by the doorway. His eyes seemed to bulge in recognition, but he didn't stray from the conversation he had been dragged into.

Olivia was seated next to Arley at the table, and across from Robard. They were talking and laughing amongst themselves, but Olivia wasn't paying much attention to them. She was dividing her attention between watching the mages in the corner and keeping an eye out for Renly, who the small group seemed to be obsessed with watching.

"Someone's infatuated."

She snapped her attention back to her table. Robard kept his gaze resolutely on Renly, not paying any attention to the other knights. She glanced past Arley and met Merek's gaze, the man snickering behind his mug of ale.

"I'm just sayin'." He placed his mug on the table, the action causing some of the ale to slosh over the rim. He didn't seem to be drunk, but the ale loosened up his tongue. "You been watchin' him all day, tryin' to stay close. You know he hates you, right?" He leaned over Arley and grinned. "What you are, what you did... it's not somethin' he's ever goin' to forgive you for." He scoffed as he leaned back to take another sip. "No-one will ever love a filthy, useless jinxflinger like you."

She turned away from him and took a long sip from Robard's ale, having again been refused a mug of her own from the barkeep. It hurt that Renly's dislike of her had stretched to his knights, that they hated her as much as he did. She hadn't done anything to them, to anyone, but they hated her all the same.

As much as the words hurt, she knew she still had people who supported her. She had Robard, and Nicolas – until the kid fell victim to the words of the other knights, at least – her mother and those at Alira's tavern, and Cassius and Osmond. She didn't need the care or support of anyone else.

By the time she looked back to the mages, they were gone. The little girl was the only one who remained.

Olivia looked around wildly for Renly, becoming a bit frantic when she couldn't find him. It took a few moments until she finally caught sight of him. He was being steered out of the tavern by John.

She looked back at the girl. Her eyes were wide, and obviously a little frightened as she looked from Renly back to Olivia. The missing mages, the frightened girl, Renly being steered out of the tavern... something was going on, and it wasn't good.

Olivia whipped around to Robard, and kicked him under the table to gain his attention. She indicated over her shoulder when Robard finally looked over, and she could see the moment that Robard came to the same conclusion as her.

He swore loudly.

The others at the table looked over to him in confusion, quickly shutting up when they saw the alertness in his gaze. Their whole table followed as Robard stood and headed for the front doors, snapping orders at Merek as he left.

"Get Maddox and Nico."

For once, Merek didn't argue against orders.

The girl reached out and grabbed at Olivia's wrist as she was darting out the doors after the others. She gave her a serious look, one that looked completely out of place on someone so young. "This is only the beginning."

She dropped Olivia's wrist but didn't look away. There was something off about her, something different from back in the alleyway. She didn't seem as scared as she was back then, almost as if there was an air of confidence around her, no matter how scared she looked.

She didn't know how long had passed, with her and the girl staring at each other, until Nicolas appeared by her side and dragged her out of the tavern.

Being away from the young mage seemed to jolt her back into the present. Her head seemed clearer and the strange feeling that came over her around the girl faded the more distance she put between them.

They ran down the street towards the sound of arguing, Maddox and Arley not far in front of them.

She almost ran straight into the back of Arley as they skidded to a stop in front of them, his eyes bugging at what he saw.

CHAPTER ELEVEN

Before her stood Renly, held back by John as he struggled hard against the older man. John didn't even flinch when he noticed them there, hardly even blinked when the knights drew their swords.

John looked more resigned than afraid. He must have been a lot stronger than he looked, if Renly wasn't able to escape his grasp. The idiot must have left his sword with his horse or back inside the tavern if he wasn't trying to reach for it. He tightened his grip and the prince winced in pain.

"Sorry," John said. "It's nothing personal."

"Nothing personal?" Merek seethed as he raised his sword. "You're holding our prince captive. It seems pretty personal to me."

"You don't understand." John flitted his gaze to his side. "It's the only way to save my people."

She followed his gaze. The older mages from the tavern leaned against the wall of a nearby house, seeming almost bored with the drama happening before them. If that little girl was being truthful, it was likely those mages had forced John's hand.

Perhaps they had given him an ultimatum – give them the prince or they'll poison his people and burn Drerimas to the ground.

The taller of the pair, with long blonde hair and a scar across her throat, stepped forwards. She had an air of arrogance about her, but she seemed youthful. Maybe she had just joined this uprising group and wanted to show off her skills. It would make sense as to why only two of them would come after someone so heavily guarded.

The mage held out her hand with her palm raised. Flames appeared, as if coming straight out of her palm.

Arley took a hesitant step back, narrowly avoiding running into her. None of them had ever had to fight a mage before, and she had a feeling that their ignorance about Drerimas was born from their knowledge that they didn't stand a chance if any of it was true.

Arley slowly withdrew the bow from its holder on his back. His hands were shaking, but he didn't back down. If he couldn't win, he would at least go down fighting.

The other mage, who was still leaning against the building, snorted as she watched him. "There's nothing you can do, boy. Think you can hurt us with that little thing?" She laughed. "We've been on the road for weeks. We haven't lost a single battle yet."

Silence hung over them as the realisation hit. The little girl was right. These mages, or the uprising group they belonged to, had been going village to village, recruiting allies or striking them down. None of them had heard anything about it.

Why had they only been sent now? Had the king heard about the past attacks and thought them to be rumours? Or was it only because they had come closer to Alira's walls that he finally felt the need to interfere?

The mages were now standing side-by-side, facing the gathering of knights, barely paying any attention to Renly and John. They must have had some sort of blind faith that John wouldn't let Renly escape, and so focused all their attention on Renly's defenders.

They either knew something Olivia didn't, or they were simply used to facing people too scared to go against them.

If they had any sort of chance in saving Renly, this was it.

Before she had a chance to approach Robard, to work out some sort of plan, hot-headed Merek darted forwards, sword held tightly in his grip. She watched as he got pushed to the side with a lazy wave of the arm, the tall blonde laughing at his foolish attack.

Maddox followed suit, quickly getting struck down in the same way.

One by one, the knights were pushed aside by the pair standing before them. It seemed easy for them, as if they weren't even trying to fight them properly, content to just beat them again and again until they failed to get back up.

Arley was the only one to make any kind of dent. He got off a lucky shot, lodging an arrow right into the blonde's shoulder, but it only seemed to anger her instead of slow her down. She had quickly thrown Arley to the ground, where he had skidded across the dirt until he came to a stop, back thrown into a large rock.

She reached out to take hold of Nicolas' arm as he rushed past her to join the fight, only to have him shake her off. "I'm not sitting out a fight just because it's not easy."

He ripped his arm out of her grasp and darted towards the injured mage. He swung his new sword and managed to catch her injured arm, the blonde not able to move out of the way fast enough. It was a deep gash, but it wasn't life-threatening.

Her friend glowered and tossed Nicolas to the ground.

Olivia growled as she watched Nicolas roll a few times, only to be stopped when he rolled straight into Merek. He stilled, and she couldn't even tell if he was breathing. The mage who threw him smirked.

Her whole body shook with anger as she screamed. Attacking the knights was one thing, but she drew the line at Nicolas. A searing pain made its way down Olivia's arms and fire appeared from her palms.

She glared at the pair before her as she hurled balls of fire towards them, again and again, without break. They ducked out of the way just in time, the fire whirling past their heads. The injured one grumbled as she patted her clothing with her non-injured palm to douse the flames.

"Finally!" The other laughed, all high-pitched and mocking. "A worthy opponent!"

Olivia aimed a fireball at her, pleased when it singed her hair before whirling past, landing heavily in the dirt behind her.

They fought back, and her attacking stance very quickly turned defensive as she cast whatever spells she could think of to deflect the attacks. She didn't have the chance to look at where the others had ended up but she hoped they scrambled behind her and away from the battlefield. It was hard enough to deflect the spells away from herself, she didn't have the strength, or the skills, to protect the knights too.

She sighed in relief when she spotted John, who had slacked in his grasp of Renly as he watched the battle, be hit in the nose with the back of Renly's elbow. The prince quickly darted out of John's grasp, his sword now drawn.

Her head throbbed, but she ignored it. The oncoming headache was nothing compared to the burning in her arm and the aching in her palm. She had a continuous tingling feeling under her skin and she felt a draining fatigue deep in her bones.

She had never fought like this, with such single-minded focus, a driving need to *win*. She had never fought against someone who actually wanted to cause her harm either.

A well-aimed blast hit her in the shoulder, and her body screamed. She felt like she had been hit with electricity as her body convulsed. She stumbled back a few paces as she tried to get her shaking under control.

This was nothing like fighting against her father in practice. These mages would kill her if they needed to. They looked like they would very much enjoy it too, judging from the wicked smiles on their faces.

She couldn't let them win. If they took Renly...

She grit her teeth and screamed, gathering every ounce of control over her body that she could. Her body stopped shaking and the warmth under her skin grew until it was all that she could feel, her pain subsiding.

Turning to the injured mage, she threw continuous balls of fire at her until she stumbled from the force of the onslaught, tripping over the uneven path. It was easiest to get rid of the weakest enemy first, so she could focus all her energy on the other one. She ignored the attacks from her friend, ignored the way it made her body scream in pain.

Once the injured mage stopped resisting, she pushed a forceback spell at her, causing her head to hit the path harshly. She fell unconscious immediately, her head lilting to the side as blood slowly pooled underneath her. She was concerned she had injured her beyond repair until she caught sight of her chest moving, just slightly.

Her friend stopped her assault to rush to her side, hand on the blonde's neck, checking for a pulse. She waited until the mage was sure her friend was breathing before she took advantage of the distraction. She aimed the same forceback spell at her, but it took a few tries until she fell beside her friend, unmoving.

Olivia breathed heavily as silence descended upon them. It was over. How she had managed to defeat a pair of mages that obviously knew what they were doing a hell of a lot better than she did was beyond her.

She suddenly felt very lightheaded, the pain hitting her all at once. She swayed a little until someone slid their arm over her waist. She could tell it was Robard from the way he smelled, and his gruff grunting as he struggled with keeping her upright.

"I did it," she smiled deliriously up at him.

Robard smiled sadly as he reached over to run his fingers through her hair. "That you did, little one."

Her body give into exhaustion quickly, going limp in Robard's strong hold.

Chapter Twelve

The first thing she smelt upon waking up was blood.

She groaned as she slowly opened her eyes. She was still in the middle of the street, propped up against the side of a building lining the path. The ground all around them was singed black, an obvious sign that a magical battle had taken place.

Renly was fine, thank the Gods. He restrained John with a piece of rope, while the man looked about ready to burst into tears, apologised over and over again to an unsympathetic prince.

Maddox had an open wound on his head. It was bleeding down his forehead and dripping blood into his eye. Merek was beside him, using Maddox as a crutch. He was also bloody, with a rather nasty wound on his elbow.

It was a miracle none of them were killed.

She sighed in relief and leaned back against the wall. Everyone was fine. A bit banged up, bleeding and bruised, but still alive. Her head throbbed, and she was glad the light had faded behind the hills, as even the soft light from the sparse street lamps hurt.

Robard sat beside her with a groan, knees cracking as he did. She laughed at the sound and regretted it immediately, the movement jostling her head painfully.

He frowned and reached out to place a hand on her forehead, "you okay?"

She hummed, leaning into his palm. "Head just hurts."

"I'm not surprised," he withdrew his hand. "Anythin' else hurt?"

"I'm fine," she said.

He hummed as he looked over her, frowning at what he found. He poked and prodded at her many bruises, frowning even more when she winced in pain but didn't complain. She was too tired to speak much, that bone-deep exhaustion from the middle of battle coming back tenfold now that she was idle.

"You did well today."

She leaned against Robard's shoulder with a soft smile. He ran his hand through her hair as she looked around to check on the others. The knights were getting themselves together and hobbling down the street, no doubt toward whatever lodging had been provided for them.

Her hands began to shake as she thought back to the battle. It hadn't been long, but the toll it took on her body was almost frightening. She had never used her magic against anyone before, other than the few training sessions with her father, and the sheer exhaustion it left her with wasn't anything she had expected.

What was more terrifying was having to use her magic to fight. The mages were knocked out cold, and all because *she* had made them that way. She knew she didn't have any other choice, that they would have continued to attack every single knight until they killed them all, but she never thought she would ever have to fight her own kind.

Gods, how naive had she been?

Robard stood, careful not to jostle her head, and held out a hand for her to take. She took it without question, stumbling a little when she got to her feet. He steadied her with an arm wrapped around her shoulder and led them down the same path the other knights had taken.

Renly had secured the few houses that John owned for them to stay in until morning. They were to leave at first light, in hopes of making it back to Alira with as little stops as possible. She wasn't sure what Renly was doing with John, something he hadn't shared with Robard either, but he was keeping the mages tied up in the room she had been assigned to stay in.

Merek and Maddox were already there when Robard had led her into the house she would be staying in. Both men were perched on the edge of the bed, tending to each other's wounds. The mages were tied up in the corner, on the opposite end of the room to the door.

She was thankful to see that both men were keeping an eye on the mages, despite tending to still-bleeding wounds. She tried to approach them, in an attempt to help them mend their wounds, but they flinched away from her and shuffled further away from her.

Resigned, Olivia collapsed onto the floor in front of the bench beside the door. Robard left quietly with a gentle pat to her shoulder.

Her stomach grumbled, but she ignored it. At least the hunger pains would aid in keeping her awake. She's sure Renly wanted her there so she could keep the mages in place by any means necessary. It wouldn't do to fall asleep on the job, no matter how exhausted she felt, or how much her body ached and begged for rest.

The blonde was darting her gaze around the room, wide-eyed and fearful. Her shoulder was messily bandaged, the white of it spotted red from the blood still spilling underneath, but it thankfully seemed to be slowing. She was surprised the knights had bothered to bandage her at all.

The other one, the brunette, was still unharmed. They hadn't been attacked after she had passed out, then. She kept her eyes solely on Olivia, unlike her friend. Her stare was blank and it was unnerving, but she never looked away.

The whole thing was unsettling.

"You sure you aren't one of them, little Olivia?" Merek snorted, staring at the brunette in disgust. "That one sure seems infatuated."

Maddox pinched the bridge of his nose, his head hung low. "*Shut up*, Merek."

"What, you sweet on her now just because she fought in one little battle?" Merek rolled his eyes.

Maddox narrowed his eyes as he peered up at him. He still had dried blood above his eyebrow, his head bandaged with what looked like bits of cloth he had found throughout the house. He looked utterly exhausted.

"She saved all our lives. Single-handedly, might I add, while we all failed." Maddox rolled his eyes. "If you're not going to show your gratitude, at least you can acknowledge that."

Olivia smiled. It was a back-handed compliment, but a compliment nonetheless, something she'd never received from the knights. She tried to thank him, but the words died in her throat.

He turned to look at her, long and hard, not any kinder than the blonde's stare from across the room. "Just because I appreciate your help, it doesn't mean I'm any less scared of you."

He turned back to watch the mages without another word. Merek followed suit, just a lot quieter. They're still scared of her, even after she had saved them. Even after she had fought against her own kind for them.

It wasn't long before Maddox and Merek fell asleep. The blonde mage drifted off not long after, while the brunette continued to stare. The quiet was disconcerting.

Renly looked haggard as he came in hours later. He seemed a lot younger than he was, and Olivia was sharply reminded of the kid that she used to know, the one that was so full of love and compassion before the fear and hate ate away at him.

Renly ignored her as he walked past, tossing his coat on the floor beside her. He sat on the bench behind her and faced the mages. He put at least a body length of distance between them, and didn't look at Olivia as he spoke to her.

"Why is she staring at you?"

She followed Renly's gaze to find him watching the brunette. She shrugged, not having a good enough answer for him. Renly must have seen the movement out of the corner of his eye, because he took it as an answer in itself.

"Where did the little girl go?"

Olivia shrugged again, still not having the answer. She was in the tavern the last time she checked, but if she was as smart as she seemed, the kid would be long gone by now.

"When did you get so good at controlling your magic?"

It was more luck than anything that allowed her to apprehend them. The blonde was weakened by both Arley and Nicolas, and she only managed to get the brunette because she took advantage of her distraction. It had nothing to do with how skilled she was.

Renly didn't push for an answer.

They were silent as they both stared at the mage, who had grown tired of the attention and settled in beside her friend. She put her head on her shoulder and closed her eyes, careful to avoid the one that was still bloody.

Renly and Olivia didn't dare look at each other now that their distraction was asleep, as if the thought that meeting her gaze meant he would have to thank her for saving him, that he would have to admit that she could use her magic for good.

Admit that she wasn't whatever monster he had convinced himself she had become.

He shifted as he turned his body more towards her, but he still refused to look at her. "If you hadn't been there, I... we would be dead."

It wasn't an apology, or a thanks, but she supposed it was as good as she was going to get from him.

He cleared his throat and stood. "Quit leaning against my bed."

She moved without question, placing her back against the front door, and kept her eyes trained on the mages. She wasn't going to let her guard down again.

Renly's breathing evened out as he drifted off to sleep, his face scrunched from his uncomfortable position. She ran over a lot of things in her mind as the room fell into complete silence, apart from the quiet snores coming from Merek.

Why was this the first they were hearing of the other attacks? How long had King Alroy known about the attacks and dismissed them? How many people had died to make these attacks necessary in the first place?

All the unknowns made her headache grow stronger.

Hopefully her father would have a better idea of what was going on.

CHAPTER THIRTEEN

They left as soon as day broke, barely allowing the morning light to filter through the trees.

Robard helped with the mages, Arley too, as Olivia helped Peter ready their horses. She was glad for the help. The sleepless night left her utterly exhausted, and it didn't help that she was still aching from getting hit during the battle.

Peter kept his distance more than usual. He couldn't even bring himself to look at her, and left as soon as he was done with a few horses, leaving Olivia to trail behind with the rest.

She idly stroked Shadow's mane, smiling as she seemed to lean into her touch. "At least you're not afraid of me, huh?"

As she was leading the rest of the horses to where everyone was gathered, she felt a presence in her mind. It was much like what she felt in the forest, and again in that alleyway, although a lot less painful. It had to be that mage child again.

She turned back to the village and spotted the young mage lingering by the back of the stables. She was wearing a travelling coat, pockets bulging with food, and a determined look on her face. Thank the Gods she was okay.

Olivia led the horses to Arley and made her way over to the girl, giving Arley some excuse about needing to pee before they set off.

She smiled as Olivia approached, peeling back her hood so she could see more of her face. "Thank you, Olivia."

"You know," Olivia studied her. "Don't you think it's a bit weird that you know my name but I don't know yours?"

"Molle," the girl smiled. "It- it's Molle."

Olivia glanced over her shoulder and watched with amusement as the knights tried to hoist the bound ladies onto the backs of their horses. "You could come back with us." She turned back to Molle with a frown. "You helped us, so Alira will keep you safe. I'll make sure of it."

Molle snorted, "can you promise that?"

Olivia didn't have a good answer. As much as she wanted to help Molle, to try and keep her safe from these Uprisers that she had managed to get herself tangled up with, she could barely promise her own safety back home.

"I'd be a lot worse off in Alira than on my own, you of all people should know that." She gave her a look. "I overheard them talking in the tavern. You've been there your whole life and they still don't like you, what kind of hope would I have? Especially after they hear about all this." Molle gave her a sad smile. "You could come with me. Get away from it all."

Gods, did that offer sound tempting. Never having to watch her back, feeling free to perform magic wherever she wanted to, never having to worry about if the empty threats became a little too real... but she knew she couldn't do that.

"I can't just run away, Molle. I have a family, friends, responsibilities. I have to protect my home and my people."

"*Your* home? *Your* people?" Molle shook her head with a laugh, pulling her hood back up. "You'll change your mind. I'll come find you when you do."

She turned around and left without another word.

As Olivia stood there and watched her leave, she couldn't help the feeling that she was watching her freedom walk away with her. What if the kid was right? Especially after they brought these mages back to Alira. The atmosphere back home was already charged. Something like this would only drive the people's hate further. Being there was about to get a whole lot more dangerous.

"Olivia! Get a move on!"

She was jarred back into reality at the calling of her name. She took one final steadying breath before turning her back on where Molle once stood. Time to face reality.

They rode hard that day, stopping only for bathroom breaks and to give the horses a breather. The mages rode with Maddox and Merek, with Olivia and Arley bringing up the rear in case they tried anything. The trek was silent, a stark difference to their journey on the way there. They didn't even stop for food, eating whatever they had packed or taken from the Drerimas Tavern as they rode.

They arrived back home long after nightfall.

Olivia was exhausted, not only from the full day's ride but from her sleepless night, and not being able to fully recover after the battle. She felt dizzy and sick, the jarring movements of the ride not helping her any.

King Alroy and her father were waiting in the courtyard upon their arrival. Cassius lingered off to the side with an anxious look, his face lighting up when he caught her gaze. Gods, she didn't realise how much she would miss him until that moment, but she was too tired to give him much more than a soft smile.

She dismounted with Robard's help, barely containing a laugh when she immediately caught her foot in the stirrup and almost fell off. Renly was reporting to his father, with Arley and Merek bringing him the bound mages.

Olivia's father gave her a once over as he approached, silently cataloguing her injuries. He clapped her on the shoulder, the heavy weight keeping her grounded and tethered to reality. "You did well, Olivia."

She yawned, wide and a little loud, her jaw clicking. He let out a gruff laugh and rummaged around in his pocket, producing a few berries and handing them over to her. They were round and dark orange in colour, completely covered in vertical lines. She knew immediately what they were.

Fatigue Brier were native to the northern parts of the Kingdom. They rejuvenated energy, one berry enough for a few hours before the crash overwhelmed the senses and the fatigue hit tenfold.

He handed her two. He must need her awake and alert for a reason. Being as exhausted as she was, she didn't hesitate in taking them. He took a step back, waving at her to follow him as he walked towards the castle entrance, the king and the other knights already ahead of them.

She spared Cassius a glance, who seemed put out that she didn't greet him. She mouthed an apology at him before following her father, hoping he would understand the need to finish this business before falling asleep for at least a year. His mouth thinned out into a tight smile as he nodded and left.

As they made it to the great hall, King Alroy dismissed everyone but Renly, Olivia, and Robard. The mages were handed over to the guards to be taken to the dungeons.

"Go, rest." He had said. "Your journey was long and much more eventful than it should have been. You served us well."

She watched as they left, one by one, shoulders drooping as they climbed the stairs to their chambers. Nicolas looked back briefly but didn't pause in his journey, rubbing out a kink in his neck as he turned the corner out of sight.

The great hall was empty this time of night, making the room feel a lot bigger and more intimidating than it did during the day, constantly filled with council members and the flurry of various servants.

King Alroy turned to face them when he reached the middle of the room, her father by his side. "What happened?"

"We encountered some resistance. John, their leader, had been manipulated by the mages we brought in." Renly rubbed the back of his neck. "They had been to some other villages in the area, tried to recruit them as well, but when it didn't go as planned..." He trailed off, face pale.

"They killed them." Robard said.

King Alroy raised a brow, "recruited for what?"

Olivia turned her attention to the king. He didn't seem surprised at the news, or particularly alarmed of the murder that occurred as the result. It was almost as though he already knew about the attacks, only curious as to the motive behind it.

The mages were right. He didn't care. Maybe they were magical communities, the ones they attacked. It would make sense, if his lack of empathy towards their deaths meant anything. It didn't make sense as to why they would suddenly attack Drerimas though, or why they would attack their own kind in the name of vengeance for their entire race.

Renly and Olivia shared a look before he spoke. "An uprising. Against you, against the Kingdom, for wrongdoings to their kind. That's what they said."

He swore under his breath. "Typical mages. Such high tempers."

Olivia curled her hands into fists by her side, but one look from her father had her unfurling them immediately. Fighting back against his degrading comment would be pointless. It would only serve to prove him right.

"How, exactly," King Alroy turned to face her. "Did you manage to apprehend them?"

Olivia recounted the battle. How she saw the knights going down and knew she had to help, exactly how she managed to subdue them. She had the undivided attention of her father the entire time, something which she rarely had these days.

The need to please her father ran so deep through her veins that she couldn't ignore it. He seemed pleased at what she was able to achieve, much to her relief. Even if it did make her a little sick to think about.

After much deliberation between the king and her father, it was decided that they would go question the mages themselves.

They gave each other a look, one with a meaning she couldn't decipher, before the King turned back to them. "Renly, Olivia, come with us."

Robard tensed and gravitated closer to her, as if his mere presence could protect her from whatever the two of them wanted from her. Olivia nudged her hand against his in silent reassurance. The mages were bound, after all, and her father was a lot more powerful than she was. They would be fine.

He seemed doubtful, but the tension drained from him as he ran a tired hand over his face. Robard bowed at the room before he turned to leave. He placed a heavy, comforting hand on her shoulder before walking off to his chambers.

Renly paid her no mind before obediently following their fathers out the doors.

CHAPTER FOURTEEN

The walk from the great hall was silent apart from the tapping of their shoes. She avoided Renly's gaze as they strode behind their fathers, twisting down corridors she barely remembered the castle had, their path only lit by the occasional candle lining the walls.

An off-putting feeling settled in her chest as they walked. It felt like a warning, that she should be wary of what she was about to find. For a brief moment she toyed with the idea of telling Renly, of sparing him the same warning she felt, but when she looked over at him he only looked determined.

The king and her father were handed candles by the guards as they entered, and led the two of them down to the very last cell. It was roomy enough for both of the captured Uprisers. She was surprised to find them both in the same cell. If it were up to her, she would have separated them, even put up some more precautions. There was no-one guarding their cell.

She understood why when she got closer. She could practically feel the magic radiating from the bars, and it certainly wasn't from the mages inside. Her father must have cast some enchantment.

She glanced up at her father, the question on her lips, but he answered before she even had the chance to ask. "Containment spell. No one with magic can enter or leave until it wears off."

She didn't even know magic like that existed. She'd never even heard of a spell that could do something like that. Must be in one of those books he's always telling her to read. She was impressed.

"So." King Alroy took a step towards the cell. "I heard a little something about an uprising."

The brunette tensed but didn't answer. Neither did the blonde from where she was practically curled into the taller one's side, her shoulder still bandaged.

The king sighed, "You didn't kill them in Drerimas. Why not?"

Again, they didn't answer.

They were scared, she could practically feel it, but they still maintained eye contact with the king when he questioned them. They weren't scared of him, then. What more could they be afraid of?

After refusing to cooperate, the king took a step back from the bars, and motioned her father forwards. He didn't seem particularly agitated from their refusal to talk, almost as if he had expected resistance. Or wanted it, from the way he phrased his questions. Lazily, like he wasn't even interested in an answer.

"Persuade them, William."

Her father took the king's position without hesitation. His demeanour changed the moment he was in front of their cell, something dark and serious coming over his face. If he wasn't her father, the clear shift in personality would have shaken her to the core.

At this, the blonde turned away.

Her father cleared his throat, "Tell me about the uprising."

They didn't speak.

"What about Drerimas?"

They still refused to answer him, but this time they truly seemed scared. Sure, he looked a lot more intimidating than the king, but he held nowhere near as much power as him. There was no reason to be scared of him any more than they should be scared of the one in charge.

Was it the magic that frightened them?

Her father sighed, much like the king had done, and raised his palm to the bars. She didn't know what spell he was casting, but the effect was instantaneous.

The brunette began to hiss and squirm, not quite screaming but in obvious pain. She screwed her eyes shut and tried to focus on her breathing, but it didn't seem to be helping.

"I'll ask again. Tell me about the uprising."

Still no answer.

He sighed and lowered his hand, but only for a moment. Olivia blinked, and the brunette was screaming.

Little cuts began to appear on her skin. She was thrashing around, trying to escape the pain, but it didn't relent. The blonde had her eyes wide open with fear, arms flailing as she watched her friend in pain. She couldn't help her.

Her father was torturing them.

Olivia took a subconscious step away from her father as the realisation hit. She didn't know he was capable of doing something like this.

She chanced a look at Renly beside her, who had his lips pressed tightly together, jaw set and eyes ablaze. He was furious at what was going on... or was he furious at the mages for not answering the questions? She could hardly tell anymore. He gave her a quick look, and she could see how scared he allowed himself to be. They were both well out of their depth.

"Fine! We'll talk!"

The screaming stopped, and the silence was almost deafening.

The blonde gathered her friend in her arms, who was still shaking from the aftermath. She didn't let her go as she began speaking, not even flinching when the brunette's blood slowly began to seep onto her clothes, mingling with the dried blood from her wounds back in Drerimas.

"We- we don't know much. The Uprisers hardly tell us anything! We're new, we haven't been with them for long. Not like—" she stopped herself, fear seeping into every part of her expression.

Olivia wasn't inclined to believe them, but the fear in her voice was definitely real. If they really were new, it was possible they were sent to Drerimas on purpose. Or they went themselves, in an attempt to prove themselves to the more important members of the Uprisers. It made sense. Capturing a high target like the prince, or one of his knights at the very least, would certainly impress them.

"Why are the Uprisers attacking villages?" Her father asked.

"The others, they were fed up with the lack of response to suffering villages. To the growing famine and disease that's been running rampant in magical communities since we were kids." She began stroking her friend's hair. "Sick of the prejudice the Kingdom holds against those born with magic. Sick and tired of knowing our king would much rather us dead than to help us."

Olivia knew of the magical diseases she was speaking of, the ones that could wipe out entire communities. She knew the king never wanted to waste his resources trying to help them, some excuse about not wanting to bring it back inside Alira's walls, even though he *knew* the disease only affected mages. She had overheard her father arguing with the king about it more than a few times.

The Uprisers should be angry. She had no qualms about that, Olivia herself was livid about it. Just because they were angry, it didn't mean they had to resort to such disturbing methods. They were extremists, damning the name of mages across the Kingdom instead of helping their cause. They were only going to cause more fighting and death this way. It wasn't going to fix anything.

It was easy enough for her to think that from where she stood, she supposed. Sure, she didn't exactly love the way she was treated by others in Alira, but she was safe. Many of her kind couldn't say the same thing.

These Uprisers were probably too far past caring about the consequences. They just wanted to make the man in charge pay for the crimes he has committed against his people, the ones he swore to protect. To make him feel the way they do.

Her father took a step back and shared a look with the king. King Alroy shook his head and gestured for her father to keep going.

The blonde caught his gesture and looked up at them, wide-eyed and scared. "No! P-please, I swear, that's all we know!"

"I don't think I believe you," the king snarled.

Her father turned back to face the cells, raising his arm like he had before, but he hesitated. *Thank the Gods*, she thought, *he's finally coming to his senses.* He turned to look at her over his shoulder, and extended arm out towards her.

Silently beckoning her to do as he had done. To torture them. The thought made her sick.

"No." She shook her head wildly. "N-no, I'm not going to *torture* them!" She spared a look at the huddled girls. "They already talked."

Her father glared at her, arm not budging. "I'm not asking, Olivia."

His tone was the same he used on the Uprisers in the cell. She couldn't help the shiver it sent down her spine, but she held her ground. "I said no."

"How disappointing."

He turned back to the cell and the screams started up again, more cuts appearing on the brunette. Olivia tried to speak over her screams, to beg her father to stop, but it was to no avail. They were just too loud.

She knew she was shaking, her hands curled into fists by her side. The sound of her screams echoed off the walls and rattled around inside her head. She wanted it to stop, she *needed* it to stop. Since when had her father become this heartless? They were his own kind, ones who had been abused their whole lives by the man at his side, and he didn't even care.

Her head began to pound, the effects of the Fatigue Brier slowly fading.

She wanted to sleep for a year, to wake up and find out this whole thing had just been some elaborate nightmare.

"Enough!"

She flinched at Renly's tone beside her, but was grateful when it stopped the screaming. Her father lowered his hand with a huff.

"We're only wasting time," Renly turned to face his father. "Even if they do know more, they're too tired and injured to tell you."

The king sighed and nodded, seeming to take his son's advice on board, and turned to talk to her father.

Renly's hands began to shake. Fear from standing up to his father, or from what was happening in front of him, she didn't know.

"We'll be back tomorrow," the king snarled at the mages, before turning on his heel and leaving, her father right behind him.

They left, but she couldn't move. Her eyes were glued to the cell, where the girls were now crying, and trying their best to comfort each other.

Her *father* did that.

She didn't start moving until Renly gently tugged on her elbow. He turned her around so she could no longer see their pained faces.

She followed Renly out of the dungeons without another word.

Chapter Fifteen

Olivia spent a long time after she returned from Dereimas in the library, reading over any book that looked remotely magical. There weren't many in the library, but she was surprised at the amount she found.

She tried to find anything she could on Drerimas, but she came up short. It was as if she had imagined the whole thing, the tingling feeling she felt before she could even see the village.

Admittedly, she had been distracted. Her mind kept wandering back to the previous night, to the dungeon. She was scared of the king's next move.

She barely slept, even after the Fatigue Brier wore off. She woke to tortured screams still ringing in her ears.

She found herself in the castle's library well past midnight, a stack of books taller than herself piled on the rickety table. No-one was around that time of night, much to her relief. It was calm and quiet, and it allowed her to concentrate a lot better than she ever could back home.

Cassius found her there a few hours after she had arrived, but didn't say anything. He simply sat beside her and looked over some of the books she had already discarded. She was thankful that he didn't question her, about the books or about her journey, and instead just sat beside her, reminding her that she wasn't alone.

It was odd to not hear him talk her ear off, but she was grateful he didn't push. He fell asleep after an hour, much to her amusement.

Having Cassius with her, conscious or not, seemed to help her a great deal. While she never found anything on Drerimas, she did find information on a lot of things she had never heard of before.

They had a whole book on wars that had been fought within the magical communities for centuries, which was definitely the last place she ever thought something like that would be.

It even detailed the Battle of Trin – an old war that occurred long before most people remembered, where fighting between the warlocks and enchanters resulted in the bloodiest battle the magical community had ever seen. A truce was formed and the term 'mage' was born, where both warlocks and enchanters could fit under the one name and be seen on equal footing. It was the most important battle in mage history.

Perhaps King Alroy had just forgotten the book was there. It seemed unlikely.

She also got her hands on a set of scrolls detailing various magical poisons, or ones that specifically targeted those with magic in their blood. From Silent Blight, a poison that messes with the chemicals in a mage's brain and drives them crazy until a cure is found, to Galanthis Serrata, a poison found within the leaves of the plant of the same name, that attacks the magical cells in the body and freezes them, killing the mage if they don't get the antidote within the week.

It even detailed Winter's Thorn. She always hated that one. It was more of a potion than a poison, and only lasted up to a day, depending on how much was ingested. They used it as a training tool to withstand torture, or to push past the initial pain of overusing one's magic. It caused a stabbing pain to be felt throughout the body, a feeling that is apparently as close to getting physically stabbed as you could get, until the potion ran its course. It has been known to make people pass out from phantom pain.

She wouldn't be surprised if it was still in use, within both human and mage communities alike. It would explain why the scrolls were still there.

She was so engrossed in her readings that she hadn't even realised when the birds began to chirp, nor when the sun started to shine through the windows. It wasn't until the doors flung open, hitting the wall behind it with force, that she looked up from her books.

Cassius didn't even stir, just turned his head away from the light that was pouring through the open door. Arley stood by the door, looking wildly around the room, exhaling deeply when his gaze landed on her.

"Do you know how hard it was to find you?" He ignored Olivia as she snorted at him. "You've been summoned by the court."

Her amusement faded as quickly as it arose. Did something happen to the Uprisers in the dungeon? Did they find out about Molle? She was still surprised that no-one had mentioned the kid since they came back.

There were so many possibilities that it made her head spin.

She slowly stood from her chair and followed Arley out the door, leaving the books where they were. She yawned and stretched, wincing at the loud popping that echoed around the almost empty room.

Arley hesitated and looked back into the room, "shouldn't you wake him?"

She turned to look back at Cassius, and laughed as he drooled onto the book he was currently sleeping on. "Let him sleep."

"You look horrible by the way."

"Thank you, Arley."

The walk to the great hall was silent, almost awkward. Arley didn't say a word since they left the library, always a few steps ahead of her, but he didn't seem angry or scared. They hadn't spoken since Drerimas, not that they had spoken much before.

Her father was waiting as they arrived, along with the entire royal family and choice members of the court. Arley whistled quietly as he passed Olivia to leave, muttering a quiet "good luck" before closing the doors behind him.

Well, that wasn't worrying at all.

"Olivia," her father gave her a sharp look. "Good of you to finally join us."

She bowed, "my apologies father, Your Majesty."

Renly chuckled from where he stood beside his mother.

"No matter." King Alroy waved a dismissive hand in her direction. "We're here because of this uprising business."

Olivia tensed. Did they talk to the Uprisers again this morning? She glanced briefly at her father before looking back to the king. She didn't hear the screams from any more questioning, but the walls were pretty thick down in the dungeons.

"Olivia," the king gave her a tight smile. "I require you to accompany Prince Renly and his knights with all of their trips outside of Alira's walls. Just until this mess sorts itself out." He gave her a sharp look. "You will defend them with your life, am I understood?"

Olivia wasn't asked if she consented to this, if she even wanted to leave the city walls during such a time. Instead, she was simply told she was going to do it, and that was that.

She was terrified, especially if this mess didn't get sorted out any time soon. The battle in Drerimas was the first time she used her magic against anyone that wasn't her father, and she wasn't sure how well she would fare the next time.

Not that it mattered, apparently. She didn't have a choice, not with the king demanding it. Besides, once word got out about this uprising, being inside the city walls wouldn't be any safer than being outside of them. The townsfolk would get more desperate to vent their frustrations, to vent through their fear, with only Olivia and her father to take on the brunt of it.

And they wouldn't dare touch the court mage.

"Understood, Your Majesty."

At least being with the knights meant protection. She needed whatever she could get.

"You will train with the knights in basic combat and personal protection." The king turned to look at her father. "You will make time to train with your father, too." He turned back to her. "You will not have the knights be responsible for your protection, but you will be responsible for theirs."

She'd struggle to fit in her hours at the forge with all of her extra duties. She wouldn't mind so much if she would get paid for any of it, but that was highly doubtful. Osmond was going to be livid.

She bowed to the king, carefully avoiding her father's gaze. "Of course, Your Majesty."

"Very good," he waved dismissively at her. "You'll be summoned when needed." He turned to face his son. "You can leave, too, Renly."

"But father-"

"Now."

Renly huffed as he walked out, checking her shoulder as he pushed past and threw open the oak doors. Olivia bowed to the room and quickly followed Renly out. She didn't make it very far until she ran straight into his chest. He was frustrated, breathing heavily with a scowl on his face. He glared as he pushed her up against the closest wall, his strong arm against her collarbone.

"Mark my words, mage." He spat the word out like a curse. "As soon as this threat is over, you'll be back to being some useless nobody in that dirty old forge." She gasped as he pressed against her harder. "No-one wants you here."

She didn't know if he meant there with his knights, within Alira, or alive at all. Perhaps all three.

She gasped for air when he pushed away from her. She rubbed idly at the bruises she was sure were going to appear within the hour. He was cruller than usual, a stark difference from the kindness he showed her the previous night, leading her out of the cells and keeping the information about Molle from both their fathers.

She hoped he was just pushing her away out of fear.

Chapter Sixteen

She landed on the ground heavily, and it took a few moments to catch her breath. She groaned and wiggled away from the sticks digging into her back. Her father sighed heavily from somewhere to her left.

"Get up," he nudged her leg. "You're lazy, unfocused. You wouldn't last a week out there."

Olivia groaned and clambered to her feet a little unsteadily. She rolled out her shoulders, making her neck crack. Her father frowned, unimpressed.

They had been training out in the forest behind their house since dawn broke. He had taken the king's word to heart and started their training the very next day. He wasn't going to waste any time. He wasn't going to go easy on her either, if the way her bones were aching was any indication.

They hadn't taken a break for food or water in the hours they had been there. It was something her father told her she should train to withstand. Just in case.

"You won't have the luxury of breaks in the middle of a battle, Olivia." He had said.

They trained until the sun began its descent in the sky, until she had tripped over the uneven ground one too many times. Her head was throbbing, her bones aching, her stomach growling.

One more hit by her father sent her sprawling. Her nose made a sickening crack as she landed face down, pain shooting across her face as the blood slowly oozed out onto the dirt underneath.

"Olivia!" His voice boomed. "You'll never learn if you keep failing! No-one else will pick up the slack for you!" He tossed a fireball at her legs, one she narrowly avoided by rolling over. He approached where she was lying, head pillowed by the fallen leaves, and hovered his face over her own with a frown. "If you fail, people will die."

His voice grew quieter, but not any softer. "It's a wonder any of you made it back the last time."

She flinched at his words.

He rubbed his face with frustration and took a step back. She slowly pushed herself up, wincing at the ache that seemed to settle in her bones at the movement. His words stung, but she couldn't deny he was wrong. It was all but a miracle she was able to stop the couple of Uprisers like she did, wholly unprepared and not at all confident in her abilities.

If she couldn't even protect herself against her own father, how could she protect anyone else?

They were interrupted by a young boy, who ran straight up to her father without sparing her so much as a glance. The kid didn't even flinch as he stopped in front of him. "The king needs you."

Her father sighed. It must have been all the confirmation the boy needed, because he scurried away without another word.

He waved a hand lazily in Olivia's direction as he turned his back on her. She bit back a shout as her nose snapped back into place with searing pain, the blood slowing to a stop. She swore under her breath, clutching at her nose to make sure he didn't break it more in his frustration.

Her father didn't even spare her another glance as he stomped out of the clearing. "Read what's in the chest by the fire before I get back."

She rubbed at her face in exhaustion, fighting the urge to just lie back down and never get back up again. It wasn't like they never trained together before all of this. She was good at handling her magic, to an extent, but apparently that wasn't good enough.

She groaned as she pushed herself up from the ground. She knew that she was training in case things got out of hand, like this uprising thing was looking likely to be. Being good just wasn't good enough, but she really did wish it wasn't so painful.

She shuffled her way towards the house, rubbing at the phantom pain of her previously broken nose. She didn't want to continue training, to read up on the boring old books and scrolls her father had. She had skimmed them countless times before and she knew they held nothing of real importance, just history and old battles, things that were completely irrelevant to her current situation.

Training is what she needed, not a history lesson.

She knew it was better to do it now rather than later, though. He was her teacher and her father, so she couldn't exactly tell him no.

Olivia groaned as she sat on the ground by the unlit fireplace and reached out for the chest. Her stomach rumbled as she fumbled with the lock. The faster she could get through all this, the faster she could go to the tavern and convince her mother to get her something good to eat.

There was only a single scroll inside the chest. She picked it up wearily and slowly unfurled it, only to almost drop it in surprise. It was exactly what she had been searching for.

She recognised the curved handwriting immediately. She had read this scroll once before, a long time ago, when she was still quite young and her magic hadn't presented itself yet. She forgot all about it after the fire. Her lips curled into a smile when she read the first word.

Drerimas.

The scroll wasn't very long, just snippets of what she's sure was quite a long series, and it was mostly focused on Drerimas. Why her father neglected to show this to her until now was beyond her.

It was the site of an old magical battle, a civil war of sorts between warring magical communities, many from both sides of the war having lost their lives. The village was abandoned in an attempt to forget about the war and the bloodshed, in an act of regret over what had occurred. It was taken over by humans many years later. It was no wonder she felt the magic so strongly there.

Olivia read the scroll over and over again, making notes in the leather-bound notebook her father had gifted her many years ago. She sat there until the sun had fully set and the lanterns along the path outside had been lit. She was determined not to forget about this place, or any place similar. Not if there was a chance something like this could occur again.

She sighed as she pushed herself up, stomach grumbling almost painfully. She kept her head down as she made her way to the tavern, too hungry and drained to fight with any of the bristling townsfolk.

She barely made it a few steps through the doors before she was being hugged tightly, a mess of black hair suddenly in her face. She winced at the pressure but clung back just as tight, breathing in the comforting scent. The woman smelt like warm bread and ale, likely from spending most of her day at the tavern.

Nyx led her over to the counter and poured her an ale with a sly wink, her long black hair braided messily over her left shoulder. Despite her long hours, her skin was still beautifully pale, and there wasn't a spot of muck on her.

"Is that little Livvy I see?" Finnian grinned from where he was manning various stoves in his kitchen. The longer he looked at her, the more his smile slipped. She didn't know how she looked after her training with her father, but she's sure it wasn't a pretty sight. "I'll make you somethin'."

Olivia grinned and slowly sipped at her ale. She pointedly ignored Finnian's occasional worried glances, and Nyx's constant staring. It would only make them worried if she told them the truth. They hated when she didn't eat, and when she trained so long that she looked like... well, like she did now.

Her mother appeared as she was finishing her ale, cutting through the awkward atmosphere. She kissed her daughter on the forehead in greeting before slapping her up the back of the head. She sent her a disapproving look as her gaze flicked down to the ale in her hands.

Olivia grinned innocently as her mother rounded the bar to start cleaning the dishes. "It's Nyx's fault."

Nyx gasped dramatically and shoved her shoulder lightheartedly. She giggled, a sound that made the tension bleed from Nyx's shoulders and brought a beaming smile to her mother's face.

Finnian slid up beside her mother and slipped a bowl of food in front of Olivia with a wink. She closed her eyes and breathed in the smell, a grin slowly pulling at her lips. Finnian's Pottage always made her feel at home. It filled her with warmth and sat heavily in her stomach, chasing away the hunger pains she often felt. He had given her a slice of freshly baked bread too, the aroma making her stomach rumble loudly.

She grinned brightly at Finnian, "you're my new favourite."

Finnian laughed at Nyx's pout, eliciting a happy laugh from her mother as they began to squabble. She ate her Pottage as quickly as her slowly numbing limbs allowed, and watched fondly over them. She loved them, all of them, and she sometimes forgot how deep her affection went until she walked through those doors.

They welcomed her mother with open arms when she was at her lowest point. She had been fired from her job in the castle after the fire, and no-one in Alira was willing to give a job to the mother and wife of the local mages. The tavern didn't care.

Most of the time, the four walls of The Sun felt more like home than her house did. It was her safety, her escape from the horrors waiting for her outside. The patrons of The Sun never insulted or abused her, rarely stared longer than a few seconds. No-one dared mess with the people serving their ale.

Garrick appeared as Finnian took her empty bowl, sauntering down the stairs with a sly grin, one that grew into a proper one when he saw her. His red hair fell into his eyes, but he didn't bother pushing it back.

He had owned The Sun since she was a young girl. He must have come into money early on, because he was still fairly young when he bought the place. He was a lot skinnier back then, and had a frown that was much more present than it was these days. He hired Finnian, then Nyx, and later opened his arms for her mother. Everything seemed to get better after that.

He had stayed behind the bar those first few weeks after he had hired her, chasing off the patrons that wanted to cause her harm. He got into a few fistfights early on, and after things calmed down a little, he would stick by her side and glare at anyone who so much as looked at her funny.

After a month, it was like nothing had ever happened.

Her mother groaned from where she was cleaning mugs, "you don't have to look so satisfied every time you come down those stairs, you know."

Garrick rolled his eyes as he approached the bar, accepting the ale that Nyx handed him before sliding it over to Olivia.

"I wish you lot would stop trying to get my daughter drunk," her mother grumbled.

There was a loud crash coming from somewhere in the tavern, followed by drunken happy cheers. Her mother left with a sigh to go pick up the pieces of whatever had smashed, much to Garrick and Nyx's delight.

Garrick snickered as he leaned comfortably against the counter, facing out towards his patrons. He reached over and ruffled her hair with a sad smile. "You look tired."

She sighed into her mug, turning to face the same way as Garrick as she put her red strands back into place. "I *feel* tired."

He hummed, "heard you've been getting some unwanted attention."

"Not more than usual," she shrugged. "Just a bit more... enthusiastic."

She could practically feel the pointed look he was sending her. "Olivia–"

"Don't." She turned to face him with what she hoped was a hard look, but he just smiled sadly at her. "Please. Can we just... I don't want to think about it."

Garrick nodded, sad smile turning into something a bit more chipper as he bumped their arms together. "Have a few more of those and I guarantee that will happen."

"Mother will be thrilled," she snorted.

They spoke idly for a while, until her mug was refilled again, as Garrick caught her up with everything she missed while she was away.

He was finishing a rather rousing tale of Nyx beating up a patron for touching a girl who clearly didn't want it, where Nyx had broken the man's nose and chased him out of the tavern, when they heard obnoxiously loud laughter floating over from the opposite side of the tavern.

They both looked up, and she rolled her eyes at the sight. Maddox was leaning against a table, grinning slyly as he chatted up some girl. She kissed him filthily before walking out the front doors.

Olivia scrunched up her nose, "gross."

Maddox was wearing a dopey grin as he turned and caught Olivia's eye. Without hesitation, he made a beeline straight towards her.

Garrick let out a low whistle. "I don't get anything like *that* upstairs."

She groaned, shoving Garrick good-naturedly as he laughed joyously at her reaction.

A shout caught their attention. Garrick's amusement faded as they saw Nyx glaring daggers at a patron who had a hand on her arse. She looked like she was going to rip his arm clean off his shoulder.

Garrick sighed, "I better intervene before I have to explain an amputee to the king."

Not more than a second passed before Maddox slid up beside her, a satisfied grin still on his face.

"Olivia!" He clapped an unsteady hand on her shoulder, which slipped straight off. She could smell the alcohol on his breath. "What're you doin' here?"

She snorted as he tried to lean casually against the bench, only to stumble a few times before gaining purchase.

"My mother works here."

He blinked emptily at her a few times before he made a face of revelation and clicked his fingers in front of her. "That's right!"

She laughed, but it didn't seem to sway him like it usually would. He just laughed back, grin wide and welcoming. He was a lot more pleasant the drunker he was, it seemed.

"You know," he gave her a dazzling smile. "What you did in Drerimas was pretty impressive."

The ease she felt when entering the tavern slowly melted away. She shrugged and turned away from him, turning instead to face the benchtop they were sitting at. She didn't want to talk about it, especially not with Maddox. She came here to escape all of that.

"'m grateful you were there," he leaned further onto the benchtop. "We'd be dead without you. 'm sorry I couldn't tell you before."

He was giving her a hopeful smile when she turned, and she couldn't help the small upturn of her lips. He had never directed something so positive at her before. "Why didn't you?"

"Huh?"

She snorted as he swayed into her, and she reached out a hand to steady him. "Tell me before. Why didn't you?"

"I don't know." He shrugged, a small frown sliding onto his face. "The prince and Merek have very strong opinions about you."

"Oh, I know." She said.

"Yeah, well." He avoided her gaze. "I know their opinions shouldn't affect me, but..."

She could practically feel the guilt and fear wash over him. He was a dedicated knight, that much she had always known. He joined before Merek and Arley did, and a while before Renly was old enough to take over. She had heard stories about him through Robard – he always thought Maddox was one of the best. A big joker, and probably a bit too invested in how much interest being a sworn knight got him, but he was loyal and strong and would never betray them.

"It's okay," she squeezed Maddox's shoulder. "I'm used to it."

"You shouldn't have to be." He frowned deeper, guilt swimming in his gaze. "The way people treat you..." He shook his head. "I know they're scared. Hell, I'm terrified. But it doesn't excuse anythin'."

She smiled sadly and slid her arm back to her side, "people do stupid things out of fear."

Maddox hummed and turned back to the benchtop. He picked up his mug and raised it to his mouth, only to find it empty. He frowned and looked across to Olivia's, which was in a similar state. His frown quickly turned to a grin as he snatched her mug from in front of her.

"Enough of this sad shit," he spun in his seat and wiggled the mugs at Finnian, who frowned but came over to refill them anyway. "Let's get drunk."

Finnian raised his brow at her in silent question. He slid Maddox's over to him but hadn't filled hers yet, waiting for her permission, to reassure him she was safe. Or to tell him she wasn't, so he could call Garrick over to throw Maddox out on his arse, knight or not.

"Why noy?" She turned a grin on Maddox, who returned it brightly.

Screw it, she thought. She deserved to let loose for once.

CHAPTER SEVENTEEN

She was late getting to training with the knights the following day.

After depositing Maddox in his chambers the night before, the knight so drunk she feared he would fall in the streets and not manage to get back up again, she had stayed up late into the night pouring over the ancient scrolls that belonged to her father. She had woken to find she had fallen asleep face-first in a scroll dated back before her grandfather was born.

She knew she had to be better, especially after she discovered that she had already known about Drermias but had simply forgotten about it.

Her bones ached from how much she had pushed herself over the past few days, and it took a lot more effort than usual to push herself to get dressed and hurry down to the training fields.

Robard was waiting for her when she finally arrived, smirking as he leaned against the fencepost by the edge of the yard. "Good of you to show, little one."

"Bite me, old man."

Robard laughed loudly, his teasing smile turning into a wide grin. He slung his arm over her shoulder and led her over to the others.

They had a less enthused reaction to her running behind. All apart from Nicolas, who grinned and waved her over, and Maddox, who looked to be nursing a horrible hangover. Everyone else simply avoided looking at her or, in Merek's case, wouldn't stop staring.

As it turns out, Merek wasn't the only one to be unfairly judgemental.

Renly treated her as if she had never even held a sword before, as if she could barely hold a branch before falling over. It infuriated her. Not only because of the time they spent together playing knights as little kids, but because of her work in the forge. It was her *job* to be able to handle the exact weapons they were training with. Hell, she had even helped make most of them. Even the training swords!

It didn't help that Maddox treated her overly kind too, probably too afraid to hit her after she saw him so vulnerable the night before.

Robard knew her, though. He knew her potential and strength, and didn't mock it. She had never been more grateful for that old man.

Training went smoothly for the most part, much to her surprise. She sparred with Nicolas and Robard, and was thankful she could work up to sparring against those who actually wanted to cause her harm rather than help her improve.

"Come now, Olivia." Renly smirked as she finished sparring with Nicolas, the boy being helped up from the dirt by a laughing Maddox. "My turn."

She braced herself for an intense start, to be beaten into the dirt quicker than she managed to flatten Nicolas, hoping he had finally come to his senses, but he went so easy on her it was almost insulting.

She would have preferred to be completely overpowered by him, to have the chance to properly fight against him and lose because he was better than her, not to win because he couldn't be bothered with her. It was completely embarrassing.

She let out a low growl as she side-stepped his lazy swing with ease. She glared, a reaction Renly hadn't expected, as he took a minuscule step away from her.

"Oh, come *on*, Renly! Is that all you've got?" She glared. "A little pathetic if you ask me."

She watched in satisfaction as Renly frowned, annoyed at being challenged in front of his men. His frown only seemed to deepen when the sounds of laughter floated over to them.

"Bad idea," she heard Robard grumble, although she wasn't sure who he was talking to.

Renly shook his head and reached over to where they kept their swords. The real swords, not the lightweight ones they were using to practise with. He threw her one and arched a brow in silent challenge. The solid, familiar weight of the sword brought her more confidence than she's had the entire day.

She caught it with ease. Who was she to reject a challenge from her prince?

"Come on then!" She grinned toothily at Renly as she stalked around him. "Fight me for real, pretty boy."

Renly grinned just as wide and slid into an attacking stance. A real stance, not the toned-down stuff he was giving her before. He twirled the sword around in his hand with ease before bringing it up in front of him.

"Bring it, mage."

She growled as she lunged at Renly, who sidestepped her quickly and kicked her in the back. She stumbled a few paces before spinning around with a grin.

"Now that's more like it!"

She held her own, but she was never as good as Renly, not when they were kids and not now. She didn't expect to be, though.

He swung angrily at her neck, only narrowly missing as she ducked just in time. She stumbled a little in surprise. She just wanted him to try, she didn't want him to take her head off.

Renly landed a blow to her side that had her stumbling and clutching at the growing pain. He used her distraction to sweep at her leg, sending her tumbling on the ground, sword thrown from her grasp and landing a few inches away from her.

She blinked, and Renly was suddenly looming over her. He held his sword to her throat and pressed, digging into her skin until she felt warmth trickle down her neck.

He had a wild look to him as he stood over her. She couldn't tell if he was angry or frustrated, with her or with the entire situation they both found themselves in. All she knew was that the look frightened her.

"You shouldn't be here," he growled. "You're a liability, and you're going to get us all killed." He pressed harder. "This only proves how weak you are without your magic to protect you."

She pawed at his wrist, trying to get him to loosen his grip. Panic was gripping her as she stared into his eyes, but all she could see was anger.

He laughed and shook his head, "sometimes I wish I never met you."

He stood abruptly and stalked off, not sparing a word or a glance to his knights, who had suddenly grown a lot quieter. Peter didn't hesitate to scramble after him.

She rubbed at her throat and grimaced at the blood coating her fingertips. It was minimal, though. Nothing too serious. She thumped her head against the ground with a groan. He looked wild as he peered down at her, like nothing she had ever seen before. She was scared of that look coming from Renly. She had never been scared of him before.

Robard came into her view, his smile not quite reaching his eyes. He offered her a hand and she took it gratefully, rubbing at her throat again as she stood. She was glad to see her fingers mostly devoid of blood this time.

He clasped a hand on her shoulder, using his thumb to rub at her collarbone. "You're not done with trainin' just yet."

She cleared her throat, as if that could rid the tremble in her voice, and stalked towards Maddox. "You're up, Dox."

He ran with the change of pace good-naturedly, teasing as he shuffled them over to somewhere less crowded. She didn't dare look at the other knights, didn't know if she could handle their looks of agreement to what Renly had said. She wouldn't know what to do if they were pitying, either.

Eventually, the others began to continue training too. They were nicer to her after Renly's outburst, didn't stare as much, and held back the biting remarks they would usually share.

Merek was unusually silent the rest of the day.

CHAPTER EIGHTEEN

"Are we there yet?"

"Quit whinin', Dox."

Olivia laughed to herself as she rode beside Nicolas. She had been training with the knights for a few days now, something she was grateful for. Maddox was warming to her, thanks to Nicolas' constant praise and Robard's protectiveness over her. Arley still didn't seem sure, and Merek seemed to like her even less than Renly did, not that she thought that would change.

She had been cornered by her father the night before and told she would be setting out the following morning with the knights. She really wished he would get better at giving her some warning about these things.

Apparently, they were out looking into something the captured Uprisers had told the king. It was surprising, as they genuinely didn't seem to know much about the Uprisers future movements, but she packed her things anyway. Her father said it had something to do with a meeting ground that the Uprisers used to keep in contact with each other. A common one, apparently. He said it would be more of a fact-finding mission than anything, but she doubted that.

It made her question if it was truly for the Uprisers, or for mages of any kind. Surely an organisation such as the Uprisers wouldn't be meeting in a commonly known area.

She didn't know what they should do if they found anyone there. Were they to apprehend them? Scare them off, wound them? The whole thing was a little too hasty in her opinion, but it wasn't exactly like she could just refuse to go.

Olivia was glad for all the extra training she had been doing, not just with the knights. She knew if they actually ran into any trouble like last time, she was much better prepared.

The past few days were completely filled with training. She was up before dawn training with her father, trained with the knights in the afternoon, and did magical study after dinner. Her brain hurt, arms ached, but she felt good. She felt muscles where there were none before, and felt more confident in her own abilities. Even if her magic could still use a bit of work.

It reminded her of the old days when she was constantly running around with Renly, training together to become the best future knights they could be. They felt like they were on top of the world and no one could touch them. She felt a pang of longing and looked over at Renly, leading the group, silent and brooding. They hadn't spoken in days, not since their altercation at training. She would have thought he felt bad about it if he didn't still look so annoyed whenever he saw her.

They could have made it to the meeting ground by nightfall, a fact that Renly kept trying to push, but Olivia thought it was a bad idea.

"What if someone's there?" She questioned. "Our presence this late might scare them off before we get any information from them."

"Like you'd know the first thing about interrogating someone." Renly was furious as he spun on his horse to look at her. "Or maybe it runs in your blood."

Olivia frowned as the rest of the knights grew silent. He knew how uncomfortable she was that night in the dungeons, how disgusted she was with her father about what he had done, but he used it against her anyway.

Before things could get too heated, Robard cleared his throat. "If we surprise them, they could move to a different location and this would all be for nothin'."

It was a challenge, clearly, but Renly gave in like he knew it was a bad idea in the first place. He either trusted Robard completely, or just didn't want to give Olivia the satisfaction of being right.

Renly's posture deflated as he gestured to a clearing up ahead and to the right. "We'll make camp here, then. It's not far from our destination."

Olivia huffed and turned away, ignoring Nicolas' imploring gaze, and the chatter of the others as they picked up their previous conversations. She followed the others as they dismounted, though she steered clear of Peter and tied Shadow close to where she was going to make camp.

She knew they were close. She could feel the magic in the air, so palpable she could almost reach out and touch it. The feeling was a lot stronger than what she felt as they approached Drerimas, and it made her a little nervous. A feeling this strong would only occur in a place frequented by many mages over a long period of time. This may well have been a meeting place for the greater mage community, used for tens, if not hundreds, of years. It definitely wouldn't be just for the Uprisers to use.

The others shuffled about, making and eating dinner, and setting themselves up to sleep, but she couldn't bring herself to join them. The last time she felt such a foreboding feeling was right before they got ambushed and attacked, right before Renly was almost taken and everyone almost died.

She was glad when Nicolas noticed her absence and brought over a bowl of food for her to eat, refusing to leave until she had eaten it all. She knew she shouldn't go without food, especially if she was expecting to use her magic, but she felt nauseous at the possibility of another Drerimas. What if there was an ambush waiting for them?

She couldn't sleep that night, wound up too tight, the magic of the place practically screaming at her for her attention.

Sliding out from under Nicolas, who had fallen asleep on her shoulder as he waited for her to finish her dinner, she shook the feeling back into her limbs. There was no point in sitting still and waiting for the feeling to go away.

She heard whispers in the wind as if some unknown force was calling out for her, and she could feel the magic tug deep inside her chest. She hadn't felt anything like this before, not on the way to Drerimas, and not back in Alira with her father. Olivia idly wondered if she should tell anyone about the feeling, but decided against it. It wasn't like Renly would believe her. Telling Robard would just start a fight between him and Renly, and Nico wouldn't understand. None of them would understand.

It felt like some sort of impossible choice, like a challenge, like there was some sort of correct answer she should pick but she didn't know what it was.

CHAPTER NINETEEN

They arrived as the sun was high in the sky, just before its peak. The others were slow to rise, knowing they were close enough that they didn't have to leave early, and as long as they only poked around for a few hours they could make it back to Alira by nightfall.

The path wound its way through trees that seemed impossibly large, leaning over the trail as if enclosing on them. There were bushes beside the trail that burst brightly with coloured leaves and berries, a stark difference from the leafless trees that loomed overhead. It seemed magical in a way, otherworldly, as if a warning that they would come across something much bigger than themselves if they continued on.

Arley veered his horse to the side of the path, eyeing the many bright berries with intrigue. They grew out towards the path, as if the berries were asking to be picked by passing travellers. She had seen these bushes before, in one of the many books she had been pouring over since arriving back from Drerimas.

Oumetta Berries. They looked sweet and innocent, as if one bite would bring a multitude of bursting flavours, but they were dangerous to ingest for both mages and humans alike. A single berry would send the body into shock, and eating a handful at once would most certainly kill you.

"I wouldn't if I was you," Olivia shook her head as Arley reached forwards to pick a berry from the bush. "They're poisonous."

"I don't believe you," Arley said.

"Do whatever you want," she shrugged, "but I can't save you once you're dead."

She smiled in satisfaction as Arley dropped the berry into the bush as if it burned him. She rode to the middle of the group, the best place to keep an eye on everyone, enemies and friends alike. She watched Robard lean close to Renly, whispering something she couldn't quite catch.

Renly nodded and slowed his horse. "We'll leave the horses here with Peter. We're outside the perimeter of the camp, so if there's anyone waiting for us, they won't be able to hear them."

The tug inside her chest was almost painful as they made their way into the camp on foot. The pressure was humming through her veins, blood rushing through her ears so loud she could barely hear anything over the top of it. It was as if all her senses were screaming at her that whatever was there was powerful, a lot more than she had ever encountered before.

She hadn't realised she had frozen in place until Nicolas reached out to squeeze her hand, encouraging her forwards with a gentle smile.

It felt odd to wander into the abandoned camp, the whole area situated around a large cave. There was an area that had previously been used as a campsite, the ground scorched in a large circle, with logged seating around it. The area was cleared of trees and debris, dirt kicked around with faded bootprints as if it had been frequently maintained.

Everything she touched felt of magic. It was as if residue of it had been left behind, and it made her hand snap back quickly. The others gave her curious glances but didn't say anything. There was nothing to fight so the knights were effectively useless.

Olivia vaguely wondered if it would have been better if she had come alone.

Renly hovered by the mouth of the cave, shuffling from foot to foot. They would have to venture inside to see what was there, but he seemed nervous. He cast a look around at his men, scattered around the abandoned campsite, at a loss of what to do.

"Alright then," Renly sighed as he turned to enter the cave. "Let's get this over with."

Olivia followed Renly closely, eyeing Robard until he let her go in front of him. If there was something waiting for them in there, it was useless for her to be at the back of the group.

She heard Arley say he'd hang back and keep watch at the mouth of the cave. It was better than nothing, she supposed, even if he couldn't do much if a mage decided to show up and follow them inside.

The further they went into the cave, the darker it became. There was nothing to indicate it was anything more than a normal cave. There were no carvings on the wall, nor was there anywhere to hold a torch for anyone who came through. Perhaps there was nothing magical there, just a place for mages to hide in case the place was discovered, or somewhere to sleep so they felt safe.

There was a soft glow deeper in the cave, far enough in that you couldn't see the entrance, the light from outside fading as the glow became brighter. They jumped down a small ledge and wandered farther in until they reached the source of light. Even this far into the cave, everything still seemed normal.

She was just about to say as much to Renly, suggest they spent more time looking around outside instead of wasting their time in some cave, when a booming voice vibrated around the walls.

"Who goes there?"

Renly, who had been walking beside her, flung his arm out to push her behind him. She let him do it out of surprise.

Olivia peered around his arm to find a woman, sitting crossed-legged with her eyes closed, wearing a small frown. She was sitting with her back to the cave walls, perched atop a large rock, looking down over whoever dared approach her. She was old, her hair long and greying.

She almost flinched at the raw power she felt radiating from her.

"Price Renly of Alira, son of King Alroy."

The mage didn't even open her eyes, like the title meant little to her, despite his family ruling over the land she resided in.

Renly frowned as he took a step towards her, despite Olivia reaching out to hold him back. She didn't notice the other knights filtering in after him until it was too late. It was obvious none of them felt the power that Olivia did, otherwise they would have been a lot less eager to go rushing towards her.

"Are you the leader of this camp?"

"Do you have any information on the threat against the throne and my father?"

"Are you a part of the uprising?"

She didn't answer any of his questions. She didn't even look like she was listening to him. Her eyes were closed and her face neutral, with no signs of recognition from anything Renly had said.

Renly huffed. It was clear he didn't know what he was doing and wasn't prepared for how to question a mage when all he had was his sword. The magic she could feel rolling off of her was strong and powerful. It felt old, like she had been around for an age, but it didn't feel threatening. If anything, it felt almost comforting.

The mage smiled and opened her eyes. She seemed amused as she looked over Renly, then over at his knights. She wasn't threatened by them, nor was she angry, that much was obvious. Her smile faltered as she caught sight of Olivia.

The mage started answering Renly's questions without prompt, her gaze never shifting from Olivia.

"The uprising is true, but it doesn't operate from here. Some mages aren't happy with how they are treated. Like criminals, for something they cannot control. They get ridiculed, beaten, abused, exiled from their own homes, chased out by their own communities. Not a single thing has been done about it."

Olivia felt a shiver run down her spine as the words rang true. Renly glared at the older mage, as if he could sense Olivia's wavering devotion. She couldn't bring herself to reply to her though, couldn't let the knights find out what she really thought.

"It's not something to be stopped, not an idea you can simply smother under boot. Their methods are harsh, and not a peaceful resolution, but it is the only thing they can think to do to keep themselves from extinction."

Silence settled over the cave. She wondered if this was serving as a wake-up call to some of the knights, a glimpse into the lives of those on the other side, or if it was only fuel to convince them to eradicate the ones that were left.

"The one least expected is the one to watch the most." The woman demanded Olivia's attention as she spoke. The words settled with a sense of foreboding. "The smaller the warrior, the sharper the sword. Remember that, young mage."

She uncrossed her legs and let them dangle over the side of the rock. She straightened her back and turned to look at Renly. "Times are changing, and the laws must change with them or suffer the consequences. This little uprising, if unsuccessful, will only be the start of troubles to come if things do not change."

Renly growled and took a step towards the old mage, his hand resting on the hilt of his sword.

The mage snorted and rolled her eyes, "believe me, young prince, I want no part in some silly little war."

"Do you know who is behind all this?" Renly didn't seem convinced by her words as he cast his gaze around the cave. "You seem to know a lot for someone who wants no part."

She turned back to Olivia, ignoring Renly's huff of annoyance at being ignored. "As a mage, this is something I'm sure you understand. I'm surprised you're not already a part of it, a young and capable mage such as yourself. You should be defending your people."

"I want no part in this, just like you." Olivia growled, her hands curling into fists by her side. How dare she assume that she would want to side with murderers, with those who would attack innocents for revenge against a king.

142

Her eyes flashed for a brief moment, and the sense of comfort she had previously felt slowly disappeared. Something shifted in her demeanour, and her previous kindness seemed to be fading, but her expression never changed. "Dearest Olivia, you are doomed to this war, even if you want no part in it. You must decide which side you are willing to defend. There is no turning back once you do."

Olivia was too stunned to respond. She knew her name, just like Molle had. The second mage she had ever met outside of Alira, and they both seemed to know her.

Renly drew his sword and stepped towards the old mage. Merek quickly followed in his leader's footsteps, and the others seemed to be doing the same, from the distinct sound of swords being unsheathed behind her.

The old mage's eyes flashed, and the cave walls began to rumble. "I've had enough. Take your knights and leave."

The walls began to shake and all the knights took a few steps back. Rocks crumbled from the walls and rolled towards the centre of the room. In the blink of an eye, the rocks rolled together, towering on top of one other until they formed in the shapes of giant beasts. There were two of them, standing imposingly in front of the old mage.

The knights barely had time to register what was happening before the beasts were set upon them.

They couldn't fight them with their swords, not when they were made from rock, and they couldn't engage in hand-to-hand combat with them either. One look at the knights confirmed that they were just as confused about the whole situation as she was.

The mage was much stronger than Olivia had first thought. Olivia herself could only animate objects that she made herself beforehand. She couldn't do anything like *this*, making them out of the elements surrounding her and forcing them to do her bidding.

Olivia rushed towards Renly and pushed him out of the way as a rocked arm swung at where he had been standing. He was stunned at the turn of events, but she didn't give him time to think about it, just nudged him towards the cave's exit.

"Go! I'll get the others!"

To her surprise, Renly went willingly. Robard quickly followed as he tugged a stunned Nicolas with him. She chased the others out after them, turning to throw spells at the beasts as they retreated, anything to just slow them down a little. She was sure they weren't conjured to kill them, but she doubts the old mage would care if any of them got a little banged up in the process of fleeing.

She hastily cast a dismantling spell over her shoulder as she pushed Maddox out of the way, a spell she had never tried to cast before, and didn't think it would have much effect. She grinned in satisfaction as one of the monsters began to break apart. A loud groan reverberated off the walls as the rocks combusted. She shrieked as bits of rock exploded towards her, scraping parts of her face and neck, and embedding itself into the flesh on her leg.

Olivia turned to cast the same spell at the remaining monster, only to come face-to-face with it. In the blink of an eye it had its stony hands wrapped around her windpipe. She clutched at the rocks around her throat as she gasped for breath. Her eyes bugged wide as she was raised off the ground.

Suddenly, she could breathe again. The arm released its grip on her, and she tumbled to the ground, the beast dismantling in front of her very eyes.

"You're not powerful enough to stop what is coming on your own, Olivia Shaw." The voice of the old mage rang out towards her. "You must devote yourself to a single cause or die trying to fight them both."

Maddox helped her off the ground and they ran. The walls shook as the entrance began to cave in.

Olivia dove out of the cave as the entrance came tumbling down behind her.

Chapter Twenty

Olivia groaned as her body flared in pain. She had been pushed to the dirt from the force of the impact and her head was spinning.

Why would the captured Uprisers ever tell the king about this place? It was obvious it had once been used as a meeting spot, perhaps to seek wisdom from the old and temperamental mage in that cave, but she didn't understand the need to mention it. There wasn't anything there other than the old mage, and it didn't seem like there had been much activity for a while, despite the magic still flowing through the soil. She didn't know why they would lie about the Uprisers ever being there.

She pushed herself to stand, stumbling a little as she tried to steady herself. The blood rushed to her head, leaving her unstable and dizzy, but Nicolas had slung an arm around her shoulder before she could collapse.

"'m fine, Nico," she grumbled, but he shook his head in refusal.

"You're definitely *not* fine."

He led her over to the tree stumps by the disused campfire, but she dug her heels into the dirt to stop them. Her body throbbed with pain, but she felt too disorientated to focus on healing herself.

Despite the mage in the cave right behind her, she knew they had to look around the camp before they let their guard down. Something about this whole thing made her feel unsettled, like the camp was hiding something more from them, but she couldn't figure out what.

Leaning heavily into Nicolas' side, she turned to find Renly. "Something isn't right. We wouldn't have been led here just for that old coot."

In the distance she heard Arley voicing his confusion over some old lady, quickly followed by a loud complaint about missing some giant rock monster attack too.

Renly sighed as he glanced back at the stoned-in cave entrance, as if it would give him all the answers he needed. It was impossible to get back through the cave with the amount of debris that was there, and even if they could, nothing new would be waiting for them on the other side. She had a feeling that the old mage wouldn't be as kind in letting them leave a second time.

He grumbled something she couldn't quite catch before making his way over to her. He waved Nicolas away before slinging Olivia's arm over his neck instead. She flinched at the contact but quickly recovered, glancing away as she caught a hurt look in Renly's eyes.

"Fine." He led a limping, slightly-disoriented Olivia away from the cave. "We'll look around, then."

As they walked around the camp, nothing jumped out at her as being out of the ordinary, and nothing particularly tugged at her magic either. Nicolas gave them a strange look but shrugged it off, taking a seat by the disused campfire and resigned himself to watch them limp around. Robard, having overheard their conversation, was the only other knight willing to help them in their search.

They stumbled around in silence. She was concentrating on everything surrounding them, on trying to hold back her pain as her leg began to throb. She hadn't even realised she had been hurt so badly until she put continuous pressure on it. She was too nervous to look at it to see how bad the damage had become.

Eventually, they came upon a large thorny bush, with vines climbing up the rockface behind it. It was around the side of the cave, well out of sight from the other knights. Her magic tugged sharply at her chest the closer they got.

She slid out of Renly's grasp and stumbled towards the rockface. Placing her hands on the rock, she felt a tingle of magic under her palm. It felt like it was asking her to look deeper. She closed her eyes and put all her focus on the pull of magic inside her, letting it guide her to do what it wanted her to. She pictured the rock under her palms, even the vines she could feel curl around her fingertips. In her mind, the outline of a door appeared in the rockface, including a small circle where a door handle would be.

She drifted her hand to curl over the handle and pressed her palm flat against the rock. If the magic wanted her to enter, that was exactly what she was going to do.

Her palm began to vibrate.

She opened her eyes to find the rockface sliding to the side, leaving a gap just wide enough for her and Renly to pass through. Renly was suddenly beside her, holding her up before she had even realised she was falling.

They stumbled through the opening and found a room. It wasn't small, either. The walls were made from stone on all sides, and the roof had fallen away in parts. There was a large stone table in the middle, wide enough to have all of the knights gathered around it at the same time. Sunlight was streaming through the exposed gap in the ceiling and shone directly onto the table.

She shared a look with Renly before shuffling towards the well used stone table. It looked a lot more like a meeting place than the space by the cave had. She turned to observe the space around them. There wasn't a lot there, just the table and some vines growing up the side of the rockface, and a small clump of moss and dried flowers in one corner. Intrigued, she slipped away from Renly and made her way over to it.

Dried flowers, leaves and fresh berries like the ones they found outside were gathered in a neat pile. Poison berries. She vaguely recognised the leaves too, knew them from a book on potions she had perused in the library.

She picked up a small selection of what was in front of her and held it towards Renly, who raised a brow. "Poison berries? The same ones from the trail?"

"Potion ingredients," she nodded. "The leaves are used for healing potions, and the berries used for salve." She furrowed her brow as she looked over the pile in front of her. "Some of this stuff doesn't grow anywhere close to here."

Renly reached out to touch the leaves, but she quickly tugged her hand away. "I don't know the effects it has on humans, and I'm not willing to find out."

"I don't get it." Renly stood from his crouched position and looked around in confusion. "Why did they go through such lengths to hide this away? There's a mage living in a cave outside, for heaven's sake."

Olivia hummed in agreement and stood, dropping the leaves and berries to the ground. She wiped her hands on her pants, leaving a red stain from the berries in its wake. She limped towards the stone table and looked over it closer.

There were various ingredients still scattered over the table, like someone had left in a hurry. The base had chipped corners and scratches all over it, proving it was frequently used. There was a hole in the middle and various smaller ones around the rim, narrow enough to hold ingredients and potion bottles. Leaning closer, she spotted a symbol etched into the middle of the table – an eye with a straight line through the middle.

She cocked her head to the side and reached a hand out towards the symbol.

It seemed familiar somehow...

The moment she touched the symbol, the magic in her veins seemed to roar to life, burning and boiling under her skin. Her limbs locked tight and she couldn't move.

Her eyes rolled in the back of her head and images overcame her vision.

The vision was blurry as it swam before her, as if she was looking through the bottom of a glass bottle.

A line of people stood before her, grinning maniacally down at her. They towered over her, so she couldn't make out their faces. She could see their grins though, impossibly wide and full of sharp teeth, the whiteness of them glinting brightly.

The voice that spoke was demonic, low and deep, and sent shivers down her spine.

"You couldn't pick a side. Everything that happened was your fault, and yours alone. They all died because of you."

The people parted to reveal a line of pikes behind them, each one with a head shoved on them.

Her mother.

All the knights.

Renly.

Cassius and Osmond.

Something shoved her in the back, causing her to stumble towards the head in the middle.

It was her father. He was still bleeding from his open neck.

"You're a disappointment, Olivia." He said. "I trained you, gave you all the knowledge I had, and you still failed. If only you had paid more attention, if only you were more capable, you could have stopped all this bloodshed. You don't deserve to be the one left alive."

Her father's severed head faded from her vision, and she felt the tightness in her limbs lift. She collapsed on the ground and all she could hear was the blood rushing through her ears. She couldn't focus on anything. Reality came back to her with such force that it left her feeling nauseous.

Renly crouched in front of her, grasping her face in his hands. His mouth was moving but she couldn't understand what he was saying, could barely even focus on his face. He slapped her cheek, but it all felt so distant.

Darkness overtook just as Renly dove towards her.

CHAPTER TWENTY-ONE

The next time Olivia woke, she was around a campfire.

She woke slowly, feeling groggy and sluggish. It only took moments for her head to throb, the pain coming back in waves.

She groaned as she pushed herself into a sitting position and clutched her head. There was shuffling next to her and she followed the sound, squinting through her headache, to find Nicolas approaching her in earnest. He was talking a mile a minute, eyes wandering over her body to check for any more wounds. She couldn't concentrate on his words, but the worry and care he held for her washed over her in a wave of comfort.

His ramblings got louder the closer he got, and she groaned, her headache growing. Nicolas trailed off with a worried look, and she felt bad for making him feel worse.

"Give her some space, lad." Robard clapped him on the shoulder before he could get too close and pulled him into the opposite direction.

Thank the Gods for that.

Robard waited for Nicolas to stumble away, sending him meaningful looks until he finally took the hint and left, before he sat down beside her. He didn't say a word as he reached over and took her cheeks in hand, moving them from side to side gently, inspecting for any lasting physical damage. He grunted, seeming satisfied, and let her go.

They sat silently beside each other as she slowly came back to herself, and waited for her throbbing to calm to a dull thud in the back of her head. She breathed out a sigh of relief when the pain finally subsided.

"Thank you." She gestured over to where Nicolas was moping around Arley, the elder trying his best to ignore him. "I didn't want to be impolite, but his voice was driving daggers into my skull."

Robard chuckled, "same as usual, then."

Olivia giggled and looked away from Nicolas, as if the boy could sense their conversation.

Robard shifted his gaze back to the dying fire. "Renly told me what happened." Olivia tensed, but Robard continued before she could overthink what that meant. "Told everyone else you collapsed while walkin' around."

"What did he tell you?"

"You found the real meetin' ground." He shrugged. "Said you touched a symbol on a table and wouldn't respond. He could only drag you away once you collapsed."

She hummed, "how long was I out for?"

"A good few hours. Longer than I'd like." He looked up at the night sky. "We arrived around lunch. It's well past dinner now."

"That's not good." She signed and rubbed at her face. "I saw..." She furrowed her brow and dropped her hand into her lap. 'I don't know. It didn't make a lot of sense."

Robard hummed and turned his attention back to the fire. She took a deep breath and exhaled slowly, letting the events of the day melt from her shoulders and into the dirt below. It wouldn't help things to dwell on what she had seen while she was still so exhausted. She didn't think she could get up even if she tried, her bones so tired they felt numb.

She stifled a yawn and leaned over to place her head on Robard's shoulder. The older man grunted, but slowly raised his hand to rake his fingers through her hair.

"I remember when you were little. You'd hang off your mother's arm in the castle halls, only lettin' go when Renly came about." Robard smiled softly down at her. "I remember teachin' you to hold your first sword. You fell from the weight of it straight away."

Olivia pouted, "you promised to never bring that up again."

Robard laughed. "You improved quickly, little one. Probably from all that sneakin' into the kitchen stealin' food. All that runnin' away made you agile." He ruffled her hair fondly before continuing the soothing strokes. "You been sittin' on that fence watchin' us train since you could barely walk."

She picked her head up from Robard's shoulder and extended her leg out in front of her. She rolled up her left pant leg to reveal a dagger holder, and produced the weapon it was hiding. It was small, the length of the bottom of her palm to the tips of her fingers, but it was beautiful.

The hilt was black and wound up almost half the weapon. A metal lip stuck up at each side of the handle to stop an accidental slip of the finger. The blade itself was sharp, with an etching of flames up one side, and the other a small inscription – 'the sun will always rise'.

Robard grinned as he reached over to run his fingers down the blade. "You kept it?"

"Of course I kept it," she smiled. "Best gift I've ever gotten. You remember when you gave it to me?"

"You were 12." Robard smiled. "Not long after the fire. I remember it well."

"As do I." She smiled sadly down at the dagger. "I had troubles with my parents, and my father was..." She shook her head, trying to dislodge the thoughts. "I hadn't gotten the job with Osmond yet and I felt so lost. You approached me, didn't care about the people that were watching. You gave me this knife, wrapped up in a bundle of dark green cloth." She knocked her shoulder with Robard's. "Haven't left home without it since."

"I didn't care. You were still my little Livvy." He leaned over and kissed her gently on the forehead. "I loved you then, and I love you now."

She sniffled, not trusting her voice to keep steady if she tried to respond.

Robard pulled her down onto his lap, "rest. I'll keep watch."

Before she could voice her complaints, he began to hum. It was an old song, one she hadn't heard in years. An old lullaby back from Robard's home town, one she hadn't heard past anyone else's lips.

The comfort of his gentle fingers carding through her hair, and the humming of his old lullaby, had her drifting off before she even realised.

Chapter Twenty-Two

They made it back to Alira early the following day.

She left the group before they could say much, just a weak smile from Robard and a worried look from Nicolas.

They'd come find her if they needed her for any debriefing with the king, but she doubted she would be necessary. Renly would be better at retelling what happened anyway, since she was passed out half the time, and she definitely wasn't about to tell the king or her father about the vision she had. It still made her head spin.

Instead, she spent the day in the woods behind her house. It felt good to be able to do this, to take some time out for herself. She was able to finally get some peace and quiet, and no-one demanded anything from her when she was out there. It wasn't until the afternoon that she was interrupted.

She had been sitting by the riverbank, the afternoon sun heating her back and easing the knots in her shoulders. She nibbled at a few pieces of bread, toasting them lightly with some conjured flames, as she dipped her feet in the shallow end of the river, resting them on a small pile of rocks under the water.

"You'll kill the fish like that."

She couldn't help but laugh in response.

Renly sat down beside her and crossed his legs. He reached down into the water, allowing it to rush around his fingers. He looked impossibly young, hair flopping into his eyes and a soft smile on his face, as if he felt the same release of pressure being there that she did.

They used to come to the riverbank a lot when they were kids. When the pressure of being a young prince was getting too much for him and he just needed an escape, somewhere close by where he could breathe and escape all the royal duties that had been thrust upon him, she always took him there.

"I remember coming here when we were young," Renly said. "We used to race each other to the deep end and take turns jumping off the rocks. It would be hours until someone came and dragged us away." He gave her an amused look. "Something about it not being proper for a prince to be playing in the woods alone with a girl."

"I remember." She smiled. "It's where I broke my arm for the first time, after you pushed me off the rocks."

"You jumped and we both know it."

They both laughed at the memory, but quickly tapered off into silence. Renly withdrew his hand from the water and stretched, cracking his neck as he did so.

"I always liked this spot the best." He looked over the water with a small smile on his lips. "It's quiet here. The water runs gently and the birdsongs ring clear." He let out a sigh. "It always makes me feel calm, safe. More myself, without the expectancy of what is and isn't proper of a prince or a knight."

She looked at him, long and hard, until she heard something splash in the water. A bird flew from the gentle ripple, flying off to chase after its friends, loudly chirping as if they were bickering.

She looked back at Renly and found him watching the birds with a soft smile. It had been so long since they had engaged in proper conversation, one that went past bickering and yelling, that actually held some semblance of happiness.

Renly had never been one for apologising. He did come and seek her out, she supposed, after everything that had happened. They hadn't spent any time alone together since the fire. It was nice, even if an awkwardness still clung to the air between them from years of separation.

Olivia looked away, "how'd meeting with your father go?"

He scrunched up his nose in distaste at the question, making her laugh. He leaned back, arms outstretched behind him as he closed his eyes against the sun. He lolled his head back and jutted his chin towards the sky.

"He took it a lot better than I thought he would. He said we should have stayed there longer, tried to draw someone out." His laugh sounded hollow. "Said I failed my duty and probably blew the whole thing." He frowned as he turned, peeping one eye open to look at her. "Told him there wasn't anyone around for miles, but he didn't care."

"No-one would have shown, no matter how long we stayed." She gave him a small smile. "The magic felt old, I doubt it had been visited for a while. Even if someone new came along, they'd have been able to sense us long before they'd have spotted us, and wouldn't have dared approach."

He seemed to ease at the words, "you don't think I messed anything up, then?"

"You did well, Renly." She said.

"I never told him about the second place we found. Not like I could make much sense of it, anyway." He shifted in his spot uneasily. "Think he went easy on me after seeing the state you were in, if I'm honest."

"I didn't have the energy to fix myself up until after we got back, and father told me to wait until I got home to do it, just in case I passed out." She laughed. "I must have looked a sight. I'm sorry."

It was rough arriving back to Alira that morning. It was true, she looked a state by the time they got there, and she was mildly embarrassed about her appearance after the displeased looks the king and her father had given her. She was still limping, and her throat ached from the attack, not to mention how much her head throbbed.

Her father had told her to go home without even offering to help her. She was much too tired to complain.

Renly didn't stop staring. He had a serious look on his face, and it startled her. Despite the situation, he looked beautiful, stretched out on the long grass. His hair fell over his eyes as the sunlight glinted off his skin.

"Your father should have fixed you himself. He shouldn't have let you leave like that. You were in so much pain, Olivia, I practically felt it and he just..." Renly trailed off.

She knew her father was tough, but he was just trying to help her. He was training her so she could help other people. Sure, his methods were a little extreme at times, and there were moments when she struggled to remember that he was doing this because he cared, but it came from a good place. She was sure of it.

"He was just trying to help me," she looked away from him.

Renly grimaced. "If that's what help looks like—"

"I didn't see you doing much better."

Renly was stunned into silence, and she could feel the weight of his stare. She rubbed at her face with a deep sigh but didn't look back at him. "'m sorry, I just... he's trying to help me, trying to teach me to be better at all of this. He wants to make sure I don't die or get any of you killed. This whole thing is a lot harder than it looks."

He was still staring when she chanced a look back, but he seemed more sad than angry.

"He's tough, but I've never been the best student."

Renly huffed out a laugh, and she was glad to see a little of the tension bleed from him. He didn't voice his agreement but he didn't have to.

It was a while before Renly spoke again. He cleared his throat as he shifted around, but never said anything. He obviously wanted to talk but didn't know what to say, or maybe he was just nervous of her reaction. Whatever it was, his indecisiveness was grating on her nerves.

A particularly loud shuffle sent a flock of birds flying away from the clearing. She snapped her head over to him and glowered. "Your nervous energy is scaring the wildlife."

"I was scared." His words came out quiet. "I thought you were going to die in that cave, then everything that happened afterwards..." His face paled. "I thought you were going to die and there was nothing I could do to stop it."

"Ren—"

"You saved our lives in Drerimas, then saved them again in that cave, without even thinking about it. It scares me how nothing my knights or I do makes even a dent." He looked at a spot behind her. "It scares me that you're more powerful than all of us."

She's sure it was supposed to come out as some sort of compliment, but it felt more like a slap in the face. He was afraid of her power. Afraid, if something were to happen, that he would be reliant on her. He was *scared* that she was better than him.

The fact that *he* was the one scared made her laugh. If anyone should be terrified, it should be her. She may be able to fight mages better than he could, but he had the power that really mattered. He could have her killed in an instant if he wanted it. In all her years, she had never thought much about it, but lately it was becoming a much bigger possibility.

"I was terrified both times I left with you, did you know? Scared to death that something would happen and I wouldn't be able to save anyone." She frowned. "But nothing left me more rattled than that day when you held your sword to my throat. I've never been afraid of you until that moment.

"Facing those Uprisers and the rock monsters, I was filled with adrenaline and the need to keep everyone safe, and I knew my enemy. When you..." She cleared her throat. "I didn't know if you were going to go through with it."

She rubbed at her neck, right where it would have scarred had she not healed herself. Knowing the conversation wasn't going anywhere, not while they were both so filled with mixed emotions, she stood from the riverbank and went to walk past him.

He caught her arm as she passed, just above the elbow. His mouth was agape when she turned to face him, but no words came out. She slipped her arm out of his grasp and left.

CHAPTER TWENTY-THREE

She knew she should be studying, trying to decipher what that vision meant, what the symbol sketched into the table represented, but she couldn't bring herself to do it. She just needed some rest from all the magic before her migraines got any worse.

After Renly came to see her by the riverbank, she spent the rest of the afternoon and the following day training with the knights. Each session was more intense than the last. Renly's fear of being incompetent against magic must have been driving him insane.

They were leaving Alira again the following morning, giving them just enough time for one last training session before they had to leave.

Apparently, the king was informed of an Upriser camp a little more than a day's ride from Alira. He needed new Uprisers to question, said the ones he already had were quickly losing their usefulness. The way he had phrased it sent chills down her spine.

Olivia sighed as she leaned back against the fence. She was watching the others train as she took a break for some water. Cassius' feet were dangling off the railing beside her, where he was cutting up pieces of apple with his knife. Why he didn't just bite into the fruit like a normal person was beyond her.

They had gotten quite close after she was tasked to shadow the knights on their trips outside the city.

She could tell he was worried about her. Despite Cassius never quite losing the ability to talk her ear off, she was comforted by the way he kept seeking her out. Whenever she wasn't busy with training or study, they always seemed to be together. It felt good to be around someone so happy and optimistic, someone who didn't care about battle tactics and magical warfare.

"The forge hasn't been the same without you. We're getting too much business now that you're not there to turn the customers away."

She snorted, "I'm sure you turn them away just fine on your own."

Cassius gaped, looking affronted. She laughed as he kicked out at her arm before rolling his eyes and averting his gaze back over the training field. "Is it going any better with them?"

"They still dislike me, but I think some of them respect me a little." She shrugged. "They're at least impressed, no matter how hard Merek denies it."

"What about the prince?"

She didn't know how to answer that question, especially not after her talk with Renly. She didn't miss the way he tracked her movements as she subconsciously reached up to her neck, before moving to run her hand through her hair instead. She hadn't told Cassius about that day, and she wasn't about to tell him now and cause him to worry even more.

"'m worried about you, Liv." He admitted. "Every time you leave with them... I'm scared you won't come back. That they might leave you out there to die."

She looked up at him, curious about his admission. Was he afraid they might kill her, where there would be no-one to protect her? She would be the last person to tell him he had nothing to fear in that regard, or that she didn't fear the same thing sometimes.

He shrugged, eyes cast downwards to stare at the apple in his hands. "Towns-folk have talked about doing much worse, and I wouldn't put it past them." He glanced up at the knights, face scrunched up. "Maybe not now, with such a threat looming over us, but the worry is still there and I can't help it."

Olivia broke into a grin, one that couldn't be helped, and nudged at Cassius' leg. "I didn't know you were such a softie."

She was glad to see her distraction worked, as he rolled his eyes and shoved her back. He could carry a conversation for days without anyone saying a word, but most of what he said was gibberish, nothing to pay much attention to. He had never shared his fears with her, about anything, let alone fears about her safety.

"You're impossible." He rolled his eyes, but still sliced off a piece of his apple and handed it to her.

She took it from between his fingers with her teeth, grinning as he scoffed and turned away, a blush high on his cheeks.

"Oi!"

Olivia snapped her head up as Maddox yelled across the field, a wolfish grin on his face. "Get back to training and stop trying to get into Cassius' pants!"

Cassius blushed deeply at the insinuation and turned his gaze to the ground, pink rising to his ears. Olivia laughed as she swallowed and pushed herself off the fence, passing Cassius the water she had been drinking.

"Try not to drive old Osmond too crazy, will you?"

Cassius flipped her off as she made her way back over to where the others were gathered.

She felt lighter after her conversation with Cassius. She felt more grounded, as if there was more to life than fighting and training and studying. It didn't make her head any clearer, but the stress seemed a little less.

Since when did he make things less of an annoyance? She was spending way too much time with the knights if Cassius was the least annoying part of her day.

Nicolas wiggled his eyebrows as she came into view, "you two seem cosy."

She shoved him, satisfied when it made him stumble. It didn't escape her attention that Renly was quiet and didn't join in on the teasing. He was glaring at Cassius, who was still perched on the fence.

"Stop interrupting my training!"

Renly pointedly ignored as she raised a brow at his words. He had never told Cassius to leave while they were training before, and he had never voiced his dislike of her watching them over all the years she had been sitting in that exact spot.

Cassius, to his credit, simply raised a hand to say goodbye before he jumped off the fence and ambled back to the forge.

Training went well after that. Merek was less of a pain than usual, and she even spoke kindly with Arley. Peter still glared at her every chance he got, but it didn't bother her too much anymore. She had been getting those kinds of stares for years. She just thought that he would be better with her now, after everything, but apparently not.

Renly was kinder too, which was more of a shock than Merek not ripping her head off. He was more compassionate, more like the friend he used to be, even though he refused to keep eye contact with her.

As the knights filed back into the castle after training, talking animatedly about gathering together at The Sun that evening, only she and Renly were left behind. It was still tense between them and she hated it. She would have much rather he curse and scream at her like he used to, because at least then she could tell what he was thinking.

Before either could say anything, someone cleared their voice behind them.

Princess Lorelle was standing by the entrance of the training fields, hands behind her back and positively beaming at Olivia. She couldn't help but grin back. Renly tried to hide his smile behind his hand as he walked away, carrying his weapons and armour over to Peter.

Lorelle ran to her and hugged her tightly before she had even cleared the field. She laughed as she hugged her back just as tight, and walked them over to the side before she let the little princess go.

"Is that new?" Olivia gestured to her dress. "Go on, give me a twirl."

Lorelle giggled and did as she was asked, spinning around so much she stumbled dizzily, a grin still plastered on her lips. Lorelle never cared about what happened between Olivia and her brother, never cared for the rumours and snide remarks she heard throughout Alira. She was much more diplomatic than both her brother and her father. She was definitely her mother's daughter.

"Can I see it?" Lorelle pouted, gazing up at Olivia through her lashes. "It's been so long!"

She knew exactly what the girl wanted to see, but she hesitated. She loved the girl, would do anything for her, but the last time she performed magic in front of Renly it hadn't ended so well.

She waited for a few moments, until she could see Peter leave from behind her, carrying an armful of Renly's things. She smiled at Lorelle and knelt down in front of her. The girl's eyes positively gleamed with pure joy at the action, and outstretched her hand towards her.

In the blink of an eye, a small, dainty dancer appeared on Olivia's palm. The heat warmed her hands, and caused her palm to singe. The reflection of the flames danced in Lorelle's eyes as she crouched in order to see it better. She giggled when Olivia made the flame dance, going up on its toes to do a little spin. Lorelle began to hum a little, the song she always used to sing while they did this, and Olivia easily made the dancer match the beat.

When Lorelle first found out about her magic, she wouldn't stop pestering Olivia until she showed her something. She always requested to see the dancer, ever since the very first time Olivia conjured it up for her. It was the first time that anyone asked to see her magic with excitement, and without judgement.

Olivia tensed as she felt someone watching them. She averted her gaze to try and discover the source, to see if she or Lorelle were in any imminent danger. She breathed a sigh of relief when she saw Renly, his eyes trained on the tiny dancer on her palm. He wasn't frowning, nor did he look happy. He left quickly when he caught her gaze, ignoring them both as he scurried past.

Lorelle tore her eyes away from the dancer to follow Renly's retreat back into the castle.

"He doesn't hate you." Lorelle looked back at Olivia. "He never really did. He was hurt and confused as to why you never told him, that he had to find out the way that he did. He would have helped you."

Olivia gave a sad smile, "he couldn't have made that promise."

"He loves you still." Lorelle said. "He's just scared that he can't protect you like he can protect everyone else."

That was hard to believe. Renly had told her something similar that day at the river, that he was scared he couldn't protect everyone else from an attack born from magic. She's not so sure he cared that he couldn't protect her from the same thing.

She extinguished the flames, and cradled her singed hand against her chest.

"When did you get so smart?" She reached forwards with her uninjured hand to ruffle Lorelle's hair. Lorelle rolled her eyes but pulled Olivia in for another hug.

"Thank you for my dancer, Liv." She pulled away, but kept her arms around Olivia. "Please be careful on your next journey."

She waited until Olivia nodded before she untangled herself from her arms and left the same way her brother had.

CHAPTER TWENTY-FOUR

They left early the following morning, but not before she grabbed some breakfast at The sun with Nicolas and Robard.

Despite the early start, she spent most of the night before in the library. She wanted a break from all the magic, but leaving with the knights again meant she needed to study, whether she wanted to or not. It was worth it, though. She had finally found out what that symbol meant.

It was in a large book buried in the back of the library, the hardcover almost too heavy to lift. About halfway through the book, beside a small paragraph, is where she found the drawing of the symbol.

The symbol had to be etched into wood, specifically from the Lunar Fove tree, before it could activate. It would only work for mages. It somehow connected with the magic in one's blood in order for it to work.

Whenever a mage touched the etching, they would see what may happen in the future. The visions were never completely accurate though, as the future changes the moment you witness it. Thus, whatever prediction was seen could never be fully trusted. Either way, It was accurate enough that mages still strongly believed in its power.

She had to push the book away before her climbing nausea became too much. What did she do to get that kind of prediction? It scared the hell out of her. She hadn't been able to get it out of her head.

It helped that there was still some consistency from before all this. Merek still hated her, and Arley still didn't seem to care either way. Peter still ignored her. It helped take her mind off things, being able to pretend that a prediction as wild and scary as the one she got could never come into fruition if everything stayed exactly the same.

The thing was, not everything remained the same, and maybe that made all the difference.

Maddox seemed to like her now, teasing her and cracking jokes just like he did with the other knights. Even Renly joined in on the friendly teasing, seeming in higher spirits than usual. It was oddly comforting, as though if something did happen, she now had people who were willing to protect her, to help her fight instead of watching her fall.

"So. Cassius." Maddox grinned.

Olivia screwed her nose up at the line of questioning, making Maddox bark out a laugh. "What about him?"

"What do you mean 'what about him'?" Maddox rolled his eyes. "He's stuck to your side lately."

Robard gestured to her wrist, "he give you that, too?"

"Who's side are you on?" Olivia glared at him.

Robard smirked and shrugged.

She smiled down at her wrist. Cassius had come to join her in the library the night before to give her a bracelet, one he had made himself. It was made from iron, and it wrapped around her wrist and up her forearm. He said it was to remind her of home, of the people who loved her, whenever she performed her magic. He said it was as close as he could get to protecting her while she was away from Alira. She loved the sweet gesture.

Robard had walked in on them as he was wrapping it around her wrist, and Cassius had all but sprinted out of the room with a furious blush.

"Yeah, he did." She glowered at Robard. "But not for the reasons you think."

Robard snorted. "Okay."

Renly rolled his eyes, a frown on his face. "'Course not."

"*Anyway*," Olivia glanced at their surroundings. "How long 'til we make camp?"

"Yeah!" Nicolas piped up from in front of her. "We stopped for lunch *an age* ago, I'm starving!"

"You're always starving." Arley laughed fondly.

"Am not!"

"Are too!"

She tuned out the childish squabbling with a fond smile. It felt good to be able to join in on the teasing now, instead of being stuck at the back of the pack, ignored by everyone in front of her.

Her smile faded as a familiar feeling crawled up her spine. The hairs on the back of her neck stood on end, and her entire body went on alert. She felt like she was being watched. She slowed her horse down, much to the grumblings of the others, and began looking around her wildly for the source. She didn't trust her feelings before, and she wasn't going to ignore them this time.

Nicolas must have seen how serious she was, because he informed Robard, and the three of them trailed behind as they tried to locate the source of her anxiety. She had all but stilled in the middle of the path, as Robard veered to the right and Nicolas to the left.

As Nicolas was venturing towards a small shrub, he stilled, and let out a high-pitched scream. A small creature jumped out from behind a shrubbery and ran off deeper into the forest. The others laughed, leaving Nicolas blushing as he ventured back onto the path again.

"Thanks a lot, Olivia."

"See!" Renly laughed. "Not everything is out to kill us. Stop being so paranoid."

They took off again without another word, their laughter echoing through the forest as Nicolas avoided everyone's humoured gazes. Maybe Renly was right. Just because it happened before, it doesn't mean it will happen again. Maybe she was just paranoid. After the cave mage and her vision, it wasn't really a surprise.

Robard kept an eye on their surroundings as they rode on, though. He trusted her entirely, even if she doubted herself.

They reached camp as the sun was slowly descending behind the trees, and Nicolas' rumbling stomach was getting too loud to ignore.

She wasn't feeling the same dread as the last few times they made camp, which was a relief. The campsite was loud with wild animals and the rushing of a nearby stream. It was comforting, the fact that the wildlife hadn't been scared away, and how peaceful everything seemed to be. Surely if this camp was as bad as King Alroy believed, the animals would have fled. They always seemed to be the first to know when danger was around.

She tied Shadow to the shadiest tree she could find and took her waterskin to fill back up. The sound she heard turned out to be a creek, a very small and narrow one, that wound around a rather large boulder. Birds were playing in the water while other small wildlife calmly drank from the bank. They didn't seem to be disturbed by her presence, or by her magic.

Olivia sat by the creek's edge and drank the rest from her waterskin before she bent to refill it. Everything seemed quite peaceful here, as if the negativity of the world surrounding it hadn't reached it yet. It was calm and she felt some of the tension bleed from her shoulders.

She hoped she could revisit sometime.

As she was refilling her waterskin one last time, a twig snapped behind her, and the animals quickly fled into the treeline. Peter appeared by her side a moment later, arms filled with various waterskins. From the other knights, she assumed. He ignored her as he filled each of them in silence. He didn't look over at her once, body tense as he couched towards the creek.

She wanted him to like her, to at least tolerate her, but bringing anything up now when he seemed so on edge didn't seem like a good idea. She stood from the bank, brushed the dirt off her clothes, and hesitated. Peter sighed deeply and stood as well, balancing the waterskins precariously in his arms.

"I'm not like them, you know." His eyes were ablaze and she took a step back on instinct. He laughed, but it sounded hollow. "I'm not blinded by you like they are. I'm not going to make that same mistake." He spits at the dirt, right beside her boot. "I still see you for what you really are, Jinxflinger."

She followed behind him as he left back to camp, almost in a daze. He was so angry at her, at what she was, even though the others seemed to be slowly warming to her. Even after she had saved his life. It was a stark reminder that not everyone was willing to overlook what she was.

Nicolas bounded over to her as they came into view of the campsite, eyes alight and a grin plastered on his face, and she found herself smiling back. His youthful happiness really was infectious.

"Liv! There you are! C'mon, you're missing it!"

She laughed as Nicolas grabbed her wrist and started leading her closer to camp. "Missing what?"

"Merek acting like a real person," he grinned.

They rounded a corner and she almost stopped dead in her tracks. Merek was sitting in the dirt, a grinning mess, as a sweet looking animal ran around him, occasionally letting him reach out and pet it before scampering off again. It collapsed in front of him with its tail wrapped around its body, its doe eyes peering up at Merek innocently. The creature was small, with a bushy tail as long as its body, and big round eyes. Its nose was small, ears tiny as it hid amongst its fur. It was undeniably cute, and undeniably foreign.

Merek looked up at her with confusion. "What is it?" He grinned as it rubbed its tail against his leg. "Can I keep it?"

Olivia laughed. She had the same reaction when her father had shown her a picture of the creature as a child. She had been utterly transfixed with it, and her father had told her that if she was this transfixed with a simple drawing of the creature she would be bewitched if she was to ever see one in real life.

"It's called a Chimercha." She shared an amused look with Nicolas. "It sends endorphins through its fur to whoever touches it. That's why Merek is so... pliable."

"But what is it?" Nicolas asked. "I've never seen one before!"

"You wouldn't have." She turned back to look at the little Chimercha with a frown. "It's usually found in domestic magical environments. It's drawn into an area by the pull of magic. They use them a lot in hospitals to cheer up the patients, to take their pain away a little."

It didn't explain why it was there, though. It wasn't generally attracted by a single person's magic, more from the soil of a large group of them.

Whatever this place was, they were definitely close.

CHAPTER TWENTY-FIVE

Merek woke with a headache the following morning, groaning loudly as he clutched his head. His eyes bugged as he saw the Chemercha and he immediately scooted away.

He glared at the others, who were stifling laughter behind their hands. All except Maddox, who was openly laughing at him. He stood in a huff and stormed off to the creek, desperately trying to hide his blush.

"Didn't know he had a soft side," Arley chuckled.

Maddox snorted, "I haven't seen him that happy in years!" He hummed into his morning porridge. "Maybe I should get him a cat."

"A cat?" Arley raised a brow. "He'd forget to feed it, and it would die within the month."

Renly laughed, having to cough before he choked on his food. "It wouldn't even last the week."

Robard reached out to pet the Chemercha, sleeves over his hand to avoid skin contact. He smiled as the small thing seemed to purr and immediately rub against his pant leg. He gathered some porridge on his spoon and tried to feed it to the Chemercha, laughing when it all but turned up its nose at the food and shrunk away from it.

"Not everythin' likes your cookin', Peter."

Peter grumbled as he took the empty pot and stomped off towards the creek.

"You said it's usually domestic, right?" Renly asked. "Drawn in by magic?"

"Usually," she eyed the little bundle of fur curiously. "I've never seen one in real life before. I thought they were extinct."

"We must be close to the camp, then." Renly hummed.

Olivia shook her head, cheeks full of food. "I dunno." Maddox threw a stick at her with a disgusted look as bits of food flew out of her mouth. She swallowed before she spoke again. "I mean, what army brings their pets?"

Arley shrugged, "an inept one?"

Olivia laughed. "I *mean*, the Chemercha is domesticated. It likes people. The fact that it could escape to approach any person it finds is a risk." She looked at the little creature. "They're good with the sick and injured, but they make people laugh, and that sort of noise wouldn't be safe entering a battleground."

"So it escaped a nearby village?" Maddox raised a brow. "The closest is half a day's ride, it wouldn't have run this far."

"You said it's attracted to magic, right?" Nicolas asked. "Couldn't it have just come here because of you?"

"Could have," she shrugged. "But it's more attracted to bigger magic made from a sizable group of mages. Something has to be close by." She looked back at the Chemercha. "It could be the Upriser camp, but..."

Renly looked from her to the creature and back again, furrowing his brows. He stood, and stretched his arms above his head until they popped. "We should get going, see if this little thing wants to lead us back to where it came from."

Maddox smirked, "Merek will be thrilled about this."

The ride wasn't a long one, only a few hours through the density of the forest. Merek grumbled the entire way about the Chemercha being with them, much to everyone's delight.

The closer they got, the more Olivia could feel the pull of magic. It was strong magic, too. She was sure if she felt the ground under her palm, she would be able to feel the magic deep into the soil, too. They weren't trying to hide, or trying to ambush anyone. They were being much too loud for that.

They saw the tents before they caught sight of anyone. There were a few scattered around a sizable clearing, all of different colours and patterns, each just as beautiful as the last. It was a stark difference to any campsite she had seen before. Most were tall and wide, a few with extra additions, while some held no walls, with things like tanning skins twinkling in the sun.

The camp held many women and children, but no men. They didn't seem like a threat. The Chemercha ran towards a small group of children, who immediately seemed more at ease upon its arrival, giggling as it waved its bushy tail in their faces. The act in itself was strange. If she recalled correctly, the Chemercha only ran like that towards those it felt were in pain, and those kids seemed to be fine.

No one in that camp was a threat, that much was obvious. It was definitely not like what the king had led them to believe.

"They're still mages." Merek grumbled as they dismounted by the treeline. "Just 'cause they're all cosy it doesn't mean they aren't dangerous." He scoffed. "The king himself told us this was a camp full of Uprisers."

Frustration boiled in her veins at his ignorance, making her feel uneasy. She caught the eye of a mage who overheard him, and smiled apologetically at her. She didn't smile back. Just kept staring.

Renly dismounted and walked straight into the camp without hesitation.

There was a sense of uneasiness about the whole situation. This place looked like a refugee camp, not some dangerous gathering of Uprisers. There were too many children, and none of them seemed to hold much animosity towards the approaching knights. Very unlike the Uprisers they had met before.

Seeing a place like this made her nervous. It would be easy for the knights, for Renly, to just leave her there. Cassius had predicted it, and she wouldn't put it past Merek to suggest it.

She trailed behind the knights like a lost little Chemercha. She kept her gaze solely on their backs instead of those around her, trying to block out the faces of the others as she passed. Up until a few weeks ago she hadn't met more than a handful of other mages in her lifetime.

They found an older mage, one with scars littering her face and what seemed to be a permanent frown, huddled a few others, deep in conversation. The way the eldest held herself, how she was constantly keeping an eye on those around her despite the serious tone of the conversation she was having, made her believe that she was definitely the one in charge.

Renly approached her with confidence, standing tall with his chest puffed out. "Are you the leader?"

The younger mages started, fearful eyes flicking between Renly and the knights, before they shrunk behind their elder. The eldest took a confident step forwards, all but hiding the others behind her with a sweeping hand. "Yes." Her eyes flicked to the golden crest on Renly's chest and raised a brow.

"I'm Prince Renly of Alira." He extended an arm out to her, but slowly lowered it when she didn't move to shake it.

She had an aurora of authority about her, like a fierce motherly protectiveness that extended out to all her people. She didn't say anything in response to Renly's introduction. Not like others always had, how they would immediately apologise and bow and do anything that Renly wanted. It was as though she had no respect for Renly or the Kingdom. She wouldn't be surprised if that were true.

Renly raised a brow at the strange greeting but didn't comment on it. "What's your name?"

"Margaret."

Renly nodded, and looked around the camp. "What are you all doing out here in the forest, Margaret?"

"I run a peaceful camp here." Margaret said. "We were all run out of our homes for having magic."

"All of you?" Robard asked, confused.

Margaret nodded. "You'd think it was illegal to have magic, seeing the amount of us here. Wouldn't you, Prince Renly?"

Renly was wise enough not to comment, but he didn't seem compelled to believe her.

"Why didn't you fight back?" Arley piped up. "Why didn't you fight to stay in your homes?"

Olivia was shocked by his question, but the other knights didn't seem to show any surprise at it being asked. It was frightening the way he was surprised that all these women, all these children, didn't just fight back against a mob of angry villagers. It was as if he forgot that attacking anyone using magic was illegal. It would see them killed or hung, and no-one would stop to ask if it was in self defence or not.

"We only use our magic to help others, not fight against those who cannot fight back." Margaret looked over her people with a frown. "A lot of these people weren't properly taught how to use their magic, how to tame it. It's a fickle thing if used incorrectly, and a lot of them didn't want to take that chance."

Olivia could practically feel the hurt and wariness radiating off of Margaret, the fear from the mages still hiding behind Margaret too. There were children scattered around the camp, young girls, innocent women. How could the knights not believe them?

Margaret didn't linger on Olivia any more than she looked at the knights, nor did any of the others around them. They didn't know her, and by all accounts it was a normal reaction, but it made her more curious and confused. They didn't know her by name, didn't recognise her like the others had. Why had the others known who she was, when these mages didn't?

Margaret stared warily at the other knights, as if she didn't quite trust them. She didn't back away but didn't stand up for herself, either. It was like she was waiting for them to make their move first, prepared for them to attack so she could defend herself.

Renly seemed to notice Margaret's apprehension, and turned to his knights. "Go look around, Robard and I will stay here with Margaret." He turned back to look at Margaret. "Is that fine with you?"

Margaret nodded stiffly. "Emonie, Malie, take these kind people on a tour of our camp, will you?"

"But Maggie-"

"*Now*, Emonie."

They nodded stiffly and scrambled away, leaving Olivia and the other knights to stumble after them. She shared a confused look with Renly, but he just turned back to Margaret, whose eyes never left Emonie and Malie.

They didn't say much. One of them, the one she assumed to be Emonie from the way she talked back to Margaret, looked the same age as Olivia herself, with short blonde hair and scars running up and down her arms. Malie looked a little older, with longer black hair and not as many scars, but she was a lot quieter. Perhaps her scars, if she had any, were more mental than physical.

They showed them where they ate, in one of the larger tents she had spotted on their ride in, and where their medical was, in a much smaller tent that held only a few cots and some bedrolls. Malie told them that they all slept differently, but a lot of them liked to sleep outside, where they could keep an eye on each other and have easy access to escape. Because of this, none of them had their own tent. Not even Margaret.

They had a forge, something that surprised her but she was glad to see. It held many hunting weapons but not much else. She assumed they didn't use their magic while hunting in case it drew unwanted attention to themselves. It was smart.

Olivia paused as they were led past a group of kids, who were running around an older mage, giggling with each other. She didn't pay attention as the others ambled off after Emonie and Malie. She was too fixated on the kids, who still seemed happy and carefree even after everything that had happened to them.

The older mage they were with was beautiful. Her hair was long and golden, tied messily in double braids, probably done by the kids climbing all over her. Her violet eyes sparkled as she laughed, and her eyes bunched up as her grin grew. Around her throat was a dark necklace, the band thick around her throat, with a small charm in the shape of the moon hanging from its middle. She was wrapped in a long maroon cloak, covering a shirt that ended just above her belly button, revealing a piercing, and dark green trousers.

She blushed as the mage noticed her, and her smile slipped. "Hello."

"Hi." Olivia raised a hand in greeting. "Sorry, I didn't mean to interrupt."

"You're not." Her smile grew. "I'm Ariadne."

"Olivia. I am. Hi." She blushed at her stumbling, internally cursing at her awkwardness. She was grateful the other knights had already moved on.

Ariadne laughed as she shifted to sit upright, much to the complaints of a little boy who had been climbing into her lap. "What brings you here, Olivia?"

Olivia waved a hand behind her, to where she assumed Renly was still standing. "Here on the king's request, actually. Came with Prince Renly and his knights."

"Oh." Ariadne raised a brow. "And they're happy with a mage riding with them?"

"They're fine with it." She knew the lie wasn't convincing, only made certain as Ariadne's smile turned pitying. Olivia cleared her throat and gestured to the kids. "You their minder or something?"

"Or something." Ariadne sighed as she looked over her flock. "These ones are orphaned. By abuse and hate crimes, mostly." She smiled as one of the kids squealed, giggling uncontrollably as her friends began tickling her. "I look after them, make sure they're fed, that they're as happy as they can be."

Ariadne seemed to be doing a pretty good job of it. The kids weren't sickly skinny, none looked particularly poorly, and the majority of them were smiling or laughing as they played with each other. The Chemercha was curled up on the lap of a little boy, who was smiling as the little animal began snoring in its sleep. His eyes seemed dull. Empty. It's no wonder the Chemercha was attracted to him.

One of the girls came skipping over to Ariadne, a pleading grin on her little face as she clasped her hands behind her back and twirled. It reminded her of Lorelle.

"Miss Ari!" She beamed. "Can you do some magic for us? Pretty please?"

Ariadne rolled her eyes with a grin, looking from the little girl up to Olivia. "Only if Olivia says it's alright."

"Oh, please!" The girl immediately turned to her. "Pretty please?"

Olivia grinned, "of course, little one."

The girl turned back to her friends with a cheer, waving a hand for them to come over and see the magic up close. It was obvious these kids were displaced too young to start learning how to control their magic. Either that, or they were too traumatised to attempt to do it themselves.

The girl didn't even flinch at the brief introduction to Olivia, either. She didn't try to act polite, nor was she rude, like so many youngsters she had seen around Alira. She had simply accepted that Olivia was there and moved on.

Ariadne giggled as a gaggle of kids began running towards her, desperate for the entertainment she was ready to provide. Once they had all gathered, Ariadne waved her hand at a bunch of fallen leaves. The leaves began to twirl in a gentle whirlwind around one little girl's head. Ariadne smiled as her eyes lit up and she giggled with glee. All the kids ran around the floating leaves, laughing as they tried to capture them with their hands.

The more she watched these kids, the more she watched the way the others in the camp foraged and cooked and did mundane activities, the more she wondered about the king's intentions in sending them there. The camp was peaceful, full of women and children who had already been displaced by violence once before. It was definitely not some high-risk battle camp that he assured Renly it was.

Did King Alroy really expect them to just take his word on it? Attack these peaceful, innocent people? To kidnap more mages for him to torture for information, just because of who they were?

Would the knights have done so if she wasn't there to be realistic about the whole situation?

Merek and Arley's booming voices floated through the air as they made their way towards her. They definitely wouldn't help things, especially not around the giggling and happy children.

Ariadne looked up at her, brow raised as she flicked her eyes between Olivia and the incoming pair. Olivia smiled tightly and shook her head, silently hoping that they would pass them by without incident.

Merek snorted loudly as they slowed to a stop beside her. *Of course* he did. "I see you're fraternisin' with the enemy now."

Olivia swore under her breath and turned to look at Merek, who was grinning wolfishly at her. The Chemercha's effects had obviously worn off.

"They're just kids." She glared at him. "Orphans, actually."

"Sure." Merek turned his grin to the little girl closest to him, the one who had previously begged Ariadne for a magic show. "Don't know what they did to deserve it, do you?"

Anger pooled inside her, and she could practically feel the frustration well up inside Ariadne, too. It was one thing to say such vile things to her, to any of the adult mage's around that camp, but to say it in front of children? Kids who had already gone through so much hatred from humans?

She reached out a hand on instinct to stop Ariadne before she even thought about getting up to confront the knights. She knew it would just make things worse, and she wasn't sure she could stop herself from fighting Merek if he attacked Ariadne.

Olivia pushed past Merek in an attempt to get the knights as far away from Ariadne and the kids as possible, making sure to knock his shoulder harshly as she passed. He stumbled from the force and immediately stomped after her, mumbling snide comments as she made her way back to where Renly and Robard stood.

"Jinxflinger!"

She flinched as Merek yelled, his booming voice startling her. "If your father wasn't who he was, you would be here just like the rest of them!"

Olivia rounded on him, fire in her eyes and frustration in her bones. There must have been something dangerous in her gaze because Merek took a step back on instinct before squaring up against her again.

"We could leave you here, you know. We could kill you and no-one would care."

Arley flinched at his words. He put a hand on Merek's shoulder to pull him back, but he shook it off, approaching Olivia until he was towering over her, his breath fanning her cheek. He looked dangerous.

"Enough, Merek!"

Someone put an arm on her shoulder and pulled her back roughly. He stood between her and Merek, back to her and shoulders tense.

Renly.

Merek threw his hands up and stalked off without another word. He disappeared out of the clearing and back to where they had left their horses, where Peter was still keeping watch over them.

She let out a shaky breath and ran a hand through her hair. The audacity that man had, to say something so despicable inside a camp full of the mages he claimed to despise. To say that he would kill her, just because of her magic?

He was either incredibly brave or irreparably stupid.

"We'll camp for the night, just to be sure." Renly turned to face her, the tension bleeding from his shoulders. "I'm certain they're peaceful. Just displaced and trying to find a place to fit in."

It made her feel a bit better that Renly could see their innocence just like she could.

Renly ran a hand through his hair as he looked at the small gathering of people who had witnessed their unprofessional squabbling. "Don't worry about Merek. I'll deal with him."

He left the clearing in the same direction that Merek had stalked off, but not before sharing a half bow with Margaret, who had watched the entire thing unfold.

Chapter Twenty-Six

She spent the rest of the day following Renly as he spoke with whoever in the camp was willing. The fact that a known mage was travelling with the crowned prince was enough to have most share information with him they normally wouldn't have.

Robard and Margaret joined them after a while, the mage not wanting to leave them alone with her people for too long, and the knight too restless to sit back and just watch.

Merek was told to stay with the horses outside of camp, his little display having caused many in camp to become wary. Peter stayed with him too, after he was caught glaring at everyone.

Nicolas and Maddox spent their time with Ariadne and the orphaned kids, which was surprising. They couldn't provide magical entertainment like Ariadne or Olivia could, but Maddox was offering piggyback rides, and Nicolas was looking on with wonderment and fascination as the kids told him wild and wonderful stories, giggling alongside them when Ariadne began casting her magic to amuse them. She couldn't help but smile at the exchange. She had never seen the knights so gentle.

The mages they spoke with all told similar stories of how they came to be displaced. Most were chased from their homes by angry townsfolk, while some left of their own accord, when tensions became too high and they began fearing for their lives.

The last few they spoke with were huddled together by the fire in the middle of camp, buried under blankets and thick jackets. Olivia was glad to see that, at the very least, they were able to keep clothes warm enough to prevent them from getting cold or sick.

One of them had long greying hair that curled around the middle of her chest. The other, a lot younger, had short black hair that hung by her jawline. She had old faded scars running across her throat, a few of them scattered across her cheeks too.

They didn't seem pleased at the disruption, and refused to make eye contact with any of them.

"The quicker you tell your stories the quicker he'll be gone." Margaret sighed, sounding resigned.

The grey haired mage sent a harsh glare at Margaret, her shoulders tense. Olivia didn't think she was going to talk until Margaret met her stare straight on. Something in Margaret's eyes must have convinced her, however, because she sighed and turned back to the fire.

"I was chased out of my village." She wrapped her blanket tighter around her shoulders. "They had axe's and scythe's and threatened to kill me if they ever saw me again. Said I was abnormal, born *wrong*." She stared, unblinkingly, into the fire. "They would rather see me dead than in their village for another day."

"Her husband was with the group that chased her out," the mage beside her said. "Threw her a bag of food and his well wishes before going' back without another glance."

The grey-haired mage sniffled, eyes still glued to the flames. Her friend wrapped an arm over her shoulder and pulled her tighter against her side. Margaret didn't seem fazed by the story, nor particularly saddened. It was eerily similar to the stories they had been told all night.

"What about you?" Robard asked, smiling kindly at the scarred mage. "Somethin' similar?"

She shook her head, a deeper frown growing on her face. "We were invaded." She glanced up. "By those Uprisers you're so desperate to find."

Renly leaned forwards, intrigued. "And?"

"They burned our village to the ground when we didn't comply with their violent ideologies." She scoffed. "They only left me alive because of my magic, knew I wouldn't run to the king because he wouldn't believe anything I had to say."

Robard frowned, "did you recognise any of them? How many?"

"I don't know who they were, but there weren't many." She sighed. "There were 5, maybe 6 of them. They seemed competent, like they had done that sort of thing before. That's all I know."

"What did they say?"

"They wanted us to join them in support of their vengeance against the king." The mage averted her gaze back to the fire. "To take up arms and demand the same respect he gives to everyone else." She flits her eyes to Renly before shifting, seeming uncomfortable. "I don't agree with their methods, but I..." She cleared her throat. "I find sympathy with their frustrations."

To her surprise, Renly didn't react badly at the mention of a sympathiser to an attack against his father. "I'm sorry."

Renly waited for the mages to look over at him in surprise before he continued. "I am truly regretful for what happened to you. I took an oath to protect you and I failed." He looked over to Olivia briefly before turning back. "I promise to do better, but I need to deal with this threat first. I cannot allow my kingdom to fall and my people to hurt just so others can vent their frustrations. I need to find these people, and I must make them stop."

She was surprised at Renly's eloquence. He never would have said those words weeks, maybe even days, ago. She wasn't sure if he really meant it now, but it was working.

The pair smiled, just a small thing, but they seemed to relax a little more in his presence. She looked over to Robard to find him wearing the same sort of confused astonishment.

The older mage smiled kindly at Renly. "Whatever we can do to help, we will. A war like this... it's not going to help anyone."

She heard a bright giggle off in the distance, a stark difference from the conversation she was having, and turned to find a little girl riding atop Maddox's shoulders with a wide grin. Olivia couldn't help but smile at the sight. She spun back around to find Renly and Robard sharing amused looks.

"Go," Renly waved his hand dismissively at her. "Have fun, make sure Dox and Nicolas aren't causing too much trouble."

She wasn't sure she should leave them, especially not when they were discussing something so serious, but she was *tired*. She was so tired of hearing the horrible things that had been done to her people, and how little the king seemed to care. If it was just one story, sure, she could understand how it slipped through the gaps without notice, but this many? With details disgustingly similar to each other?

She couldn't hear any more of it. Not tonight, at least. She slowly stood and left.

Maddox was still carrying the same little girl on his shoulders when she arrived, but with an extra two small boys handing from each arm, all of them squealing with delight as he spun them around.

"Liv!" Nicolas grinned as he held his arm out for her to take. He was sitting on the ground, surrounded by children, all gathered around an amused Ariadne. "C'mon! You're missing out on a magic show!"

Olivia laughed, but took his outstretched hand anyway and sat beside him. "Every day is a magic show for me, Loggerhead."

Nicolas grinned through the insult before he turned back to face Ariadne. She was conjuring water from one of the children's waterskins and forming it into different shaped animals. She felt herself relax the longer she sat there, Nicolas pressed comfortably to her side, as the kids screamed out requests for different animals. She felt her magic hum in contentment and settled inside her.

It brought her a sense of comfort she hadn't felt in years.

She leaned her head on Nicolas' shoulder and looked out over their small gathering. Ariadne had a little boy curled into her side, fast asleep. Maddox was letting the little girl down from his shoulders, wincing as he straightened his back, and Nicolas had a small gathering of children using his legs as a pillow. The Chemercha was still with the same little boy as before, who was starting to look a little more content.

The girl who had been riding atop Maddox's shoulders came bounding over to Olivia, completely ignoring Ariadne as she made the water form into a giant whale, squirting the kids with its blowhole.

"Olivia!" She grinned as she sat in front of her, a respectful distance away. "Can *you* show us some magic now? Miss Ari always shows us the same old boring stuff."

"Hey!" Ariadne grumbled. The whale combusted and sprayed the giggling children.

The girl turned to Ariadne with a shrug. "It's true." She turned back to Olivia with a pout. "It's always so childish, never anything grand and amazing!"

Olivia raised a brow, "I'm best at small things, little one, so I might be a little too boring for you too."

"I don't care!" The girl pouted. "Please show us!"

Olivia shook her head with a smile, and looked over her shoulder at Ariadne. "She always like this?"

Ariadne shook her head. "Mattie's on her best behaviour today."

Olivia laughed and looked back at Mattie. She looked up at her through her lashes, still pouting and trying her best to look cute to get what she wanted. It was working.

Maddox sat on the ground beside Mattie with a teasing grin. "Yeah, Olivia, show us what you've got."

She glanced at Nicolas for help, only to find him giving her the same grin as Maddox.

She sighed, "fine."

Mattie cheered, and the others quickly turned away from Ariadne to gather around Maddox and Mattie with matching excitement.

Fire would be her best bet, if she wanted to really impress. Anything other than that would run the risk of embarrassing herself with a half-cocked spell. Fire dancers were probably still going to be a bit boring for the likes of Mattie, who had grown accustomed to simple magic. Nicolas may have found it mesmerising, little Lorelle too, but it wasn't enough.

These kids needed something bigger. They deserved something exciting.

It gave her an idea.

Olivia grinned at the little girl and held out her palm. She closed her eyes and waited until she could feel the fire lick down her arm and up through her palm before she opened them again.

Above her palm sat a dragon made entirely from fire. It was almost as big as Mattie's head, its mouth open as it breathed the same fire it was made from. The heat from the creature warmed her face.

Mattie was positively beaming, the fire reflecting in her wide eyes. Maddox shared the same look of excitement, his teasing smile gone as his jaw hung open, and Nicolas wasn't much better. Olivia couldn't help the grin that came over her face at their reactions, at the amazement in their eyes where she was so used to seeing distaste.

She looked over to find Ariadne smiling fondly at her, rousing the little kid in her lap to show him the dragon. It was the first time she ever really felt proud of showing off her skills. The first time she had ever done it willingly for an audience of more than one.

Soon her dragon faded and Mattie shook herself out of her daze. She immediately started to beg for more, for anything she was willing to give them. Soon she had requests flying at her from every direction, from the kids to Ariadne and even Maddox.

She spent what felt like hours with them, showing off every piece of novelty skill she had ever learned, determined to get them to grin wider and laugh louder. She just wanted to bask in their glow, in the entertainment her magic was providing them.

A community like this, with fellow mages coming together to live in as much peace and comfort as they could, made her longing for the same kind of accepting community even stronger. She felt a sudden surge of anger as she remembered King Alroy's determination to capture and kill these very same mages.

Olivia was glad when Ariadne captured the children's attention to get them ready for bed. She knew her line of thinking wouldn't lead anywhere good, and she didn't want to alarm the children by letting her magic slip and get out of control.

They camped out that night. They gathered their things to sit around the fire, their beds made from gathered leaves and holey bedrolls.

Maddox didn't stay with the children, instead making his bed by Arley, who was camped out close to the edge of camp. Nicolas stayed with them, though. Not like he had much choice, with the way that Mattie and her friend Annora kept tugging at his arm, begging him to stay.

Olivia made her bed closer to Ariadne, where she could keep a close eye on Nicolas and the children. She knew Nicolas would stay with the kids even if she left, but he would feel a lot safer with her being there. The boy and his Chemercha slept snugly beside her as Ariadne slept on her other side, bundled up with various children clinging onto her.

Olivia reached out a hand to gently run through the boy's curly hair. Both him and the Chemercha purred happily at the contact. She smiled fondly down at him and turned over, only to be faced with Ariadne's sad smile.

"His name is Hamlin," Ariadne's smile faltered as she looked at the little boy. "He's had a hard time, as I'm sure you can tell. He only seems at peace when the Chemercha is near him." She looked back at Olivia. "He's only been here a few months, came wandering in on his own, all dazed and refusing to talk. I've tried to weed him off the little creature but they keep finding their way back to each other."

Olivia glanced over her shoulder. The Chemercha was pressed completely to Hamlin's side, its nose under his chin and the boy's arm over its body. It looked protective over him, like it would deter anyone from touching him. She had never heard of a Chemercha being that attached to a single person before.

She turned back to face Ariadne with a sad smile. "I'm glad he has the Chemercha, at least."

Ariadne nodded but didn't say anything more on the matter. She frowned, looking away from Hamlin and turned to face the fire.

"I was displaced many years ago." Ariadne tore her eyes away from the fire to look back at Olivia. "I gained my magic from my grandparents. It skipped a generation, so my mother was human. My grandparents died when I was little. When everyone found out about my magic I was chased out of town, not only by my village, but by my parents too." She frowned. "I bounced around from village to village, getting threatened or run out of every single one. Eventually I stopped trying. I almost starved to death before Maggie found me and brought me to her camp. It was only a few strong back then, but she saved me."

She glanced down as one of the children began to stir. She ran her hand through his hair to calm him, and pressed a light kiss to his forehead. She smiled when the little boy immediately stopped squirming and nuzzled closer to her chest.

"We were forced to move constantly because Maggie's old campsites kept being spotted and attacked." Ariadne kept her gaze on the little boy in her arms. "I only found stability this past year when we grew enough in numbers that we could defend ourselves if we needed to. We had enough magic to shield our entire camp in the event of an attack, until most of us could escape." She smiled fondly down at the kid. "We found this place, and I... it's the first time I've ever felt loved and supported by a community. By a family." She glanced back at Olivia with a wobbly frown. "I'm terrified of all that going away."

Olivia reached out and grabbed her hand tightly. "I will do everything I can to protect you and your family. I promise."

Ariadne laughed, but it sounded hollow. "Do you really have that much influence?" She snorted when Olivia fell silent, but squeezed her hand anyway. "It doesn't matter. I'm grateful for your help, Olivia, whatever it may be."

She fell asleep feeling the most accepted, the most protected, she had ever felt in her life.

CHAPTER TWENTY-SEVEN

Olivia felt optimistic about reporting back to the king for the first time. She knew he couldn't deny the camp's peacefulness if she reported their innocence in front of the court. She trusted Renly and Robard to back her up, Maddox and Nicolas too after the night they had with the children.

The way they found the camp, the stories behind them being there, left little for the court or even the king to complain about. After all, you can't kill orphaned children and not get a bad reputation for it, and that wasn't something the king needed right now.

It didn't go as smoothly as she had hoped.

They met the king, her father and the council in the great hall as soon as they squared their horses away. Some errand boy she had never seen before was waiting to inform them by the stables, all twitchy with nervous energy, before he ran back to the safety of the castle walls. It was odd, all of them being requested, not just herself and Renly.

Her optimism faded with every step she took towards the grand hall. Renly began to frown, and the lively chatter from the others faded into incoherent murmuring.

"Ah, there you are."

The same twitchy messenger boy pushed open the large oak doors for them, gaze focused on the floor as the knights trickled in.

Her father stood beside the king, face pinched as if they had been discussing something unsavoury. The council sat around the large table at the side of the room, the surface covered in papers and mugs of what she assumed to be ale.

"Sorry father."

Olivia stopped in the middle of the room beside Renly, with Robard on her other side, and the rest of the knights gathered beside him. The air in the room felt charged.

"No matter." King Alroy frowned as he peered past them. "Nothing to bring back with you?"

Olivia clenched her jaw at the insinuation but didn't comment. He was looking for the mages he expected them to capture from the camp.

"No, father." Renly tensed beside her. "You seemed to have been fed misleading information. The camp we were sent to was full of orphaned and displaced mages, not a battle camp of Uprisers as suggested. These women and children hold no threat to yourself or the Kingdom, and know little of the Uprising."

The king narrowed his eyes. "Well, that's very doubtful. The information was obtained through very persuasive manners." Olivia cringed as she remembered how persuading those methods could be. "How sure are you?"

"Certain."

"I'm sure they weren't as innocent as they seemed." King Alroy hummed. "Their words of being displaced by fear or negligence may very well have been exaggerated. They're a camp full of mages and should be watched closely."

"Here, here." The council agreed. King Alroy puffed out a little in the support so eagerly given.

"They should be eliminated," one of the council members, with a long white beard, said. "Just in case."

Olivia couldn't help as her mouth fell open in surprise. He was talking about a *massacre*, and happily too. She glanced at her father and saw him stony-faced, his jaw clenched tightly and his hands balled up in fists, but he didn't say a word. He didn't even try to defend his people.

Luckily, King Alroy waved off the suggestion with a scoff. "That's illegal."

He didn't mention anything about how horrid of a suggestion it was, of the shock of someone casually mentioning the murdering of the people he swore to protect. Olivia was mortified at the concept, at the fact that someone on the council could even think something like that was acceptable, let alone try to encourage it.

"The places they came from are likely to be underdeveloped." The king continued. "We can't control the views of everyone in the outlier villages, and it's not on our heads the way they reacted." He turned to look at her father. "You feel safe here, don't you, William?"

He froze, and his eyes widened, but he quickly regained his composure and gave a nod. "Of course, Your Majesty."

King Alroy then turned to look at Olivia, eyebrow raised. "And you, Olivia?"

She barely held back a laugh at such a question. He must have known how horrible it was for her to grow up with magic under his rule, with the townsfolk taunting and threatening her around every corner, with the knights acting as if she didn't exist unless it was to join in the taunts. It felt far from safe. Spending the little time that she did in Margaret's camp, she felt safer there than she ever did inside the city walls.

"Um."

Renly snorted at her eloquent answer, but she wasn't sure what she was supposed to say. She knew he wasn't being serious in his question, that he didn't really care either way, but she had this sudden burning urge to tell him exactly how she felt. She knew it might only serve to threaten her even more, but she felt the need to stand strong for all those displaced mages who couldn't. For the promise she had made to Ariadne.

Her father glared at her, and let out a low, growling warning. "Be very careful with your next words, child."

She could feel the tension in the room. Her father's words held an undercurrent of a threat, one that he would likely follow through with depending on her next actions. She felt the steady eyes of the king and the nervous energy in the room, all awaiting her answer.

Now wasn't the time for bravery, it seemed.

"Of course, Your Majesty. I feel very safe here." She gave a bow, lowering herself to face the floor so she could bite back the nausea clawing up her throat. Once her nausea surpassed, she stood back up much straighter than before, gaze ahead and not daring to make eye contact with anyone.

"Very good." The king nodded, before turning to his council. "Now, what shall we do about this possible threat?"

It was decided that watching the camp too closely may send them into a panic, and may prod them into an attack. Olivia didn't bother reminding them that the camp was entirely peaceful, and they wouldn't dare attack while they had children with them – neither did Nicolas or Maddox, who she knew felt just as protective over those kids as she did, because they all knew how valued their input would be.

Her father was tasked to visit the camp every week or so to check up on them and make sure they weren't lying about their innocence. King Alroy didn't trust them, didn't think they were as innocent as they seemed, and everyone else seemed to agree with his decision.

Not for the first time, she was incredibly suspicious of where he had gotten his initial information from, and why he trusted it so blindly. He valued the word of his informant more than his own son, it seemed. Or perhaps he was just desperate, eager to get his hands on whatever mage he could find, to paint them as an Upriser and squeeze information out of them that they didn't have.

The only silver lining was that her father would be the one to go to them. She was glad that it was another mage, and not Merek or a council member with something to prove.

She left the moment that they were dismissed, walking straight out the doors after Renly, only not running ahead to keep up appearances of respect in front of the court. Her hands were shaking. Her whole damn body was shaking, in an odd mixture of anger and fear.

Maybe she would have been better off staying behind at the camp like Merek had suggested.

Robard tried to hold her hand, to stop the trembling, but she jerked away from him. Everything was crashing down around her all at once and she needed a distraction. She needed to hit something.

He withdrew his hand with a frown. "Are you okay?"

She couldn't bring herself to look at him, so she stared at the wall instead and shook her head. There was no point in lying to him, not when she couldn't even keep the emotion off her face. She was furious at the comments made about her people, disappointed that she proved to King Alroy that those mages were no threat but he still didn't believe it.

She was terrified of the way things were headed.

Renly stood in front of her, blocking her view, and leaned down to look her in the eye. He was concerned, she could see the worry clear as day on his face. He searched her eyes for a few moments before he sighed and stood, turning to the others. "Training in a few for anyone that wants it."

Olivia was surprised enough to look over at him. She felt validated at the frustration she could feel dripping off of him. Maybe some more training is what they all needed. If anything, it would be a good excuse to beat the hell out of something.

"I have better things to do." Merek left in a huff, storming off down the halls and weaving through mildly concerned servants. None of the others followed after him. She was surprised that the rest wanted to stay.

She went hard during training, building up a sweat within the first few minutes.

Maddox and Arley teased that she was finally getting good, that soon she wouldn't even need her magic to be a good fighter.

She knew they didn't mean it to sound the way that it did, like she would be dead by now if not for her magic, but she still felt the sting from their casual words. Like her magic was something to look down on, like she was weak without it.

It made her spar harder, faster, meaner. She wanted, *needed*, to prove them wrong. The only real challenge she got was from Renly. He didn't hold back, and gave just as good as he got. This time, though, it wasn't enough.

Olivia hit Renly hard, again and again, until he was beaten to the ground. She put her sword to his throat as he lay on his back, defenceless. She was puffing as she looked down at him, holding the sword steadily. A perfect mirror to what he had done to her not that long ago.

She made eye contact with Renly and immediately withdrew her sword, the fog of her anger fading away. One hand lifted to run through her hair. She was surprised to find her hand rather steady, a far cry from the trembling mess she had been before. "Sorry, Renly."

Renly blinked up at her, before a slow smile made its way to his face as he pushed himself to stand. "Now you know what you're capable of."

He picked up his sword from where it landed beside him and left without another word. She distantly heard Arley laugh about the prince losing to a girl.

She was stuck in place, still looking at the spot where Renly had been lying moments before. She had beaten him, and he hadn't even let her win. He had even been... proud of her? It all made her head spin.

Maddox clapped her on the shoulder, making her jump. "You can beat the little prince over there, but you still can't beat me." He grinned as she turned to look at him, sword twirling around in his right hand. "I'm not afraid of a little magic."

She grinned. This was going to be fun.

CHAPTER TWENTY-EIGHT

She awoke to a bad smell in the morning, much earlier than she usually arose. She didn't have to search long before she found the source of the smell – it was her. She had forgotten to bathe since before she left for Margaret's camp.

It was probably time to do something about that.

She stretched with a yawn and made her way down the stairs to raid the cupboards, only to find them bare. She didn't have to be quiet as neither of her parents were home, but that wasn't much of a surprise these days. Her father was probably still at the castle, where he always seemed to be, and her mother either hadn't come home yet from the tavern or was there early to help clean the place up.

She gathered an armful of clean clothing and left for the river. It was relatively secluded there, as not many people were brave enough to venture to the backyard of the mage they feared so much, but it worked to her advantage. She didn't have to fret about being watched, or if someone would steal her clothing. It was just her and nature.

There was a wider area of the river that was almost circular, the stream running more gently than in the other parts, and deep enough for the water to reach her midsection. It was the perfect bathing spot, and one she frequented.

The water gently lapped at her skin as she bathed. She enjoyed the sounds of nature all around her, of being completely alone and at peace. Sure, sometimes she enjoyed a nice hot bath, something that was getting easier to achieve the better control she had over her magic, but she would come outside to bathe more often than not. The crispness of the water woke her up a lot faster than a warm bath ever could.

She ducked under the water to wet her hair, the greasy feeling flowing down the stream with the running water. She stood, flicking her hair out of her eyes as she came up for air, when she heard a twig snap behind her.

There went her peaceful morning.

She turned around with exasperation, but her words of annoyance got caught in her throat.

There was a girl lingering in the morning darkness, the light barely bouncing off her red hair. She couldn't make out who it was, but she could feel the magic in the air. It wasn't anyone who lived in Alira.

Olivia took a step towards the girl with intrigue but misjudged the slope. She slipped on the mud underfoot and hit her head on the side of the bank. A sickening crack rang across the quietness of the forest as her nose throbbed, warmth blooming from it moments later. She clutched her nose as she scrambled up onto the bank. If the bathing didn't wake her up, the pain certainly did.

The girl didn't advance, so Olivia chanced a look up through her fingers. Who she saw was almost surprising enough to send her back down the riverbank.

Molle.

The girl sighed as she approached her. Olivia must have been a pathetic sight for the young girl to look at her like that. Naked, dark hair dripping over her eyes, clutching a bleeding nose – and *she* was the one that everyone knew the name of. It was almost laughable.

Molle reached out a hand towards her, before she seemed to think better of it. Her eyes lost their spark but she never lowered her hand. Before Olivia could even blink, the girl grabbed hold of her nose and snapped it back into place without warning.

"Shit!" Olivia grit her teeth against the searing pain. "What was that for?"

Molle shrugged with a sly grin.

The pain slowly subsided, and Olivia spared Molle a look. Not for the first time she wondered how advanced the mage training was supposed to be. Molle knew leagues more than Olivia did, despite being so much younger than her. Being raised in a sheltered community, with a reluctant teacher, obviously stunted Olivia's learning.

She dried herself with a wave of her hand and got dressed. Molle didn't look like she was inclined to leave anytime soon, and Olivia would much rather talk while she wasn't naked.

"What are you doing here?" Olivia asked as she pulled on her shirt. She winced at the phantom pain as the material brushed against her nose. "What do you want?"

"You."

Molle looked determined and entirely too serious, something that made Olivia almost frightened. She wanted... her? Even after such a pathetic display?

"Me?" Olivia asked.

"You have to leave." Molle took a step towards her, and Olivia had to fight every instinct not to back away. "You don't have to fight. Just run as far away from Alira as possible. You're too powerful to be stuck fighting a war you don't want to be in."

"I–"

"Olivia." Molle's look sharpened, and this time Olivia did flinch. "Do you really want to fight against your own people to defend those who don't care about you? Who only care about what your magic can do *for* them?" She scoffed. "I understand why you don't want to fight, but I never pegged you for an idiot."

"Alira is my home, they *are* my people." Olivia bristled at the insult. "The methods the Uprisers are using are wrong, you know that."

"Is it?" Molle asked. "Is it so wrong to defend your people when they're dying in the hundreds? Just for being born? Being executed and exiled for something they never asked for? Someone has to take a stand!"

Olivia flinched, but not at Molle. Her argument was solid, as much as she hated to admit it. She didn't doubt their motives, not after everything she'd witnessed, after she's heard the flippant way the humans talk about killing what they don't understand.

But the Uprisers were extreme, that much she was certain of. Their methods, not caring about the casualties, mage and human alike, made them almost as bad as the treatment they were fighting against. Her father had made sure she knew the dangers of acting on anger and rage with her magic. He always said that kind of magic could poison you, make you convinced the world was a dark and horrible place that needed saving by whatever means necessary.

"These people have done nothing wrong," Olivia said. "King Alroy should be the one punished, not his people. If I don't help protect them they will all be slaughtered for the same reason that we are. They didn't ask to live under a tyrant."

Molle scowled, and it made Olivia pause to question her. This girl was a stark difference from the timid little thing she met in Drerimas. She had a frustration and determination she certainly didn't have back when they first met, and it hadn't been long since they parted.

She squinted at the girl, as if staring hard enough would give her all the answers she needed. The kid had been terrified of the Uprisers, sick of their methods. She had even helped to save Renly from them.

What changed since they met?

"You're making the wrong choice, Olivia." Molle huffed, taking a final step closer until she was standing right in front of her. "Things are moving quickly and you should leave while you still have the chance."

She escaped through the woods before Olivia could even process her final words of warning.

"Remember. A golden cage is still just a cage."

CHAPTER TWENTY-NINE

Olivia disappeared to study in the library after her talk with Molle.

She wanted to forget all about it, to bury herself so deep in her studies that she wouldn't have the time to dwell, but the conversation wouldn't leave her mind.

What had happened to that poor girl since she was left all alone in Drerimas? Perhaps she had tried to flee the Uprisers but had been caught, had been conditioned to believe the lies that they were spreading. She was young enough to be easily impressionable, so it wasn't an unrealistic thought.

If she had insisted that Molle came back to Alira with her, would she have been safer? Would she have finally escaped the clutches of the Uprisers? Would the king have kept her in the dungeons alongside the others they captured?

All the possibilities made her head spin, and it became almost impossible to focus on anything she was trying to read.

It didn't matter what could have been, nor what had happened to that poor girl. She was a part of the Uprisers now by the sounds of it, if not just a sympathiser.

Did she have it in herself to slay a child if it came down to it? She didn't know if she could. She didn't know if she could kill *anyone*. But she wasn't as naive as she once was. Not after Molle's parting warning, after the words of the old mage in that cave, nor the hallucination she had seen.

She wasn't dumb enough to think she could fight in a battle and not have to hurt anyone. To think that no-one would be killed. She didn't want anyone from either side to die. She knew she didn't want to join a side that would kill in vengeance for years of neglect and violence, who would slay innocent people because they had been hurt.

She didn't want to side with those who had committed the atrocities in the first place, either.

Perhaps Molle was right. Sure, she had her family and her friends in Alira that she loved, but she had suffered under the king's rule for so long. She knew the king, and after everything was over, she couldn't be sure that he wouldn't banish her, no matter the outcome. She couldn't be sure he wouldn't publicly execute her either, to prove that no mage was safe in his Kingdom, no matter how close they were to royalty.

She couldn't turn her back on her people based on what *could* happen, though.

Neither side winning would be particularly favourable for her, and that only made her decision that much harder. Gods, the whole thing made her head hurt. If only she had someone to tell her what to do, to assure her a better outcome that didn't make her sick to the stomach.

She needed help. Something more divine.

Edgehaven!

She could have hit herself for forgetting such a place. She'd only read about it fleetingly in one of her father's dull old books, but it was as good a shot as any. It was supposed to be a place to seek guidance and absolution for mages of all walks of life. It was used by mages for centuries, or so they'd said.

It supposedly offered answers, and that was the one thing she needed the most. Honestly, at this point, anything would help. As long as it wasn't like the last gathering place she'd been to, she didn't see the problem in trying.

She huffed and let her head fall into the book open on the table. Why couldn't anything just be simple?

Renly, of course, chose that exact moment to walk through the door. He only took a few steps into the room before pausing. She groaned when she heard him try to stifle his laugh. "Alright, Olivia?"

She grumbled, face still muffled by the pages, and threw up her middle finger. His laughter rang throughout the empty library, and a little of the tension bled from the room.

"Up you get," she heard the table squeak, and suddenly there were arms around her shoulders, hauling her into an upright position. Renly was perched on the table, his legs propped up on the seat beside her. She caught a glimpse of a teasing smile before it was pulled into a tight frown. "Gods, you look awful."

"Thank you," she batted his hands away from her. "Real charmer, you are."

His gaze raked over her as he looked for any injuries, intense enough to make her squirm, and he sighed when he saw nothing physical. He didn't seem any happier at that discovery, though. She's sure she looked a sight, as stressed out as she had been, hidden away in the dusty old library without any fresh air. She could practically feel the dark circles growing under her eyes.

She didn't mean to worry him. He had enough on his plate without having to be concerned over her. Things were getting tense though, tenser than usual, and if she was to leave for Edgehaven she'd have to do it soon. Today, before anyone could get wind, before anyone insisted they accompany her.

Renly must have been able to sense something, because he frowned. "Where are you going?"

It was frightening how well he could still read her.

She hesitated to tell him. For one, he was human, and she didn't know the punishment of telling him about such a place. Besides, it wasn't as if she could tell him she was off chasing some story about a magical place that would clear away her doubts. He'd think she was crazy.

On the other hand, he had shown her kindness lately, something she hadn't seen from him in such a long time. He trusted her when he could have ignored her and simply followed his fathers commands. She didn't want to lie to him.

She shrugged, gaze glued to the table. "You might not see me for a day or two."

Renly hummed, "I'll try not to do anything drastic while you're gone."

She snorted, "you better not."

She looked up to meet Renly's eyes. His immediate acceptance of her leaving was shocking. After all, he knew the Uprisers were closing in, and he knew that many mages had tried to convince her away from Alira. The trust he was showing was unexpected, but appreciated.

Maybe she should tell him. If something were to happen to her... well, it wasn't like he could come save her, but it may stop him worrying. On the other hand, telling the crowned prince that she was seeking assurance to fight alongside him instead of running away would only lead to more questions, more doubt of her loyalty, and that wasn't something either of them needed right now.

She needed to do this, and she needed to do it alone.

She gave Renly a tight smile and stood. If she didn't leave now, the journey would be a long one, and she knew she shouldn't be leaving the city in the first place. Anything could happen while she was gone.

Her hand was on the doorknob when Renly spoke up, sounding a mile away.

"I trust you, Olivia, but you need to have faith in yourself."

She quickly took her leave before she did something humiliating like hug him.

CHAPTER THIRTY

She gathered enough food in a saddlebag for a few days on the road and left through the woods that afternoon.

The ride wasn't supposed to be an overly lengthy affair, situated just as far away as Drerimas was, but in the opposite direction. She could have stopped a few times on the way, but she wasn't about to make the journey longer than it needed to be. She was risking enough by leaving in the first place.

She only stopped to rest and feed Shadow before continuing on again. She expected the journey to be more... perilous? Nerve-wrecking? Perhaps she had made too many trips with the knights so she expected things to go haywire at least once. She was pleasantly surprised when everything went according to plan.

The path she expected to take was direct and free of humans and bandits. The streams detailed on the maps were exactly where they were supposed to be, and there was no-one to try and steer her off the path. It was peaceful, riding in silence with only the soft sound of the path under Shadow's hooves and the flittering of wildlife to keep her company.

She was a little nervous that she might ride straight past what she was looking for without even noticing, though. There were no detailed pictures, no finer details on the map she found past lakes and mountains. She didn't have the slightest clue of what it should look like. Only that she would know when she saw it, whatever that meant.

She needn't have worried, as it turned out. She felt a strong tugging in her chest the closer she got, guiding her way. The trees became grander, as if the soil had unnaturally strong nutrients to feed the roots, and the branches hung over the path. The wildlife was abundant, with deer drinking from the stream running by the path, and birds chirping happily as they flew through the trees.

The beauty of it was beyond anything she had ever seen before. The water from the stream running through was impossibly blue, the giant stones surrounding the clearing covered in growing moss. Red leaves from the surrounding trees lay fallen by the riverbanks.

The place seeped peace.

The sun was dipping below the towering trees as she finally arrived. It wouldn't be long until the area descended into darkness. Somehow, the lower light made the place even more breathtaking.

Renly and Nicolas would really love it here.

She shook her head to dislodge the intruding thought. They were part of the reason she was there in the first place. All of the knights, really. Having any of them with her would only ruin the peace.

Olivia sighed and led Shadow further down the path. It became more treacherous the further they rode, as if a warning for those who weren't supposed to be there. The trees seemed to close in on them, and she almost had to duck just to make it through. Sticks clung to her hair as they made it to the other side.

The red tint of the leaves seemed to grow darker, and branches poked out at unsuspecting travellers.

A river seeped into the middle of the path, blocking it completely. It was much wider than the stream that welcomed her as she first entered the clearing. The path didn't continue on the other side. There were mossy stones lying in the middle of the river as the only safe way to cross. The bottom seemed impossibly deep with no end in sight.

If either she or Shadow took a wrong step in that water she wasn't sure they could make it out.

It seemed as if this was the end of the line. This was it.

She knew she had to cross, though. As beautiful as it was, this place was definitely not what she was searching for. She could feel it. The tug in her chest told her that what she was searching for was across that river.

She led Shadow slowly across the large rocks, taking extra care to make sure neither of them slipped and fell into the water.

A wall of rock was the only thing that met her on the other side. There was no way around it. Two obscenely large, mossy rocks marked the only entrance she could find. The gap between them was tight, but it seemed the only way in or out of whatever waited for her on the other side. The tug in her chest became stronger, practically pulling her to the rocks. She definitely found it.

With a deep breath, she squeezed through the rocks, Shadow stubbornly following her in before she had the chance to tell her to wait for her there.

It wasn't as narrow as it looked from the outside. As soon as she committed to walking through, it was as if the rocks parted ways for her, and she hardly needed to squeeze at all.

Gods, she loved magic.

On the other side was what she could only describe as paradise.

She thought the water was pure and blue on the other side? There was a large pond with bright blue water that seemed to sparkle in the dying light, situated right in the middle of the clearing.

The other trees were beautiful? The leaves adorning the huge trees here were red, orange, and pink. An array of bright and pale colours surrounded the bank of the pond and spread throughout the clearing.

On the other side of the pond was a gigantic, towering figure carved out of stone. It depicted a lady, beautiful even in stone, with her arms open wide to welcome the travellers to the area. She was leaning over slightly, the top of her head close to towering over the edge of the pond. Beneath the lady was an opening to what looked like a cave.

Olivia didn't need any more hints than that.

"C'mon, Shadow."

She led Shadow along the rocky path over toward the cave. Behind the statue was a large branch, fallen sideways with rope attached to it, and a large trough with clean water underneath. For travellers horses, she assumed.

Olivia went to attach Shadow to it without a second thought, but paused just as they approached. She didn't know this place, no matter how innocent it seemed, and she shouldn't just blindly be following its rules.

Shadow nudged her gently in the side, her nose leaving a wet streak down her arm, and nodded towards the fallen branch with a huff.

Well, if Shadow thought it was trustworthy enough. She never had a reason to distrust her judgement before. She attached the rope to her halter and turned back to the cave.

The closer she got to the cave, the more imposing it seemed to be. It was much larger than it looked from a distance. The entrance was wider, and what she could see inside was a lot deeper than she had suspected. Small in comparison to the towering statue, she thought vaguely.

She came here for answers, and she was damned if she was going to turn back just because it was unexpected. Taking a deep breath to steady herself, she made her way into the cave.

It was deep, with a few levels down into its deepest parts. Water was cascading down the walls, seeming to run down the side and pool at the very bottom of the cave, where a large body of water sat. The water was glowing in the darkness, much brighter than the pond outside.

As she made her way further into the cave, she could see cracks in the roof, little holes letting in pockets of dying light to guide her way down to the bottom.

There was a small space by the centred part of the water. The stone was indented in a few places, some parts deeper than others, where she imagined many mages before herself knelt down to peer into the water. To seek the same absolution Olivia herself was there for.

She did just as they had done, kneeling down in the more prominent dents and peering into the water. She felt closer to her ancestors like that, surrounded in loud calmness, in such a peace she had never felt before. There was no fear in a place like this. She wished she could stay forever.

In the few things she found about seeking guidance in an environment like this, they all told of the same things. To speak your worries into the water's face, to ask for guidance and absolution, and help would be given in return. It was all very vague in how it worked, in the form she would get her answers in, but she supposed that was part of the mystery. If everyone knew, it could easily be fabricated into tricking other vulnerable souls.

She really, really hoped this wasn't a trick.

Olivia leaned further over the water, until she could see her reflection shining back at her, clear enough to be mistaken for another person. She didn't have time to dwell over how insane this whole thing was, so she just had to get on with it. She cleared her throat, squeezed her eyes shut, and spoke.

"I'm worried I'll fight for the wrong side." Her voice cracked, as if just speaking the words out loud was enough to get her killed. She knew it was likely if she was kneeling anywhere else. "King Alroy is so full of hate it's hard to ignore. But... but the Uprisers are drastic. They're killing their own in the name of vengeance." Olivia ran a shaky hand through her hair. "Both sides are equally as guilty. I don't know what to do. I can't abandon my Kingdom, but they have done wrong by my people... but my people are turning into murderers. What should I do? What side should I take?"

Her hands were shaking and her mind was racing, but the water was just as still as it was before. Her reflection blinked back at her, hands shaking just as hard as they were in real life, gaze just as lost as she was feeling.

This was stupid. A big, stupid mistake. Speaking her worries into a *pond* in hopes that it would, what? Speak back? She was an idiot. Coming here was a huge, stupid risk.

She sighed and pushed against the stone, reading herself to leave. Between one blink and the next, the water began to ripple. She immediately leaned closer in fascination as the ripples became more frequent. She was almost too surprised at what was happening to pay any attention to it.

A woman's voice spoke from the water, calm and serene, as if speaking to a spooked child. "Olivia Shaw. The one who will win the war. Those who are the most in need are the ones filled with terror and hatred. In order to save your people, you must defeat your own."

The ripples faded to the edge of the water, and the next time she blinked it was just as calm as it was when she entered the cave.

That was it? That was the guidance she travelled so far to get? *That* was supposed to clear things up for her? Was this some kind of twisted joke?

Olivia let out a scream of frustration as she fell on her hands and knees by the water's edge. She barely held back her frustrated tears.

What the hell was any of that supposed to mean?

She made her way out of the cave and back to Shadow in a daze. The growing darkness outside made it hard to see anything, the only light source coming from the glowing water inside the cave, and the slightly duller glow from the pond outside. The moon was hidden through the trees and the towering statue. There was no way she was getting out of that clearing tonight.

With a sigh of defeat, she led Shadow to a spot by the pond. It made for the perfect camping spot, the trees thin and sparse by the water's edge, with plenty of room for Shadow to roam.

Even through the anger and frustration, the sense of safety still washed over her in waves. It was as if her magic knew this place was truly safe, and allowed itself to completely surrender to its warm embrace.

She spent the night in silence, the only sound coming from a few bugs and Shadow, quietly nibbling at the grass behind her. It was a rare, peaceful night without the bickering and fighting of the knights to disturb her. She liked the silence.

She was lulled to sleep thinking over the words from the cave. In order to save her people, she had to kill her own. Which side were her 'people' and which were her 'own'? It said she was the one who would win the war like it *knew* her already. Was that why those mages knew her name?

Despite everything, was she willing to pick a side and condemn the other?

It seemed, either way, she was doomed.

CHAPTER THIRTY-ONE

The words stuck with Olivia the entire journey back.

The same fear that she lived with every day was not something she wished upon anyone. Not even Merek.

It was easier to convince and persuade a man like King Alroy, his only power coming from his position and his men, than it was to try and reason with someone who could set her alight with one flick of the wrist.

It was a realisation that sat uncomfortably with her.

Was she really going to fight for a side that persecuted her kind? That wanted them all dead, that joked about their genocide? Perhaps the outcome would be much the same on either side. Either way, one of them would always live in fear.

She found herself outside the dungeon gates before she even realised she was back in Alira.

She hardly remembered the ride at all, so overcome with thoughts and questions that Shadow's good sense of direction was likely the only reason she made it back at all. She didn't remember putting Shadow in her stables, or walking across the courtyard. She knew it was already nightfall, though, as she heard the distant drunken cheers she had long ago associated with the night shift at The Sun.

There weren't even any guards placed outside the dungeons, much to her surprise. She knew there weren't any other prisoners apart from the Uprisers, who were being held in cells specifically designed to keep them in, but she still expected at least someone there.

Letting herself through the entrance and down the stairs that led to their cells, she wondered if talking to them would help her in any way, or only cause to confuse her more. Surely these mages, the ones that have claimed to be mistreated by both sides, would help her find the lesser evil. It wouldn't hurt to speak with them.

She faltered when she finally reached their cell.

One of the Uprisers was curled up in the corner of the cell, unmoving. Smudged blood stretched out across the middle of the cell to where she lay. The other was majorly malnourished, all but skin and bones, staring out at her with nothing behind her eyes. Like she'd given up.

It was the brunette, the one that liked to stare.

The smell was putrid, and only got stronger the closer she got. Part of it was from the opposite corner, the one they were obviously using as a toilet, though most of the smell seemed to be coming from them.

She knew they weren't innocent. They had tried to kidnap Renly, tried to kill herself and the knights, but to be treated like this? They weren't acting in their right minds back in Drerimas, may have killed Renly if she wasn't there to stop them, but she found it hard to give this sort of treatment justification.

She went to unlock the barred doors, unconscious of her own actions, when she felt a hand tugging at her elbow. She turned in a daze to find Renly, who tugged her back a few paces. She went willingly, guided by Renly's confused and concerned gaze.

"What happened to her?" Renly turned to the conscious Upriser.

"Dead." She coughed, and it sounded painful. "Few days ago. Thought it'd make me talk." Her gaze slowly shifted to Olivia. "Don't know why. Told 'em all I know. Long time ago, too." She gave a toothy, lifeless grin. "Think they just like watchin' me squirm."

Renly glanced over at Olivia, the same shock she felt written plainly across his face. If she hadn't been feeding the king any information, where was he getting it all from? Was any of it even real?

Renly tensed as he looked back at the cell. "Did my father do this to her?"

She shrugged, "indirectly." She scoffed, grin slipping. "Not like any of this shit is new. She just got the short end of it."

Olivia frowned, "not new?"

The Upriser tilted her head and looked between the two of them. Silence hung over the room until she cracked another grin and cackled to herself. She seemed crazed. Having your dead friend sitting in a cell with you would do that to you, she supposed.

"Oh, you don't know?" She shook her head, still laughing. "That's hilarious."

She slowly stood, pushing herself up off the cold concrete floor with a groan, and limped towards the bars. She stopped just before she reached them. She stared directly at Olivia as she spoke, words coming out as a whisper.

"You think you guys are bad? What, they send you on a few wrong trips, tell a couple of lies?" She laughed darkly. "You don't know how good you have it." She curled her hands around the bars and grinned. She didn't even flinch at the pain Olivia knew she must have felt. "None of you would last a moment with the Uprisers."

Renly flexed his arm and pressed against Olivia's front. He curled his hand around Olivia's wrist, arm pressed hard across her chest, and all but growled at the cells. She wasn't sure if he was stopping her from moving forwards, or trying to protect her against the deranged Upriser.

She inside gave a dull laugh as her hands fell from the bars. Her cocky grin slipped and she fell back to the floor in a bundle of limbs. She seemed defeated. "Just kill me already."

"What?" Olivia asked softly.

That wasn't the reaction she expected. Laughter, maybe. Screaming and cursing? Absolutely.

Asking for death? Far from it.

"I can't take it anymore!" The Upriser hollered, her gaze back on Olivia. "I'm already dead anyway."

"I–" Olivia swallowed the lump in her throat. It was obvious that she was fading, that she really wasn't going to last much longer in that festering cell, but she wasn't a killer. She *wasn't*. "I can't."

She screamed in frustration as Olivia turned her back on her and walked away. "Please! You can't leave me here!"

It took all the willpower she had not to take the dead mage out of that cell, to not provide the other some food and water. She knew she couldn't help, even if she tried.

"Olivia! Don't leave!"

Olivia trembled as she heard the Upriser sob, as she screamed out after them and begged for death. She flinched, and the only thing that stopped her from turning around and giving her exactly what she wanted was Renly's hand on the small of her back, a steady and supportive weight pushing her forwards.

They tumbled up the stone steps and weaved through passageways, and out the back entranceway. The moment her feet touched grass she doubled over, throwing up everything she had been holding back. Renly didn't move, his guiding hand on her back now rubbing slow circles, his other hand holding back her hair.

That Upriser wasn't afraid of them, wasn't afraid of ending up like her friend. She was scared of being let go and being handed back to the Uprisers. She needed to stop this war, to stop the suffering, and she wasn't about to help those who would do something much worse than whatever was happening in that cell.

The Uprisers needed to be stopped. By any means necessary.

"We're headed out again the day after tomorrow."

Olivia slowly righted herself, wiping her mouth with the back of her hand. Renly slid his arm around her waist to keep her from falling. "Where?"

Renly shrugged, "Father spoke of a battle camp nearby, hardly half a day's ride."

She snorted, "a battle camp like the last one?"

Renly blushed and looked away from her, "he said you didn't need to come."

He drummed his fingers against the skin of her waist in the silence that hung over them. If the king wished for her to stay behind, something must be afoot, and she wasn't quite sure if staying behind would be good for her. Not after what she had just witnessed down in the cells.

She had never felt bad for Renly before, not with the way he lived, with the money and power he had. Now, though, with all this uncertainty hanging over his head, with constant conflicting stories of who his father really is... he must be suffering.

Renly tightened his grip and sighed, "look, Liv–"

"Don't."

She allowed herself to lean against Renly's shoulder, thankful when he didn't push her away.

"I don't need your pity." She felt him take a deep breath, as if readying himself to argue, so she looked up at him and pinned him with a glare. "You don't need to apologise, either. You've done nothing wrong. *None* of this is your fault."

"Only if you admit it's not yours either," he said.

She couldn't stop the small smile that crept onto her lips. She knew he was right. He didn't know how detrimental his father's prejudice would become, and she had no reason to think she should have studied her magic any more than she had, not while she lived right under the nose of a man who hated it.

There was no point blaming themselves. It was well past that, and it wouldn't do them any good to start pointing fingers now.

Renly squeezed her waist once more before he slipped his hand away. "I want you with us when we leave." He cleared his throat and quickly looked around, as if to make sure no-one was listening. "I don't trust you to be safe here alone."

He slid his palm against the middle of her back and gently guided her away.

"Come, let's get you home."

Chapter Thirty-Two

"How long is this goin' to take?" Merek groaned. "Next time I'm staying in Alira."

Maddox snorted, "and do what, sit in the The Sun all day while we do all the work?"

"Oh please," Merek waved a hand dismissively at him. "You have Olivia, you don't need me too."

"You make a good point." Maddox turned around on his horse to face her, a teasing grin on his face. "Why can't we just send Olivia and Your Highness over here out on their own? Maybe Nico too, get some experience in him, and Robard, so they don't die from their own stupidity."

Olivia gave him the finger, but Maddox just cackled and turned back around to continue his conversation with Merek.

Only a day had passed since her fateful trip to Edgehaven, but things only seemed to be getting worse. Her father had been sent to check back in with Margaret's camp, despite the fact that they had only gotten back from their camp less than a week ago. Her father seemed suspicious, but he left without a word, which only served to worry Olivia more.

True to Renly's word, Olivia wasn't told a single thing about the knight's new trip.

She came with them anyway.

It wasn't like she had to be very secretive about it, though. Her father was gone, mother was still working long shifts at The Sun, and Cassius was all but living at the forge with all the orders they've been getting since everyone heard about the Uprisers.

There wasn't anyone left to miss her.

She scrunched her nose as she scanned the treeline. The air felt stale as they continued to ride, and the trees seemed a little more lifeless than the ones they had already passed. It felt odd, like an ache deep in her chest.

It felt as if there used to be magic flowing through the land, but it was ripped out. She had never felt something like this before.

She glanced over at Renly, "something is wrong."

She smelt it moments later.

Burning.

She whipped around to stare at the path ahead of them, all her senses heightened. Smoke was billowing towards them, trapped from rising any higher by the thick coverage of trees.

She set off riding towards the smoke before she even realised what she was doing, ignoring the screams from Renly and Robard to slow down and wait for them. There was blood rushing through her ears, a steady beat of *danger danger danger* running on a loop in her head.

When she reached the clearing, she stopped so suddenly she was almost thrown straight from her horse. She heard Maddox swear as he skidded to a halt to avoid running straight into her.

The clearing was littered with bodies. There was a tent burning in the near distance. Women, men, children. All dead. It was eerily similar to the nightmares she'd had about finding Margaret's camp in the exact same way.

She barely made it off of Shadow before she threw up into the bushes.

The air filled with the stench of ash and bodies. The image still played out in front of her even as she clenched her eyes shut. She felt someone rub circles onto her back, whispering words of comfort in her ear. She rose slowly and wiped the back of her hand across her mouth. Robard slid his hand off her back with a grimace.

Olivia took another long look over the camp from beside Robard, who had clasped her shoulder with a steady hand. The feeling was grounding, stopping her from bolting like she very much wanted to.

Most of the camp didn't seem to be on fire any longer, just a smouldering wreckage left behind from the attack. Ash littered the ground from tents and material disintegrated from the flames. Clothes were half burnt off the bodies lying around the clearing, some covered by parts of structure that had burned down around them, others with their clothes melted to their skin.

They seemed so innocent. It felt exactly the same as when she entered Margaret's camp. The echoes of the children's laughter still seemed to hang in the air. The thought almost made her sick again.

"Liv," Renly softly called out.

She dragged her gaze over to him. He was standing on the opposite end of the clearing, the fire from the tent behind him reduced to smoke as Nicolas and Arley stomped out the last of the flames. Renly was gesturing to one of the bodies in front of him.

"She's alive."

Olivia shook off Robard's hand and made her way to Renly. She walked slowly, so as not to tread on anything, or anyone.

The woman was barely alive. Her lower half was covered by a post, some of the wood having pierced through her stomach. It seemed fatal, the blood pooling under her wound at an alarming rate.

Olivia crouched beside the woman, who was muttering something too soft for either her or Renly to hear. She reached out a trembling hand to clutch Olivia's own. A streak of blood trickled down her wrist as the woman clasped her hand tightly.

She couldn't even tell the woman's hair colour. The blood stained everything a deep red.

"Uprisers."

Renly made a noise as he crouched beside Olivia, a determined look on his face. "Did they do this to you?"

The woman tried to nod, only to wince in pain and squeeze Olivia's hand tighter. The movement triggered a coughing fit, and blood began to seep from the corner of her mouth. Olivia reached over with her free hand to gently wipe the blood away. It earned a small smile from the woman, even though the action only caused the blood to smear across her cheek.

"They came out of nowhere, demanded we join their fight. Attacked when we refused." She craned her neck as much as she could to take a look around her. Her gaze settled on a small girl lying a few steps away. Her lip quivered, and a tear slowly made its way down her face, smearing the blood even more. "They didn't care that they were slaughtering their own kind."

This wasn't just any village the Uprisers burned down, but a mage village. It was concerning that they held such little regard for their own kind. They hadn't even tried to convince them, either. Just seemed to attack at the first chance they got. No wonder the mage in the dungeon was terrified of being handed back to them.

"I–" The mage coughed once more, the sound coming out rough and deep. "I don't regret it." She squeezed Olivia's hand as tight as she could until Olivia looked down at her. "Dying like this is better than suffering with them."

She watched the light fade from her eyes as she took her last, shuddery breath. The weight in her hand turned limp.

Renly pulled her to stand and turned her away, steadying her as they stumbled away from the massacre behind them.

Chapter Thirty-Three

It took a little while for Olivia's panic to fade, but she still couldn't get her hands to stop shaking.

When she could think a little clearer, she marched right back into that clearing and picked up a shovel. She wasn't about to leave them to rot amongst the smouldering wreckage of their village.

She could barely see through the tears as she dug that first grave.

The others watched her for a while until Robard started to help, then Nicolas, and eventually the rest followed suit. There was no grumbling from Merek, no light teasing from Maddox. Just the sound of shovels digging into the soil.

Fresh nausea hit as she rolled a child into one of the graves. The little girl didn't seem much older than Mattie. She was eternally grateful that Margaret's camp at least had her father there with them.

It was odd to be with the other knights in silence as they did something for her. They could have easily walked away, or sat and watched her dig, but instead they helped. All except Peter, who had hung back to watch the horses.

A large amount of the bodies were buried beneath the dirt now, and the few that remained looked a lot less gruesome than the ones she had first seen. Small lumps raised out of the ground signalling the amount of graves they had dug. It saddened her that she didn't know their names to mark up the graves, that no-one would know the identity of any of the mages that lay beneath.

She watched as Arley helped Maddox lower an older woman and a small child into the same hole. A mother and her son, she supposed. They had been holding hands. Nicolas barely missed the grave as he emptied his stomach contents at the sight.

The knights were all covered in mud and blood, the mixture seeping deep into their clothes. The air reeked with the smell of sweat and blood and smoke.

She tore her gaze away from the others and picked her shovel back up, determined to get it done as quickly as possible so she could leave, and hopefully never return. Before she could get a good grasp on the tool, she was suddenly overtaken with full-body shivers. The hair on the back of her neck stood on end and her body tensed.

Abandoning the shovel, she cast her gaze to the treeline. There wasn't an inch surrounding the clearing that was free of trees, that didn't have somewhere that enemies could hide. She didn't have eyes on either Peter or the horses, and she held out hope that he was merely hiding from whatever she could sense was coming, and hadn't fled with their only means of transport.

If he had, then they were screwed.

"What is it?" Renly appeared by her right shoulder, his shovel still in hand.

"I don't know," she latched her gaze onto a small movement through the trees.

The movement came closer to the treeline, close enough for her to make out it was a person. Tall, slender, menacing. A rustle of leaves came from a few feet beside them, and another person slowly emerged, much the same as the last. More rustling was heard behind them.

They were surrounded.

"Great," she hissed as realisation struck her.

The mages hadn't been left as they were because the Uprisers had moved on. The magic that still lingered wasn't just from the dead villagers. The Uprisers were still there. Waiting for them.

She turned her panicked gaze to Renly, who looked incredibly confused. The others hadn't even stopped digging yet, completely oblivious to the danger they were in. They had to get out of there. Now.

"It's a trap," she told Renly forcefully.

She was glad to see recognition quickly flick across his face. The others had slowly stopped digging upon noticing their hushed conversation. They were all huffing, clearly tired from exertion, and still caked in mud and blood.

Was this what the Uprisers were waiting for? To attack them when they were too exhausted to fight back? What cowards.

"What should we do?" Renly was glaring at something in the treeline behind them. "We're surrounded, aren't we?"

Olivia hummed.

There wasn't much they could do in their state other than run, but they were completely surrounded, and she still didn't know where Peter and their horses were. The knights couldn't fight off two lowly Uprisers back in Drerimas when they weren't so tired, when they had much better odds. They had no hope now, with many more enemies surrounding them, especially when they were all practically weaponless.

If they tried to escape and fight in the trees, she would be surprised if anyone made it out alive. As much as she hated to admit it, the Uprisers had the upper hand.

The frustration seeped into her bones and made her shake with anger. They had killed all of these innocent mages, *children,* just to get to them. It was despicable.

She couldn't save the lives of these innocent mages, the least she could do was help her people escape. Magic tingled under her skin and seemed to nudge at its confines, as if begging to be released, to be able to do *something.* If she could just help them escape, she could deal with these Uprisers herself. If not, well, at least the others would be safe.

"I see Peter."

She followed Renly's gaze to find Peter, lingering deep in the forest, all of their horses beside him. He hadn't run.

There was only one Upriser in the vicinity of where he was standing. She was tall and slender, smiling with a cruel upturn of her lips. She seemed cocky and overly brave, just like the others had looked when she faced them back in Drerimas.

If they could just get past her, the other Uprisers were too far away to scramble after them before she could cast something to protect them, and they'd have a clear shot at the horses. They'd be long gone before anyone could get to them.

She returned her gaze back to Renly, a plan slowly forming. She hadn't performed this kind of magic more than twice before, and it had never involved anyone but herself, but it was the only shot they had. They were too surrounded to try anything else without sacrificing anyone in the process.

"On my word, take the knights and run." She gave Renly a sharp look. "You get on those horses and you flee. No looking back."

Renly looked ready to argue, but he must have been able to see the determination on her face, because the argument faded just as quickly as it came. He reached forwards with one hand and softly cupped her cheek. His hands were rough and calloused, but warm.

"I trust you, Liv."

He slowly dropped his hand and turned to the others, no doubt to signal for them to prepare to follow his lead. She turned her back to them. The Uprisers had fully emerged from the forest now, all in full display. She didn't recognise a single one of them, but their cockiness sent a shiver down her spine.

The youngest one, standing right in front of Peter, was still covered in blood from the atrocities she had just committed. She clearly hadn't used just her magic to kill. Anger quickly boiled as the girl grinned, her shrill laugh echoing across the clearing.

She didn't hesitate to send an ice shard straight through her head. The laugh cut off sharply as she fell to the ground in a heap.

She didn't give herself time to think of what she had done, just turned back to the Uprisers, who were standing in shock. "Now!"

Olivia harnessed every inch of power she could feel rushing through her veins and projected it outwards, until a sheer blue bubble grew around herself and the knights. The warmth of it felt good, like a comforting presence reminding her that it was working, that it would protect them.

The force field was holding.

She was glad to hear the knights run the moment she told them to. One of the Uprisers cursed loudly as they began throwing spells at her shield in an attempt to wear it down. She never practised holding the shield against an attack, and they were tearing it down much faster than she had hoped.

Her hands were shaking as she looked off to where the knights had been escaping. Most had made it to their horses, a few already making their escape through the trees.

Renly was dragging Nicolas over to his horse. His arms wrapped strongly across the younger's chest as he tried to fight back. He was screaming for Olivia, his arms stretched out to her as Renly pulled him back, until Robard finally came to throw Nicolas onto his saddle.

She gave them a smile as she felt her shield weakening.

"Foolish girl," one of the Upriser's spoke. "They were never the target."

She felt a sharp pain in her head, and the last thing she saw before she blacked out was the back of the horses as they fled.

CHAPTER THIRTY-FOUR

She groaned as she opened her eyes, only to shut them again from the brightness, the light making her head throb. She slowly reached up to grab at her head, surprised to find something sticky there. She lowered it to find fresh blood.

"She's awake."

Her arm stung as she was shoved forwards, and she quickly fell from the lack of stability, landing with a painful thud. With another groan she lifted her head and squinted through the harshness of the light to take in her surroundings.

In front of her stood a few Uprisers, all seeming entirely too smug. The one in front of her was perched atop a crate, her legs dangling over the edge. She smirked as she took a huge bite from her apple.

They seemed to be in a camp of some sort. Others milled around outside the shelter she had been thrown into, and many other structures surrounded them. She wouldn't be surprised if this was the famed Upriser battle camp the king had been so sure he'd found multiple times over.

Behind her was what looked like a pig pen. It didn't seem very imposing, the wooden gate only standing at her waist. Now, however, it held a handful of people, all bloodied and bruised. She didn't get a good look at any of their faces before her head was forcibly turned, hard enough to send a sharp pain back through her temple.

The Upriser atop the crate laughed as she was shoved face-first into the dirt again, only to get pulled back into a sitting position by a harsh tug of her hair. She could feel blood slipping past her lips.

"They say you're the one we should be worried about," she shook her head. "Pathetic."

Olivia spat blood at her dangling legs.

The Upriser chuckled in surprise, her eyes lighting up in mirth. "I do love a fighter."

The others by her side laughed along with her. She had a commanding presence, sitting atop her crate and looking out over her prisoners, parading around food that the others obviously didn't have the privilege of getting. She was well-built, with black hair that cascaded down both shoulders in a pair of loose braids. There were white markings on her face like battle paint. She had obviously been at that mage camp – there was dried blood still splattered all over her clothing, but she didn't seem to care.

She was terrifying.

Olivia would be surprised if she wasn't the one in charge of this whole thing. She didn't blame the Uprisers from Drerimas for being so terrified of her.

"Who are you?"

She laughed, "that's not what you should be worried about."

"Is that so?" Olivia quirked a brow.

"You can, if you want to." She shrugged. "Getting leverage over me won't make a difference."

"You're not the leader?"

She let out a bark of laughter, as if it were the funniest thing she had heard in a while. "Me? In charge?" She pointed to herself with the hand still holding her apple. Her laughter tapered off as a serious look overtook her face. It made Olivia want to scramble backwards with the ferocity of it. "If I was in charge we would have already won."

"Enough, Enid."

Enid slid to the floor and abandoned her half-eaten apple on the crate. The dark look faded into something of displeasure, but she stood to attention. She may not be in charge, but that voice...

Molle strolled over towards Enid, dressed in full battle gear. Chainmail clung to her chest and thick shoulder pads adorned her shoulders, but she had not a scratch on her.

Olivia let out a sigh of relief at seeing her unharmed. She knew she would be somewhere in the area, as it had only been a few days since their meeting in the woods, but why did Enid seem to obey her? Unless...

She laughed as she watched Olivia piece it all together.

Molle was the Upriser leader.

"Took you long enough," Molle picked up the discarded apple and took a bite, much to Enid's displeasure, before turning back to Olivia. "Enid's right. You don't really live up to your reputation, do you?" She wiped the juice from her chin with the back of her hand. "No matter. You're here now, and those pesky humans can get what they deserve without... undesired interference."

Gods, if only she had listened to her father, then none of this would have happened. He always insisted on having at least one mage in Alira, even though she wasn't as trained as he was. If she had just remained behind, like he would have wanted, she would still be there to defend it from attack. Thankfully her father would be making his way back to Alira by now.

"You may have me, but you don't have my father." Olivia snarled at the girl, baring her bloodied teeth. "You're still screwed."

Molle cackled, and out of the corner of her eye she spotted a captured pair flinch at her words. It took her a moment to realise why they were so familiar, then it hit her.

Margaret and Ariadne.

She felt dread claw into her bones at the sight of them, bruised and beaten. Her father would never let them get taken like that. Did the king even send him to their camp in the first place?

Molle commanded her attention with a click of her fingers. She gestured to Enid beside her, and watched as she retrieved something heavy out of a saddlebag that hung by the crates. "I have a little gift for you."

Enid tossed the object towards her. She watched as it rolled along the uneven ground, and came to a stop as it nudged her dirtied knee.

Her father's severed head stared up at her through unblinking eyes.

Nausea clawed up her throat as the feeling of dread clutched at her heart. She felt the ground beneath her start to quake, felt the rage build up inside her, past all the numb distress. Her father had never done anything to deserve to be killed like that.

She looked up at Molle with disgust. She couldn't give in to her fear, or her heartache. She would have to deal with those feelings later. That's what her father had always taught her.

She just had to kill the kid and the rest of her stupid uprising first.

"I trusted you!" She moved to stand, but her hands shook too much for her to gain purchase.

Molle just smirked, and the Upriser hovering over her dragged her back so suddenly she lost her bearings. They gripped her hair so tightly she felt strands rip from her head, and she was tossed harshly into the wall among the other prisoners.

As soon as the gate closed behind her, she felt her magic still. The humming under her skin faded until all she could feel was the devastation and the anger. It must have been enchanted, just like the cell back in Alira. It made sense as to why none of them had managed to escape.

She let out a scream of frustration and stared daggers at where Molle was still biting into her apple, unbothered.

"I'll kill you! I'll end you for what you've done!"

Molle just laughed as she left, the others filing out after her. "Your father tried, and look where that got him."

CHAPTER THIRTY-FIVE

When she finally stopped shaking, she found herself between Margaret and Ariadne, with no guards or Uprisers in sight. Ariadne was raking her fingers through her hair as she cradled her to her chest. Margaret seemed more alert, her thigh touching Olivia's in a silent reminder that she was there.

Her father's head was gone.

They told her that most of their camp escaped to safety thanks to her father. There was no mention of what happened to the ones who didn't escape, but most of the children made it out alive, led by Emonie. Ariadne spoke of how bravely Mattie acted, helping as many as she could before running off through the trees with Annora.

Olivia breathed out a sigh of relief, "always knew that kid would be a leader."

"Stubborn thing," Ariadne scraped her nails against Olivia's scalp. "Probably would have stayed if Annora hadn't begged her to run."

"Do you know where they would have gone?"

Ariadne shook her head. "In an event like this, we all have different places to go. Just in case, you know?"

Olivia frowned, "so you'll never see them again?"

"Maybe not," Margaret shrugged. "But I have faith. It's for the best if it keeps them safe."

They're silent for a while after that. Olivia shuffled out of Ariadne's lap to lean against the wall so she'd have a better view of their surroundings. She didn't recognise any of the other Mages with them, not that she expected to. They must have raided a few different camps alongside Margaret's.

None of the Uprisers ever came back to check on them. Probably too confident in their containment spell.

She hated how she didn't know how the others fared. Not only those who escaped Margaret's camp, but her knights, too. Nicolas' screams wouldn't get out of her head. She needed to get out of there. She needed to get back to her people, to make sure everyone was safe. She needed to warn them.

This camp wasn't far from Alira, as far as she could tell. Judging from the distance they rode that morning, and knowing the Uprisers were on their way to Alira, she would guess they were a few hours from home, at most.

"Damnit."

Margaret and Ariadne were huddled together by the fence, as far from the others as they could get. They were staring out at where some Uprisers had gathered together. Ariadne's face had gone pale, Margaret's tight and displeased.

"What is it?" Olivia strained to hear what they were discussing, but they quickly left as soon as they noticed they were being watched. "What did they say?"

Ariadne ran a trembling hand through her hair and shook her head, "you're not going to like it."

"Alira." Margaret turned to face Olivia with a sympathetic look. "They're going to attack at first light."

Olivia cast her gaze to the sky. It was pitch black, with a crispness to the air that told her it was well into the night. First light wouldn't be too far away. Alira had no chance if she couldn't escape in time.

Renly, the knights, Cassius, Osmond, her mother... they would all be dead. Just like her father. Just like her prediction said.

She closed her eyes tightly, in an attempt to quell the anger she felt. Had they not taken enough from her? Her father was dead, and now they wanted to kill everyone else too?

She struck the ground with her fist, which sent a searing pain pulsing up her arm. Her rage was bubbling inside her. Gods, what she wouldn't do to have her magic back, just so she could make that spiteful kid *pay*. She let out a scream of frustration.

"Oh, Liv." Ariadne moved closer to her and took her trembling hand in her own, gently thumbing the blood from her knuckles with a sad smile. A sense of calm washed over her, and if she didn't know any better, she'd think Ariadne still had a hold of her magic.

She took a deep breath and tried to calm herself as much as she could. She would be no use to anyone wound up this tight. Her hands shook a little less when Ariadne entwined their fingers together.

"I have to leave," Olivia looked over at Margaret. "I need to warn them. They have no chance without my help. *Our* help."

It was one thing to get back to Alira on her own, but there were so many more Uprisers than she imagined, and she knew that she would hardly make a dent by herself. She might be able to stop a couple if she was lucky, but she needed help. Magical help.

Margaret and Ariadne were her only hope.

"I can't–" Margaret frowned. "No. I *won't* help him." Her gaze darkened. "He is no king of mine."

"Listen, Margaret, I truly understand why you hate him," she pleaded, "but not everyone in Alira is like him. They don't deserve to die for one man's mistakes, as horrid as they may be."

Margaret stared at her for a long time, but didn't say anything. If she couldn't convince her to help defend Alira, she would have no choice but to go alone. Her father would be displeased to learn she died for nothing.

That was if she could make it out of camp in the first place.

Perhaps she needed to try a different angle with her.

"My family is there," Olivia could feel her lip begin to wobble, all her anger fading into tears of desperation. She wasn't just talking about her mother. "Please. I'll do anything."

"Fine, I'll help you." Margaret pinched the bridge of her nose and sighed. "I'm doing this for you, not for that bastard king. You owe me."

"Yes, of course!" Olivia nodded. "You won't regret this."

"You're just like him, you know. Your father." Margaret said. "He told me the same thing."

"What did he say?" She asked.

"He told me I shouldn't lose faith in the people of this Kingdom, even if I've lost faith in the man who rules it."

She felt a tear make its way down her cheek, but she didn't move to wipe it away. She hadn't known her father was capable of that kind of compassion. She didn't think he would be so tolerant of people who were against his king. If anyone was going to receive his kindness, however, she's glad it was Margaret.

"Getting out of here will be a cinch now that we have you," Margaret waved a hand dismissively over her shoulder. "You know the woods around Alira, don't you?"

"Like the back of my hand," Olivia nodded. "But-"

"I know the way well enough to get you to the outskirts, but you will have to lead us to Alira's border. I have a spell I've been practising, but I'm not strong enough for an area of that size." She flicked her gaze between Olivia and Ariadne. "I'll need both of your help to pull it off."

"But-"

"Ari, when we get there, you'll have to warn them. Find Renly, he knows what you look like, and he'll believe you. I can't trust that they will let Olivia leave once they find her, not if they know there's a threat like this coming."

Ariadne nodded dutifully, "yes, Maggie."

"Then we-"

"*Margaret!*"

Margaret raised a brow, "I thought you wanted my help?"

"I do." Olivia said. "But how are you expecting to get out of here? I felt the magic drain as soon as I entered. I've seen this magic before. There's no way we can get out of here."

Margaret flicked her gaze to Olivia's boot, "they didn't search you, did they?"

Olivia furrowed her brow in thought, "I don't think so, but I was unconscious most of the time."

She wriggled her toes as she discretely rolled up her pant leg. She could feel a blade in her shoe, and the one that Robard had given her was still strapped to her ankle. She had been too distracted with everything that happened that she didn't notice them still there. She gazed up at Margaret and grinned. Their oversight would definitely work in her favour.

"Didn't check me either," she grinned back. "They're strong, but they're overly confident."

"I'll act as a distraction," Ariadne hugged her knees to her chest. "You're both much better at that stuff than I am."

"But how will this achieve anything?" Olivia asked, confused. "We still can't get out of this stupid pen."

"Easy," Margaret shrugged. "As I said, they're overconfident. They messed with the spell so they could enter if they needed to. It would be pointless to have prisoners if they couldn't torture them."

"They modified it?" Olivia raised a brow. "I didn't think you could do that."

"You didn't?" Ariadne sounded shocked. "It's not easy, but of course it's possible."

Margaret looked suspicious, "your father would have known. He didn't teach you that?"

She shook her head with a frown, "probably didn't think I could handle it."

Margaret hummed but didn't comment, even though she still seemed suspicious. It didn't matter. It was in the past, and her father was dead.

"Yes, well." Margaret shook her head. "They modified it. Any mage can touch the barrier and enter on will, but will need another mage to open the gate so they can exit again. We just need to make one of them open it for us, that's all."

"That's all?" Olivia scoffed. It was like asking for the impossible.

"Yes," Margaret rolled her eyes. "The spell will remain broken so long as that gate is open. Simple." She gave Olivia an odd look. "That kid was right. You don't know nearly as much as you should, not for your age."

She was going to reply, something bitter on the tip of her tongue, when Ariadne interrupted them with incessant tapping on Olivia's shoulder, her other hand inconspicuously pointing outside. "What about him?"

They looked over to where she was pointing. An Upriser was leaning against the building across the way, a smirk on his lips as he pelted passing Uprisers with small, sharp rocks. He cackled as one hit a young girl in the face, and aimed another at her back as she hurried away.

"He's the one," Margaret confirmed. "If we're going to hurt any of them, it might as well be him."

Something uncomfortable settled in Olivia's stomach. She wanted them to pay, and she *really* wanted them to hurt, but they were victims, just like all the mages were, and they didn't deserve to die.

She carefully avoided thinking about the young Upriser back at the camp she just came from, with a shard of ice through her head.

No-one in Alira deserved to die either, and the Uprisers wouldn't stop without being forced to.

It didn't take much for Ariadne to entice the man over to them. They had moved to sit in front of the gate, so he would have no choice but to approach them from that direction. It was out of her hands now. If Margaret and Ariadne were going to go through with it anyway, she should help. If they got hurt, their blood would be on her hands.

Margaret was right. He was cocky, and came waltzing over with a wolfish grin on his face. He only had eyes for Ariadne as he leaned on the gate. He licked his lips as his gaze ran over her body, and it was enough to make Olivia feel sick. Ariadne grinned, though, and twirled her hair around her finger. Her eyes were dull but her grin was blinding.

He didn't seem to notice. Or if he did, he didn't seem to care.

"You're a pretty little thing, aren't you?" He leaned forwards, far enough to brush his fingertips against Ariadne's cheek.

Ariadne giggled and leaned into his touch. He withdrew his hand, and she attempted to follow, only to pout as it got out of reach.

"It's too bad I'm stuck in here," she looked up at him beneath her lashes.

"And why's that?"

"We could have some fun," she licked her lips with a sly smile. "Couldn't we?"

The man seemed to be turning her offer over in his head, his grin still stuck on his face. He cast a look around him, as if to make sure none of the other Uprisers were watching him. Not only was he overconfident, but he was stupid as well. It was a wonder he had stayed alive as long as he had. To be fair, though, she could imagine Maddox falling for the exact same thing.

"I'm sure we have some time."

He opened the gate in haste, his grin widening. Ariadne took a step back and forced the man to step inside to follow her. The moment he did, Margaret lunged at him. She wrapped her hands around his neck and pulled him backwards.

Olivia took out her knife and lunged at him. She averted her gaze as she heard it hit flesh. He screamed in pain, but she didn't stick around to see how badly she had injured him.

She grabbed Ariadne's hand and ran, trusting Margaret to be right behind them.

They made it out of the camp unscathed, the yelling of the Uprisers trailing behind them.

CHAPTER THIRTY-SIX

They managed to make it to Alira while it was still dark. Only a few Uprisers had caught up with them along the way, but they dealt with them swiftly.

She led Ariadne and Margaret to the woods outside her house. It was as good a place to go as any, and if anyone followed them there, they wouldn't be directly exposed to the townsfolk.

"Is this it?" Margaret looked around them with a doubtful expression.

"This is it," Olivia confirmed. "Just ahead is the river that flows by my house, and if you follow the path beyond that you'll find the city centre."

Margaret hummed and turned to Ariadne. "Follow the path and find the prince. Give him warning of the attack then come straight back, okay?"

"Got it," Ariadne nodded. "Where would he be?"

"If he's not by the training fields, he'll be in the castle. They're both along the path." She reached out a hand to place on Ariadne's shoulder. "If you can't find him, find any knight you can. They all know your face, and they'll know something's wrong."

She only hoped Ariadne wouldn't be unlucky enough to run into Merek.

Ariadne placed a soft hand atop Olivia's with a gentle smile. "I'll come back for you. I promise."

"Hate to interrupt," Margaret dragged Ariadne away by the arm. "But you need to go. They're coming."

Olivia closed her eyes and concentrated on her surroundings. Margaret was right. She could sense strong magic approaching, and it didn't feel as far away as she had hoped. They were definitely running out of time.

When she opened her eyes, Ariadne was already gone. Olivia knew how the townsfolk could be, and if she didn't find Renly or the knights before anyone else found her... a shudder ran through her at the thought. She hoped Ariadne would be alright.

Margaret paced, a ball of nervous energy. There were a few scrapes and bruises she hadn't noticed in her panicked haze at the Upriser camp, and she had no idea if it was from her initial capture or her escape. The blood seemed dried, at least.

She still hadn't told Olivia exactly what the spell was that she needed her help with. Honestly, Olivia was sceptical she would be much help. Sure, her magic was getting better, but there was no way she was anywhere close to Margaret's level. She doubted she was as good as Ariadne, either.

What if she wasn't good enough? What if she failed them, and she was the one to get everyone killed? The only reason Margaret and Ariadne were even there was because she had asked them to be.

"I can hear you thinking from here," Margaret grumbled from where she stood, staring down at the river.

"This spell," Olivia cast a look towards where her house should be. They were too far out for her to see it. "I'm not sure I can help."

"It's simple." Margaret waved a dismissive hand at her. "It's exactly like the spell from the Upriser camp, only... better." She turned away from the river to look at her. "There's just nothing physical to cast the spell onto. Like a magical barrier, but instead of preventing any mage from coming or going, it strips them of their magic, even if they leave."

"How is that *simple*?!" Olivia gaped. "Is that even possible?"

"It's old magic, but there's never been a need to cast something like that." Margaret shrugged. "The small scale spell works just as well, and it's much easier to cast, easier to control."

"Right." Olivia hummed. "How does something like this even work without anything physical to cast onto?"

"That's where you come in," Margaret pointed at her. "You said you know this land, that you're an expert. We use you to picture in your mind the perimeter of Alira in exact detail, and we use that map to cast the spell."

"Okay?" Olivia was doubtful. They would rely solely on her memory in order for this to work, and she hated to know what would happen if she didn't have it exact. She had never even heard of a spell like this. "Is it permanent?"

"You mean, will your magic come back?"

Olivia bit her lip and nodded.

Margaret seemed to soften at her nervous look, "you'll be fine, Olivia. The spell will last only a few hours, it will be well gone by sundown. Probably."

"Probably?" Olivia questioned. "You mean you don't know?"

"Well, no." Margaret looked sheepish. "I've only ever practised on a small control group. Nothing of this size, and nothing of this strength."

This plan was sounding worse and worse. She must have been able to see her doubt, because Margaret scoffed. "You're welcome to try whatever backup plan I'm sure you have."

She needed to trust Margaret more, especially if something like this was going to work. From what little she spoke of it, they would need the combined magical strength of all three of them if they were to pull this off. Not trusting Margaret would only lead them to failure.

After all, Margaret and Ariadne were helping only because Olivia had asked them to. They knew what would happen if Alira fell, but saving a king that had only caused them to suffer surely wasn't high on their priorities. They could have been long gone by now, and the Uprisers wouldn't bother looking for them. If it wasn't for her, they could be tracking down whoever was left of their camp, but they didn't. They stayed to help her. She knew the danger they put themselves in by staying, and she was being incredibly ungrateful for their sacrifice.

Olivia sighed, "What do we have to lose?"

A sharp pain prodded at her mind, and a sense of dread washed over her. She hadn't been focused on their surroundings, too busy trying to decipher Margaret's plan to pay it much mind, and the moment she tried to sense the approaching magic it hit her like a brick.

They were already here.

"You're too late."

She took a few steps back to stand beside Margaret. Molle stood before them, still dressed for battle, with a pair of Uprisers by her side. Not only had she not sensed their approach, but she hadn't heard them either.

Molle picked at her fingernails. The dirt underneath them was a little too red for her liking. "Whatever you're planning isn't going to work."

Margaret scoffed, "and how would you know?"

"By all means, go ahead." Molle shrugged. "But I've already given the order to attack."

The Uprisers that flanked her on each side were tall and imposing, and incredibly intimidating. They seemed much more capable than that cocky Upriser they used to aid their escape. For one, they had muscles, like they were capable of fighting without just relying on their magic. She was thankful that she didn't spot any physical weapons on them.

She was sure that Molle was bluffing. If she had sent the order to attack, they would have heard the screams by now, or the warning bell at the very least. The forest was still blessedly silent.

Molle was smirking, as if she had already won.

"Why are you doing this?" Olivia glowered at the girl. "These people are innocent, they aren't the ones who hurt you!"

"No-one is innocent!" Molle screamed. "They blindly follow a king that would watch us suffer and die without lifting a finger to help! No-one does anything!" She laughed, and it sounded deranged. "If we don't do something, nothing will ever change."

"I get it!" Olivia shouted back. "But these people have never killed anyone, never left anyone to die! Your issue is with the king, not his people!"

"Right," Molle scoffed, her lip upturned. "And how well have they treated you?"

Olivia flushed. Molle was right, the people of Alira had never been kind to her, ever since they discovered her magic. She felt threatened and scared almost every day she was inside those walls. The only time she had ever felt truly safe was being surrounded by other mages, far from Alira.

That didn't mean those people deserved to be killed. They didn't deserve to be tortured, to be subjected to the exact same thing that her kind have suffered. She knew exactly what the Uprisers wanted to do with King Alroy, with all the humans that had ever harmed them. The cruelty would only lead to further retaliation by the humans, and war would run rampant throughout the land, decimating everything and everyone in its path.

If the Uprisers won, the Kingdom would be lost. She couldn't allow that to happen.

Olivia took a step towards Molle, "I can't let you do that."

"Oh, sweet girl." Molle gave her bodyguards a commanding look. "You've already lost."

The Uprisers immediately started throwing spells at Olivia and Margaret before she could take more than a few steps towards them. She dove to the ground to avoid a low-flying spell and crawled to the closest tree that would give her cover.

The two of them cast whatever spells they could at the approaching Uprisers to keep them back, but it wasn't as effective as she had hoped. She peeked out from safety only long enough to cast before she ducked back for cover. Spells whizzed past her, close enough that she could feel the heat of the magic singe her ear.

She was terrified, shaking as she cast forceback spells towards the approaching Uprisers, just to give herself and Margaret some breathing space at the very least, but it didn't stop them. They just kept coming.

She bit back the frustrated tears that tried to spill over her cheeks. What had she gotten herself into?

Molle hadn't moved from her spot further back in the forest. She looked almost bored as she watched the fighting, but she didn't lift a finger to help. She looked like she would rather be anywhere else than having to deal with them.

One lucky hit from Margaret sent one of the Uprisers tumbling to the ground, and it was easy to deal her a final blow, the fallen mage too disorientated to focus on fighting back.

After that, the other Upriser fell just as quick.

She didn't feel as satisfied watching them fall as she should have.

Molle growled in frustration as she looked down at the Uprisers with distaste. "If you want something done right, you have to do it yourself."

She stepped over the dead bodies of her friends without a backwards glance, as if she hadn't been too concerned with their deaths. The thought made her shake with fear. She wouldn't spare them any mercy if she didn't even care about her own uprising.

Molle raised her hands, and left them outstretched towards herself and Margaret as she continued her approach. She could see the magic forming before her very eyes, in a way she had never witnessed before. It was as if Molle was drawing magic from around her, holding onto it until she had enough to attack with some lasting damage. Her eyes were narrowed and sharp, the purple in them sparkling. The magic she was drawing was stronger than she had ever seen.

Olivia shared an alarmed look with Margaret. How were they supposed to counter something like this? She was strong, more than Olivia had imagined she could be, and it was suddenly very apparent why she was the leader. It was obvious why the Uprisers were terrified of such a young girl.

The few spells that Margaret and Olivia managed to cast bounced right off her armour to land in the dirt behind her. Not a single one caused her any damage, not even the ones aimed at her head. She must have enchanted her armour against magical attacks. They were useless against her.

Molle's grin grew wide as she stopped her approach, her hands shaking with the energy she was holding onto. This was it. There was no way they were going to survive something like that.

"I hate that it had to come to this, girls. We could have ruled so well together–"

Her words cut off as she dropped to the ground. Seconds passed, but she didn't move. With a deep breath, Olivia inched out of her hiding spot to creep closer to her, and peered down in surprise. Her eyes were wide open, and she wasn't breathing. Blood pooled from the dagger lodged in her head, so far in that the hilt was the only part showing.

Molle was dead.

She hadn't thrown the dagger, and she hadn't seen Margaret move to get hers either. She looked back at her to check, only to find Margaret staring slack-jawed at the person standing behind her.

Olivia followed her gaze to find Renly, Ariadne and Nicolas standing behind where she had been hiding. Their chests were heaving, as if they had run to get to them. Just in time, too.

Renly smirked at her stunned expression, but she saw relief cross his face as their eyes met. "What, you think you're the only one Robard ever gave a gift to?"

The warning bells chimed loudly in the distance before she had the chance to answer.

Molle hadn't lied. The Uprisers were attacking. They were too late.

Renly paled as he looked from Olivia to Margaret. "I trust you have a plan."

CHAPTER THIRTY-SEVEN

Ariadne ran over to Olivia, worry dancing in her eyes. She fussed, asking if she was alright as she checked over every inch of her for injury. She pushed Ariadne back, if only from the stares she received from both Margaret and Renly, one amused and the other less so.

Renly and Nicolas had been out on the training fields with Osmond when Ariadne had found them, requesting every spare piece of weaponry the forge had so they could be prepared for what was coming.

It had taken a little longer to leave, however, when King Alroy found them and demanded to know why a stranger was seeking an audience with the prince. Renly had to all but plead with his father in order to get back to them in time. Good thing too, because she's not entirely sure how long they could have held Molle off for.

It was almost embarrassing how easily Renly had been able to take her down.

A high-pitched scream came from the town square, and jolted her back into reality. They needed to act quickly if they had any hope of taking the kingdom back before everyone in it was dead.

The longer she stood there, the more her body ached. Fighting off the Uprisers, and being as scared as she was, had obviously kept the fatigue and pain at bay.

"Ren," she stumbled towards the prince. No matter how tired she was, she couldn't stop now. "We'll all be useless against an attack while performing this spell. Will you-"

"We'll protect you." Renly placed a grounding hand on her shoulder. "I promise."

It had been a while since she believed a promise from Renly so easily, but she knew he had no reason to lie. He never would have come back here with Nicolas and Ariadne if he wasn't prepared to help her. He wasn't his father. Renly actually cared for his people.

"Yeah, Liv." Nicolas grinned brightly over Renly's shoulder. "You'll save us, so we'll save you in return."

The way he said it, like it was the easiest thing in the world for him to believe, made a hopeful feeling settle in her chest. He was too pure for his own good. She hoped he didn't have to die for her.

"It's time."

Margaret and Ariadne were holding hands, and the leader seemed a little annoyed at how long she was taking. Ariadne had her spare hand outstretched for Olivia to take, still wearing a kind smile. In the face of everything, she remained as kind and gentle as ever.

She would be such an easy person to love.

Olivia approached Ariadne and firmly grasped her hand. She could do this. If both Margaret and Ariadne were confident about this, then Olivia could be, too.

"Just like we discussed." Margaret waited for Ariadne to nod before she turned to settle her gaze on Olivia. "Picture the perimeter as clearly as you can, okay? Put all of your power into that invisible line. Ariadne and I will be able to sense that barrier, and we will add our own magic to it."

Olivia gulped and nodded, "okay."

Margaret gave a sharp smile, "let's kick some Upriser arse."

With a calming breath, and a quick squeeze to Ariadne's hand, she closed her eyes.

It was now or never.

She cleared her mind completely, and replaced it with only the perimeter surrounding Alira. She made sure the line she pictured was in front of where the three of them were standing. It would only lead to disaster if she miscalculated, and the spell was only half-complete because she accidentally rendered them powerless before they could finish.

She projected her magic out to feel the Uprisers inside the perimeter, and bit back a gasp. There were a lot of them, much more than she feared. The townsfolk didn't stand a chance.

The books and scrolls she had read told her of the dangers that came with performing big magic like this, but they never explained how much it would hurt.

She felt every one of her magical cells boil over, as if scorching fire was poured directly onto her skin. It felt like her magic was trying to burn holes into her skin to escape, and the longer she focused, the more it hurt.

The pain was excruciating, more than she's ever felt in her life. More than she ever could have imagined. Her eyes snapped open as she felt fire flow down her back, the pain so intense she felt little control over her body.

She felt weightless, the only tether she could feel to reality was Ariadne's harsh grip on her hand. Looking down, she realised why.

She was *floating*.

"You're doing great, Olivia!" Margaret looked fearful, but there was no denying the determination in her eyes. "Keep concentrating!"

She took another steadying breath and dug deeper inside herself. She pushed past the pain and the throbbing warning signs of overusing her magic, as clear a warning to stop as any. The impossible pain only seemed to grow. Every cell in her entire body was screaming at her, every limb felt heavy and dead. Gods, did she want to stop. But she knew she couldn't.

Every single person in Alira needed her to succeed.

She let out a scream as the pain worsened. She felt like she was on fire, and her head ready to explode, a simple migraine turning excruciating. The pain was more than one person, and she knew she was drawing the pain of every Upriser in Alira. Her heart was beating impossibly fast, her bones felt like lead.

Renly's eyes bugged wide in alarm when she couldn't stop screaming.

Why the hell didn't Margaret tell her the pain would be this bad?

Before it became too much to bear, she felt it lessen, as if someone was helping her carry the weight of it. She knew that it must have been Margaret and Ariadne joining her. The magic flowed faster, and she felt more of it drain from her body. As the pain ebbed, her exhaustion grew.

Suddenly, the pain subsided into a dull throb and she dropped from the air, landing in a crumpled heap on the ground. She barely registered the pain as she collapsed in on herself. If she were to perform one more piece of magic, she felt like her entire body was going to explode.

She vaguely heard Ariadne ask if it had worked, but she blacked out before she could hear the answer.

There wasn't anything left for them to do if they had failed.

CHAPTER THIRTY-EIGHT

Olivia blinked awake to a dull ache. Her entire body felt like lead, and she was too exhausted to move. She was starting to get a little fed up with the amount of times she woke to pain.

She slowly looked around herself without moving her head. There were copious amounts of cots around the room, a makeshift infirmary back inside the castle if she had to guess, and almost all of them were occupied. Some of the cots had sheets over the heads of their occupants.

Maddox was in one of them, down the other end of her row, one leg bandaged from ankle to knee. He didn't seem to be in much pain, to her relief. There was a grin on his face, despite his leg braced on a stack of pillows, as he flirted with the blushing nurse by his side.

He caught her eye and she looked away before he could call out to her, the movement quick enough to shift her head. It sent searing pain to her temple and she shut her eyes against the pain, letting out a quiet groan. She's tired of feeling so injured all the time.

Something nudged at her leg, and she slowly opened her eyes again. Cassius was sitting in an uncomfortable looking chair by her side, his feet up on her cot, nudging her own. His arm was in a sling, and there were cuts and bruises all over his face. His clothes were caked in dried blood, but he grinned at her.

"I can't believe you're sleeping at a time like this."

She snorted and nudged Cassius' foot back, who laughed. He looked pretty banged up, wincing as he shifted around in his chair, but he didn't look as bad as she feared he would.

"You look like shit." Cassius rolled his eyes, but she levelled him with a look. Just because he seemed to be fine, it didn't mean he wasn't injured in ways she couldn't see. "Are you okay?"

Cassius' carefree mask slipped, and he seemed more in pain than he did before. He cradled his arm a little closer to his chest and curled one of his feet under the other, but he still wore a small smile. "I look a hell of a lot better than you do."

"Cass–"

"I'm *fine*, you worryguts." Cassius wrapped one of his legs around her own, his gentle smile growing in size. "If it wasn't for you, I'd be a lot worse off."

She let out a breath she hadn't realised she'd been holding. "So it worked then?"

"Idiot, how do you think we're still alive?"

Truthfully, she knew the spell must have done something, especially if this many people were still left alive, but she had collapsed before she was able to know how successful it had been. Just because she stole the magic from their attackers, it didn't mean they were useless.

According to Cassius, the Uprisers fell easily without their magic to help them, especially after Renly got word out about how Molle had fallen. Luckily most of them had not been too skilled in attacks that involved an actual weapon.

Her thoughts suddenly drifted to Ariadne and Margaret, and no matter how far she stretched to look around the room, she couldn't find them, and a feeling of dread washed over her. What if the king had gotten to them? What if they had been mistaken for Uprisers and were struck down?

The spell must still be in effect, because she couldn't feel them anywhere.

"They're fine." Cassius turned her gently with an arm on one shoulder, and pushed her back into the pillows. "Margaret and Ariadne, they're both fine. Prince Renly told the king what they did, and he offered them to stay."

"The king did?" She raised a brow in disbelief. "King Alroy asked mages to stay in Alira?"

"I know!" Cassius snorted. "They haven't given their reply yet, but I would be surprised if they stayed. Nicolas took them to find some food."

Cassius hadn't outgrown the need to use titles since they met, and she was pleasantly surprised to know he got on well enough with Nicolas to drop them.

"Nicolas, hey?" She smirked. "Where's the respect for your knights, Cassie?"

He kicked her leg hard, his blush hidden behind one of his hands. She gave a small yelp as the motion sent shockwaves up her exhausted limbs.

"Bastard," she muttered under her breath.

Settling back into the pillows with a sigh, she allowed herself to really feel her injuries. She was bone-tired, her limbs too heavy to move very much, and her head still throbbed. She glanced down and saw her arm in a sling, but she couldn't remember how she injured it.

Everything hurt.

"How did I get in here? I can barely move."

"The prince carried you after you collapsed. He refused to leave your side until King Alroy called him away." He laughed. "Quite the sight, if you ask me."

"Which I didn't."

He went to kick her again, but thought better of it, and simply rolled his eyes as he settled into his chair. He was still smiling, however, so she counted it as a win.

They sat in silence after that. She drifted off after a while, lulled to sleep by her tired limbs and Cassius' rhythmic breathing. She woke with a start after not long at all, sweat clinging to her forehead. She had dreamt of her father. She feared his empty eyes would haunt her forever.

Cassius seemed concerned, but didn't press. She was glad he could read her so well after such a short time of knowing her. He simply brushed her hair away from her sweaty forehead and settled back into his spot.

Renly appeared after she awoke for the second time. She hadn't seen him at first, too groggy from her sleep. It was only after Cassius prodded at her bruised arm until she fought back, kicking out at his injured leg, that she saw him.

"Good to see you're both healing nicely," Renly smirked. He stood beside Cassius, pulling his chair away from her until his legs slid off the bed and thumped on the ground.

It was good to see Renly. There wasn't a drop of blood on him, and his clothes were free of dirt and debris. He looked just as royal as ever. He was unharmed, and relief flooded through her so quickly she felt lightheaded.

"I should go check up on Osmond." Cassius stood from his chair with a knowing smile. "Last I saw he was still carrying wounded from the battlefield, your mother along with him. I'll make sure they take their rest."

She winced as he limped away. She felt guilty that she hadn't spared Osmond or her mother a thought since she woke up. It didn't surprise her in the slightest that they were perfectly fine. If she was to bet on anyone to stay alive to the end, it would be the two of them. Both were much too stubborn to die.

"C'mon," Renly held out a hand for her to take. "I want to show you something."

He helped her out of bed gingerly and led her down the corridor to the landing that overlooked the main square. Thankfully, after her rest, her limbs didn't feel quite as heavy.

There were obvious signs of a magical battle everywhere, from charred walls to the massive indents in the ground. It could have been a lot worse. If only they had gotten there earlier, the outcome could have been a lot better, too. If they had escaped earlier, had managed to perfect that spell before any of the Uprisers had caught up to them, perhaps no-one would have been killed.

"Why are you showing me this?"

"You stopped this from becoming much worse." Renly squeezed her waist from where he held her steady. "You saved countless lives today, Olivia."

"Sure looks like it," She scoffed.

Renly shook his head. "Father is eternally grateful for what you sacrificed for Alira. For *who* you sacrificed. As am I."

Ariadne and Margaret must have told him about her father while she was unconscious.

She muttered out her thanks, and averted her gaze to look over the battlefield.

"He wanted to thank you by awarding you your father's old title." He chuckled when she scrunched up her nose in distaste and glared at Renly. The thought of becoming part of the court made her feel physically ill. "Don't worry, I told him that doing so would only drive you away."

Renly shuffled as he moved to rummage around in his pocket. Eventually, he found what he was looking for and held it out to her.

A brooch. A *Knight's* brooch. The Bayard Crest shone brightly in the morning sun.

She took it with weak and shaking fingers. "Is this real?"

"I had to fight my father to let you have this, with my mother and Lorelle's help, of course." Renly hummed. "It's not as if he could deny your skills, or your dedication to his people."

She felt tears start to well and sniffed them back. After everything she's seen, everything she's done, she wasn't going to cry over a damn brooch.

It felt good to be recognised for her actions, though. It felt even better to finally achieve what she had always longed for. Although she didn't like all the death and destruction that had to happen for her to get there.

"So it's really happening?" She glanced up at Renly. "I'm a knight now?"

Renly bowed his head with a teasing smile, "welcome to the ranks, Dame Olivia."

"Merek is going to be thrilled."

Renly snorted, "I'm sure he'll get over it."

She slipped the brooch into her pocket and looked back over the battlefield. The future was uncertain for her. She couldn't guarantee this new position would change Alira's perceptions of her, that they would be favourable over her newly knighted status, especially after an attack like this.

Having her father gone wouldn't help matters either. It was a thought that left her chest aching.

They may not grow to like her, but she would protect them all nonetheless.

Until her dying breath.

www.ingramcontent.com/pod-product-compliance
Lightning Source LLC
Chambersburg PA
CBHW030612120726
47904CB00006B/1872